# Cast of (

**Haila Troy.** A former model, now [...] month to . . .

**Jeff Troy.** An unemployed adman and wisecracking amateur detective.

**Ralph "Mac" MacCormick.** An amiable photographer, owner of Photo Arts and the Troys' best friend. Haila calls him "Huck Finn with shoes."

**Julie Taylor.** A stylist at Photo Arts who thinks the world of Mac.

**Erika Fleming MacCormick.** Mac's rich, blue-blooded wife.

**Isabelle Fleming.** A wealthy society matron and Erika's mother.

**Kirk Findlay.** Mac's assistant, who everyone knows has a crush on Julie.

**Harry Duerr.** The capable set builder at Photo Arts.

**Lee Kenyon.** When he's not modeling, he's a tap dancer at a Manhattan dive.

**Jim Snyder.** Lee's friend, who models to support his golf habit.

**May Ralston.** A healthy blonde model, a bit on the narcissistic side.

**Madge Lawrence.** A quiet, dark-haired model with a shadowy past.

**Robert Yorke.** A matinee idol, slightly over the hill, who also models.

**Miss Frances Frost.** Julie's neighbor and best friend, who keeps turtles.

**Lieutenant Wyatt.** An NYPD homicide detective.

**Lockhart.** His sarcastic assistant.

Plus assorted cab drivers, elevator operators, neighbors, and agency owners.

# Books by Kelley Roos

## Featuring Jeff & Haila Troy

Made Up To Kill (1940)*
If the Shroud Fits (1941)*
The Frightened Stiff (1942)*
Sailor, Take Warning! (1944)
There Was a Crooked Man (1945)
Ghost of a Chance (1947)
Murder in Any Language (1948)
Triple Threat (1949)
One False Move (1966)

\* reprinted by Rue Morgue Press
as of April 2006

## Other mystery novels

The Blonde Died Laughing (1956)
Requiem for a Blonde (1958)
Scent of Mystery (1959)
Grave Danger (1965)
Necessary Evil (1965)
A Few Days in Madrid (1965
(Above published as by Audrey and William Roos)
Cry in the Night (1966)
Who Saw Maggie Brown? (1967)
To Save His Life (1968)
Suddenly One Night (1970)
What Did Hattie See? (1970)
Bad Trip (1971)
Murder on Martha's Vineyard (1981)

# If the Shroud Fits

A Jeff & Haila Troy mystery by

# Kelley Roos

Rue Morgue Press
Lyons / Boulder

The Rue Morgue Press
P.O. Box 4119
Boulder, Colorado 80306
800-699-6214
www.ruemorguepress.com

Printed by
Johnson Printing

PRINTED IN THE UNITED STATES OF AMERICA

# Meet the Authors

Kelley Roos was the pseudonym used by the husband-and-wife writing team of William and Audrey Kelley Roos who, like their contemporaries, Frances and Richard Lockridge, wrote about a husband-and-wife detective team. Photographer (though he tried his hand at other careers) Jeff Troy and his future wife, actress Haila Rogers, were introduced to the reading public in 1940's *Made Up To Kill*, the same year that saw the birth of the Norths. They received a five hundred dollar advance for their first effort and never looked back.

Eight more adventures featuring the Troys appeared before they abandoned the series in 1966 (there had been a 17-year vacation from the series between book eight and book nine). The books, laced with wisecracks and filled with screwball humor have the feel of a 1940s movie comedy. In fact, the third Troy mystery, *The Frightened Stiff*, was filmed in 1943 as *A Night to Remember* with Loretta Young and Brian Aherne playing the Troys. They wrote numerous non-Troy mysteries as well and received an Edgar for the 1960 television play, *The Case of the Burning Court*, based on the novel by John Dickson Carr.

William Roos was born in Pittsburgh, Pennsylvania, in 1911, and he was graduated from Carnegie Tech in Pittsburg where he was enrolled in the drama department with an eye toward becoming a playwright. It was there that he met Audrey, who was studying to be an actress. Born in Elizabethtown, New Jersey, in 1912, she had been raised in Uniontown, Pennsylvania. After graduation, Audrey took a touch-typing course (William never learned) and two headed for New York City. Audrey eventually gave up her dream of becoming an actress and decided to write a detective novel. William soon became attracted to the idea as well and initially the two would plot their books over drinks in the evening. At first they wrote alternate chapters and then passed them on to the other for rewrites. Eventually, William wrote the entire first drafts but, with William still unable to touch-type, Audrey always had the last word.

They lived in Connecticut and Spain as well before finally settling in the late 1960s in an old whaling captain's house on Martha's Vineyard, where Audrey died in 1982 and William in 1987. For more information on their lives and collaborations, see Tom and Enid Schantz' introduction to The Rue Morgue Press edition of *The Frightened Stiff.*

# Chapter One

IT HAD STARTED RAINING about six o'clock, a cold blue October rain that slashed horizontally against the windows and swirled across the roof. In the living room, warm saffron-colored lamplight and the log fire's crackle and snap waged a losing battle with the dreariness of the dark that was swallowing the city outside. The sulking wind and the squealing sound of tires on wet pavements below all added their bit to my already mounting nervousness.

I had spent the last two hours giving Jeff ten more minutes to come home; ten minutes before I began divorce proceedings or calling New York's long list of hospitals to see if any attractive young husbands had been spoiled by skidding trucks. I was consoling myself with the thought that all new wives act this way when the panicky rapping came at the door.

"Who is it?" I called.

"Julie! Julie Taylor!"

"Come in, darling."

Julie stepped just inside the door, her teeth chattering, her coat soaked and shapeless with rain. Little rivulets of water ran off her hat and drops of it clung glistening to the ends of her short brown hair.

"Haila, is Jeff here?"

She sounded as if she had run nonstop all the way from the Battery to Ninety-third Street; as if, on top of that, she had taken the four flights up to my apartment three steps at a time.

"Julie!" I said, "is someone chasing you or …"

One good look at Julie Taylor's face made me stop abruptly. It was her eyes I think that had done it. There was alarm in them and something very close to fear. Then I noticed that her little turned-up mouth was grim and

7

that her last summer's freckles, which took Julie until Thanksgiving time to dissipate, stood out against the unnatural paleness of her face like the bumps on dotted-Swiss.

She glanced over my shoulder into the apartment. "I must see Jeff, Haila." Her voice was almost unfriendly in its tenseness. "Where is he?"

"Out looking for a job. ..."

"He'll be back soon? You're expecting him?"

"Julie, for heaven's sake, what's wrong? What's happened to you? Sit down and tell me!"

She hesitantly crossed the room, holding the soggy little ball that was her gloves tight in one hand, and sat on the edge of a hassock under a rain-blurred window. I made a move to take her wet things, but she drew her coat closer around her.

In a muffled voice Julie said, "Something happened today, Haila, but ..."

"At work? At Photo Arts?"

"Yes. Yes, it was ..." Her words trailed off. With a half-angry gesture she shoved her hat back from her face and looked up at me. "Haila, I'm sorry for seeming so stupid. But now that I'm sitting here, and you're sitting there, waiting for your husband ... everything so normal ..." She forced a smile at me. I got it. Everything so normal; me waiting for Jeff. But I didn't encourage her evasion by answering her smile. She went on impatiently, "Well, can't you see? Now I don't think that what happened really did happen. It ... it couldn't have. At least, I can't tell you it did. You'd think I was silly, hysterical. You'd advise me to get married." Julie jumped up, shrugging her tweed coat into position, yanking her brown hat down over her forehead. She started toward the door. "Forget that I burst in here like an idiot, will you, Haila? Forget all about it."

I stepped in front of her. "Julie, you came here to see Jeff. You're in some kind of trouble and you thought that he might be able to help you. That's it, isn't it?"

She moved quickly around me, her hand was on the doorknob. "I'll tell Jeff all about it," she said, "some other time."

"Are you sure some other time won't be too late?"

Julie swung around to face me. The look of terror was back in her eyes again. Her hand, still on the door, was rigid with strain.

"Haila," she said, "you know what a darkroom is."

"Of course."

"It was in one of our darkrooms up at Photo Arts that it ... that it happened."

"Start at the beginning, Julie."

She took one unwilling step back into the room and sat on the wooden arm of the nearest chair. "All right. All right, Haila. I've said too much now not to go on. We took a picture this afternoon. Or rather, Mac took the picture with the rest of us trying to keep out of his way. It was the Cottrell Silverware ad."

"Cottrell Silver! Then Mac's in the big time now!"

"This was his chance to get in the big time. It had to be good. It had to be the best thing he's ever done. We shot it in full color and went the limit. A wonderful set. We have a new man since you've been around who does them for us. Harry Duerr. And he's good, awfully good. Erika found him several months ago and sent him to us. The set was perfect. And we had floral arrangements by Helen Viking and dining room furniture by W. and J. Sloane and glassware by Jensen. And Cottrell Silverware all over everything."

"And a beautiful star of stage, screen and radio endorsing?"

"Better than that. Mrs.. Isabelle Fleming."

"No!"

"Yes. High society is better for silver than Hollywood."

"But Mrs. Fleming, Julie! I thought she wouldn't endorse the Bible. Not publicly, anyhow."

"Mac arranged for her to pose for this ad."

"But how?"

"I thought you knew, Haila. Mrs. Fleming is Erika MacCormick's aunt. You remember Erika, don't you?"

I remembered Erika all right. It would have been impossible to forget that face and figure. But I hadn't known that she came of such illustriously social stock. So Mac MacCormick had got all that and a gate into the four hundred too. Not that he would even consider swinging on that gate.

I said, "Go on, Julie."

"Besides Mrs. Fleming we had five models. We ..."

"Julie," I interrupted, "let's get to the darkroom."

"Yes." There was a silent moment while Julie took one long breath, then rushed headlong into it. "It was after the picture had been taken. I wanted to check on all the props I'd rented, and on the silver, before any of them got a chance to be lost. I'd left my list in the darkroom. On the shelf right over the sink. I knew exactly where it was and I was in a hurry to get it. I suppose that's why I didn't turn on the light when I went in. Besides, you ... you get out of the habit of turning on the lights in the darkroom ..."

"I'd just reached the shelf and was picking up my list when I heard the sound. I don't frighten at sounds; I'm not usually nervous nor jumpy. But this ... this was a sound that I wasn't supposed to hear. I felt that; I knew it. When you hear a noise that has danger in it, you can sense that danger somehow."

"I know."

"I turned around. The door that I had come through had been closed behind me. Not from the outside, from the inside. There ... there was someone in that darkroom with me; someone who didn't want me to know who he was. He didn't speak; he didn't move. He just stood there quietly, close to me in the darkness."

"And that sound you heard? That was the door being closed?"

"I guess so. It must have been. All I knew for sure was that I wasn't alone. Someone had come in before me, had been standing there in the dark waiting for me. He'd let me come in and cross to the sink and then just ... closed me in there with him. I ... I stood there, frozen."

"Julie, it might have all been a practical joke. Kirk or Mac ..."

"Kirk and Mac aren't practical jokers, Haila."

Julie was right; there was nothing practical about those two, not even their jokes. Furthermore, Kirk Findlay, who was Mac's assistant, had been spending each working day and overtime for the last year adoring Julie. And scaring girls out of their wits didn't lead them to altars.

"What happened then, Julie?"

"I whispered, 'Who is it?' There wasn't any answer. A beam of light hit me in the face. It shocked me, so that I put my hands over my eyes and turned away. When I looked again the light was gone. The room seemed darker even than it had before. I stood there waiting. Waiting for something to happen, hands to come around my throat, something to hit me on the head, anything. But nothing did, nothing at all. I stood there so long ... seconds or minutes or hours, I don't know ... so long that I began to wish something would happen. Anything that would break that awful stillness."

She stopped to swallow. Her voice was dry and almost cracking. She dug her teeth into her lower lip to stop its quivering.

"I didn't scream; I couldn't. I didn't even try to get out, for I knew he was there between me and the door. And there still hadn't been a sound nor a movement. It was then, I think, that I first noticed it. An odor, a strange odor, and yet somehow it seemed to be one that I knew, that I should recognize. I guess it was that smell that jerked me out of my trance. I don't know why, but it did. I pulled myself together and made a dive for the wall switch. I got the lights on, but the room was empty."

I started to protest. "But, Julie ..."

"There was no one in the room, Haila. There wasn't even a sign that anybody had been in it, except for that odor. That's all I know." She looked down at her tightly clasped hands. With an effort she jerked them apart, made them lie loosely in her lap. "Whoever had been in the room with me had slipped out while I was blinded by the flashlight."

"But didn't you hear him go? Didn't you hear the door open and close?"

"Perhaps I did. I can't remember now. All I know is that I didn't see him go or realize that I was alone."

"Then, Julie?"

"Then I stepped out into the hallway. There was no one there either. I went quickly through the studio and the reception room and all the dressing rooms. Nobody had left; the models were all still dressing. That is, all except Mrs. Fleming. She was going home the way she was; she was saying good-by to Mac in the reception room. Kirk and Harry were in the studio busy with a camera and some lights. Everything perfectly ordinary and usual. Everyone calm and placid. Not one of them looking as if he had just finished scaring me to death in the darkroom."

"What did Mac and Kirk say about all this?"

Julie pulled the creases out of her forehead with a tired hand. "I didn't tell them. Suddenly it seemed too silly to bother about. 'Someone was hiding in the darkroom,' I'd say to them, 'and he flashed a searchlight in my face.' Sounds dopey, doesn't it? I knew they'd laugh at me. They'd so what me and I'd never hear the end of it. But all the same I was too upset to stay there. I told Mac I had a headache and I went home. And in about an hour I'd decided to forget the whole thing."

I said gently, "Then why did you want to tell Jeff? What made you do that, Julie?"

Her hands clenched again. "That odor. That strange odor in the darkroom. I didn't realize what it was until after I got home, until just a little while ago. It was chloroform."

"Chloroform!"

"Yes. I'm not mistaken. I know for sure."

"But couldn't it have been something else? Something you use for developing pictures, or for color?"

"No, It was chloroform."

"But, Julie, why? Why would anyone ..."

"Yes, why," she said flatly.

"Robbery, maybe ... chloroform's been used for that!"

"No, Haila, not robbery."

"But, Julie ..."

"Listen! This thing was planned. And whoever planned it could be sure that his victim was going to be at the studio this afternoon. But he couldn't be sure that a certain person was going to bring along five thousand dollars or the pearl necklace. Or the secret formula. No, Haila, I don't think that person in the darkroom was there to steal; he was there to murder."

"Murder, Julie!"

She smiled grimly. "There aren't any butterflies in the darkroom. Or dogs too old to live."

"Who would want to kill you, Julie, who …" I became completely inarticulate.

"No one tried to kill me, Haila. I know because he had every chance to do just that … and he didn't. He must have realized when I spoke that I wasn't his … his intended victim. The flashlight in my face was to make sure."

"Julie, you're jumping to conclusions, you're …"

"I'm afraid I'm not! I think that I stumbled onto a murderer." She rushed on. "I can't prove it to you, Haila! I can only tell you what happened and what I think. And I think that someone was meant to come into that darkroom this afternoon and be killed."

"But who, Julie?"

She didn't answer, just sat there looking at me, her eyes filled with a look I couldn't understand. It might've been more fear, or it might have been merely uncertainty. At any rate it prompted me to offer her some brandy.

"No, thanks, Haila," she said. "I'm all right."

"And everyone else is, too," I said in an attempt at cheerfulness. "Everyone left the studio alive and well, didn't they?"

Julie brushed the back of her hand wearily across her eyes. "I left before anyone else did. But I suppose they were all able to get out on their own power. I would have heard by now if one of them had been killed."

"Then everything's all right, isn't it?"

She leaned forward in her chair, her lips tense. "Haila, just suppose for a minute that I'm right, that someone did attempt a murder at Photo Arts this afternoon. And he missed. Will it stop there, Haila? Do you honestly think he'll let it stop there?"

I avoided her eyes. "How many people were there in the studio this afternoon?"

"Counting Kirk and Harry and Mac and me, there were ten."

"Ten people! Julie, you can't follow those other nine people around to see that they aren't harmed, nobody could. Even the police wouldn't do it if you went to them. I know they wouldn't. They haven't time to bother with possible future crimes."

"I could warn everyone who was at Photo Arts today. I could tell them what happened to me."

"Yes. You should do that. And that's all."

"Then after that I must just sit tight and watch the obituaries in the daily papers for further developments?"

"What else, Julie? What could you do? What did you expect Jeff to do?"

"I don't know." Julie's sigh had the trouble of the world in it. "Just assure me, the way you have, that there's nothing to do, I guess."

"But, darling," I said helplessly, and then stopped. There wasn't anything to say, let alone anything to do. But ... what if Julie were right! If there's the merest suspicion that a killer is at work, you just can't sit and wait. If only Jeff were here! When he came it would be all right. And in the meantime I could at least make a pass at using my own brains. "Julie, tell me. What models did you use?"

"Miss Leonard at the Models Bureau sent three of them. The others, two young men, we got from John Powers. I don't think that you'd know any of them, Haila."

She was probably right. My days as a Powers Girl had ended long ago. I hadn't done any posing for years, not since I had started getting enough acting jobs to keep me alive.

"Well, there were Kirk and Mac and you," I said. "I know the three of you. And Mrs.. Isabelle Fleming, whom the social climber in me would give an arm to know. And this Harry Duerr and five models. Ten people who include one murderer and at least one victim."

"Yes." Julie's voice had gone limp.

"Did anything happen, Julie, while you were taking the picture, or before or after it?"

"Nothing unusual."

"Nothing at all? Think hard, Julie."

"Well ... well, maybe. Everyone was nervous. On edge a little. But that was because of Isabelle Fleming being there. You know, all that money and prestige and position in the same room. We were all terribly impressed, afraid we'd say 'ain't' or something. Except Kirk. He was his usual bounding self. Mac had to step on him or he would have playfully slapped Mrs. Fleming and asked her how she felt."

"But there was nothing strange at all? Nobody seemed upset, no tension between them?"

"Yes, there was tension," Julie said wearily. "Mac was acting like a double-crossed thunder cloud. He growled and fussed all the time."

"Our Mac MacCormick was acting like a ..." I repeated frowning.

Julie gave a tired nod. "You wouldn't know our Mac anymore. He's ..." She stopped herself quickly. "I was glad when the darn picture was over. But it wasn't because of Mac or any special tension. It was just Mrs. Fleming. And if I said it was anything else, I'd be overworking my imagination."

She walked restlessly over to the fireplace, holding her hands out to the flames. Without turning, she said, "Haila, let's stop. Let's pretend nothing happened and perhaps nothing will. I'm ... I'm so terribly tired."

"Will you have some brandy now, Julie? I think you could use it."

"All right. But just a little, please."

I was on my way to the corner where the liquor cabinet stood, when the phone rang. I answered it and then, with one hand smothering the mouthpiece, turned to Julie.

"It's for you," I said.

She pivoted to me and once again her face was flooded with alarm. Slowly, as if she were moving against her will, she crossed the room and lifted the telephone.

I could make nothing out of the ensuing conversation. Julie's answers were mostly monosyllabic and there was no visible change of her expression as she spoke or listened. When she hung up she placed the phone carefully back on the desk.

"Something went wrong with the picture we took this afternoon. We have to do it over again tonight. At nine." Her voice was calm, almost disinterested.

I said, hesitantly, "They're using the same models, Julie?"

"Yes. The same ones."

"And ... all of them can come?"

"Yes. Miss Leonard and John Powers were able to reach all of them for us. They'll all be at the studio at nine."

Relief poured over me like a needlepoint shower. "There! You see, Julie? It's all right, nothing's happened."

"Yes. Nothing's happened." She said it softly, between her teeth. She moved over to the window and pressed her forehead against the pane. Her fingers strummed upon the glass.

"Julie," I said, "don't you see. ..."

She wheeled around. "Oh, Haila, don't *you* see! Yes, it means that everyone's all right now, that nothing I was afraid of has happened yet. But we're going to take that Cottrell picture again. The same people in the same place. Now do you see what it really means? Our murderer's going to be given another chance!"

"Julie ..." I said.

She repeated, "Another chance. He muffed it this afternoon. Maybe tonight he'll do it more expertly."

Her dead calmness prodded me like a sharp fork. "Julie, you've got to go up there. Right away, now! You've got to tell them what happened to you this afternoon, you've got to warn them!"

"Yes." She was buttoning up the still-soggy coat, her eyes searching the blackness of the night outside. "They've been trying to get in touch with me for almost an hour. I'll have to hurry." She started for the door, stopped there and hesitated a second. "Could you ... could you come with me?"

"Julie, you're frightened, aren't you?"

"Yes. I wish Jeff were here."

I put my arm around her. "I'll try to find him, Julie, I'll get busy on the phone. Wait a few minutes and we can all go up to the studio together."

She glanced at the clock above the mantel and shook her head. "I can't. I've got to go now. I've got to tell them. ..."

"Yes, I know. All right, I'll find Jeff. And as soon as I do, I'll drag him up to Photo Arts."

"We've moved, you know. The Graylock Building. Thirty-seventh floor."

With a feeble attempt to jeer, I said, "The Graylock Building, Julie. A murder wouldn't have the bad taste to get itself committed there. It's much too swanky."

She didn't smile. Her head nodded a brief good-by at me as she slid out of the room, and then I heard the quick taps of her high heels as she hurried down the uncarpeted stairs. Without thinking, I started after her. Then I checked myself, went back into the apartment and began the laborious task of tracing Jeff. It was no go. I should have known that. When Jeff was job hunting he might be in Detroit interviewing Edsel Ford or offering his services to the delicatessen proprietor around the corner. I started pacing the floor, winding up at last before the splattered window and drumming on it with my knuckles as Julie Taylor had been doing a little while before.

The rain was driving down with a new violence. From somewhere in the west came the crack and then the muffled rumble of autumn thunder. The wind whistled in the narrow cavern of Ninety-third Street. And fifty blocks downtown, according to Julie, a murder had been arranged.

But there was nothing I could do about it. Jeff was the member of the Troy family who had a way with murders. All I did was tag along at his side. Without a side to tag along at I was worth less than nothing. There was no reason for me to stick my nose in and my neck out. I might better stay here and wait for Jeff.

Besides, I told myself emphatically, the whole thing was fantastic, that's what it was. There was nothing to it. Poor little Julie. She had been working too hard. Neither Mac nor Kirk realized that besides fulfilling her official title, which was stylist at Photo Arts, Julie was their errand boy, secretary, bookkeeper, office manager and bartender, all rolled into one.

Overworked and overtired, her imagination was playing tricks on her. It had happened often to me. After four weeks of grilling rehearsals, the excitement of an opening night, fear of those demoniacal critics and a case of jittering stage fright, some of my choicer thoughts would have terrified an ogre.

But on the other hand ...

On the wet pavements the Park Avenue traffic lights cast untidy reflections that slithered from red to shiny green. My mind kept changing with them. Stop ... Go ... Stop ... Go ...

I ran through the hall into the bedroom. While I struggled into an old raincoat I managed to scrawl a terse note to Jeff.

With an unpleasant shock I had realized that my reasoning, comforting as it proved to be, was no good. For no matter what pranks had been played on me, imagination didn't do such things to Julie Taylor.

I started for the Graylock Building.

## Chapter Two

AFTER SHAKING THE RAIN from my hat brim, I opened the door on which PHOTO ARTS was emblazoned in proud gold letters and found myself in an Office Beautiful of a room. Pale green walls and thick velvet green carpet. A labyrinth of indirect lighting spotted low chairs with vanilla upholstery, a divan so graceful that it seemed to grow out of the floor, a stunted table, long and narrow, with white-shaded lamps on either end. Just off center, a desk, a big smooth thing of blonde mahogany, held only a bunch of yellow and brown fall flowers in a squat pottery bowl.

Not much like the first desk that Photo Arts had given Julie Taylor. It had been an old scratched table that Mac MacCormick had picked up for a dollar-forty in one of those secondhand places. Without even a warning squeak, it would quietly crumple to the floor like a tired hound and Julie's old typewriter and all her paraphernalia would slide into her lap. Mac would shake his head reprovingly and say, "Please be a bit more tidy, Miss Taylor. Kindly nail your desk together and take a letter." Then he and Kirk would dictate some lengthy missive to their congressman, accusing his wife of unbecoming conduct, of using paint and powder and throwing her cigar butts in the municipal reservoirs.

In those good old days Photo Arts hadn't occupied the most desirable corner of the Graylock Building's thirty-seventh floor. Then it had been just one large musty room on East Thirty-third Street. They had done more business with the three gold ball corporations in those days than with any advertising agency. But it never seemed to bother them. They'd sit around in the big barnlike studio, Mac and Kirk and Julie, and whoever else happened to have dropped in, and drink cheap bourbon out of Dixie cups and talk. Net always intelligently, but always amusingly.

I was one of the models who called on them at regular intervals, not so much in the hope of getting a job, but because somehow while you were there you forgot that your rent was unpaid and that you weren't becoming America's greatest actress as quickly as you had dreamed. Many a time I had left that studio believing that my rent *was* paid and that I *was* America's greatest actress. And it hadn't always been the bourbon; it had been Mac and Kirk and Julie.

It was a mystery how they managed. They'd pawn their cameras to pay their models and then borrow back the pay to redeem the cameras. And somehow they kept that cycle from breaking down.

But all that had been before Erika had come along. I was there the day that Kirk had proudly introduced Erika to Mac and I had seen that romance begin with the moment Mac and Erika shook hands. It was wanting to marry Erika that had made Mac settle down and try to amount to something. And from the looks of the reception room he had.

Stepping across a long narrow corridor, off which, no doubt, were the dressing rooms, darkrooms, drying rooms and all the other rooms needed to take a picture, I pushed through double doors into the large, brilliantly lighted studio.

Despite the foreboding Julie had planted in my mind it seemed to me like any other prospering picture mill. Photographic equipment, cameras and lights were everywhere. There were piles of props, ranging from a horse-hair sofa and a perambulator of 1910 vintage to a slick drugstore fountain, a streamlined kitchen sink and a surfboard. In the center the set, a magnificent dining room, was semi-encircled by more cameras and more lights. In the corner stood the most anachronistic note in all that modern science; Julie's old battered desk and the decrepit paper cup container that the boys must have sentimentally lugged to their new cathedral.

From somewhere out of all the confusion of inanimate objects and the restlessness of waiting models, popped Kirk Findlay. As he stormed across the studio toward me I realized how good it would have been, under other circumstances, to be back with this big oaf and his pal, Mac.

"Haila Rogers!" Kirk's hand squashed mine tenderly.

"Haila Troy," I corrected him smugly.

"That's right. Have you seen Jeff since the wedding?"

"Not very clearly. Where's Julie, Kirk?"

"Around." Kirk's rust-red hair still stood on end and everything about him still sparkled the way it always had, his eyes, his teeth, even his ears. "Look, Haila, you were in a show! We saw it. Mac and Erika and Julie and I."

I shook my head. "Not that many seats were sold, Kirk."

"We all sat in the same seat."

From Kirk's state of mind it didn't seem possible that Julie had told him and Mac about her afternoon's adventure. Or perhaps she had and they, as she had feared, had laughed it off. But my first step, I decided, would be to confer with Julie.

"Haila!"

Mac was advancing upon me and I wouldn't have traded his yelp of delight for a Nobel Prize. He pumped my arm so dry it practically began to flake.

"We've missed you, Haila," he said. "Sorely. Where's Jeff?"

"I can't be sure, but I think he's looking for a job."

"A job for you?"

"For himself," I boasted.

"You've ruined him already, Haila."

"I didn't know Jeff lost his job," Kirk said. "That's tough. Right after you got married."

"Oh, no. Right before we got married. But he didn't tell me until afterwards so that I wouldn't worry. He saved that news for our honeymoon. That's how thoughtful he is. Dear Jeff."

"Did that damn advertising company fire him?" Mac asked.

"Yes. And he told me he was on a vacation."

Kirk grinned. "Why'd they give him the gate?"

"He told the boss that advertising was a Lorelei to the poor man's purse. That people bought radios when they should buy bread. His boss didn't have a bread account so he fired Jeff."

Mac shouted with laughter, not sounding or looking a bit like the double-crossed thundercloud Julie claimed he had been imitating of late. If Mac resembled anything celestial it was a cirrus, not a thundercloud. His wonderful homely face still wore that gleeful expression that made female models offer to pose for less than the minimum five dollars. It was worth it just to be within range of his small-boy eyes that crinkled at the corners when he smiled. At that moment I finally realized who Mac MacCormick really was. He was Huck Finn with shoes on.

"Kirk," he was saying, "let's impress some people by introducing Haila to them."

They each took me by an arm and dragged me gently across the studio. If I was to be forcibly detained from finding Julie and getting on with our crime prevention program, I was determined at least to do some ground work on these people I was about to meet. My first stop was May Ralston, a healthy blonde animal who shot a vermilion tipped glad hand in my direction and then went back to looking for pictures of herself in a current magazine. She could hardly have been Julie's would-be murderer. I doubted if those pouting lips could form a word as long as "chloroform" distinctly enough for a drug clerk to understand. Nor could it have been either of the next two people to whom I was introduced. Foul thoughts of violent death surely never lurked behind the clear blue eyes and typical American Young Man faces of Jim Snyder and Lee Kenyon.

Neither of them broke my record of never having met a man who admitted that posing was his career. Kenyon was quick to assure me that he simply used modeling to supplement his professional dancing. Jim Snyder used it to supplement his amateur golf.

Over the dancer's well-padded shoulder I suddenly saw Julie. She was standing in the set beside the dining table. Her hands were busily moving silverware and china. But her eyes were on me; she had been waiting for my attention. After a glance to see that no one was noticing, she slowly shook her head and placed a finger across her lips. Then, as if to squelch any attempt on my part to go to her, she turned and left the studio.

So she hadn't told Kirk or Mac! And I wasn't to tell them either. But why? What had happened?

My groping for answers to those questions was interrupted by my two escorts. They dragged me away from Kenyon and Snyder toward a man who stood quietly in back of Julie's old desk. He looked so shy that for a moment I thought he was going to hide behind the desk instead of stepping in front of it, as he finally did.

"Haila," Mac said, "this is Harry Duerr."

"So you're Haila," Harry said. "I've heard about you. Your name and the good old days are synonymous around here." His voice was as gentle as his gray eyes. He was about thirty, very tall and awkward because of his height. I liked him immediately. He was a relief after the masculine glamour I had just been subjected to by Kenyon and Snyder. But as I saw May Ralston staring at Harry I thought that maybe I wasn't the only gal who could do without glamour in a man.

Then I met Robert Yorke. "I've been very impatiently waiting my turn," he said, "to meet this beautiful young lady."

I could've kicked myself; I simpered.

"This is Haila Troy, ex-Rogers," Kirk said. "She's in the theater, too, Yorke."

"Are you in the theater, Mr. Yorke?" I asked. It was a silly question. Everything about him suggested an actor. In fact, suggested a modern Francis X. Bushman. And Mr.. Yorke was probably posing at the moment instead of acting because he was too handsome to be believed. The trend nowadays is toward more realistic male attractiveness. Spencer Tracy.

For a second Yorke's Prussian blue eyes and long lashes, his sleekly waving black hair, his straight nose and beguiling smile almost made me forget what had brought me to Photo Arts. I had to see Julie immediately.

Murmuring excuses, I slipped from between Kirk and Mac and started in the direction Julie had taken. When Mac tried to delay me, I put my foot down. "Mac! I really have to see Julie! Girl stuff!" That stopped him.

A flash of burnt-orange smock that Julie was wearing over her brown skirt attracted me into the reception room. At my entrance Julie looked up with a start from the list she was studying. She went quickly to the door that I had come through and closed it.

"Julie!" I said, "what's happened?"

She answered me in a low voice. "What about Jeff?"

"I couldn't locate him, but I left a note ..."

"Not so loud, Haila, please ..."

"Julie, you haven't told Mac and Kirk!"

"No."

"I thought not. But, Julie, you've got to. Immediately!"

"No. Listen, Haila, I was all wrong about this afternoon. I made a mistake." She rushed on, attempting to smother my exclamation of surprise. "Yes, Haila, believe me! It was just my nerves; I was making a mountain out of a molehill. It was silly of me. ..."

"Julie," I cut in, "you don't have nerves and you aren't one to inflate molehills. Something must have happened to make you change your mind about this afternoon. Tell me what, Julie."

"I can't. It involves an explanation that ... an explanation that I can't give you. You or anyone else. But," she added hastily, "it has nothing to do with murder, nothing at all."

"I still think you should tell Mac and Kirk ..."

"No!" Julie was folding the slip of paper over and over again, creasing it with her nails. "Not now. After the picture's been taken, I'll tell them. I can't now."

"But Julie ..."

"Haila!" She raised her eyes to mine and they were very candid. "Haila, I'll tell you this. The picture we're taking tonight means more to Mac than just crashing the big time. It means everything. It's got to be good, perfect. And it has to be delivered to the agency tomorrow morning. Don't you see ... if I burst out with all that stuff about this afternoon, Mac would be too upset to do his best? Why, Mrs.. Fleming might even refuse to pose and ..."

"Julie, no picture can be more important than preventing a crime!"

"Haila!" Julie's look at me made me ashamed of myself. "Do you think that if I thought there was the slightest chance of anything happening, I would stand quietly by and ... and let it happen?"

"Of course not. I'm sorry. But I wish you'd tell me what all this is about."

"Not just now. And you mustn't say a word to Mac or to Kirk. Or anyone. Promise me, Haila, please!"

"All right, Julie, you know best. I promise, but ..."

The door from the outside hall was pushed open by a woman of about sixty-five, whose close-cropped gray hair, thin nose and narrow light green eyes were displayed with proper regularity on the society pages of almost every newspaper in the United States.

I didn't need Julie's "Good evening, Mrs. Fleming," to tell me who she was.

Isabelle Fleming nodded briefly and walked quickly through the reception room toward the studio. She seemed displeased. Julie followed her and I, without the slightest twinge of conscience for my curiosity, followed Julie.

"Ralph!" Mrs. Fleming summoned Mac to her in a voice that was soft and controlled but it rang through the high-ceilinged room with surprising clarity. "Ralph, what's the matter? Why are we taking this picture over again?"

Mac hesitated. "I'm sorry, Mrs. Fleming. There was a slipup this afternoon ... an oversight."

"It was my fault," Kirk said quickly.

"No, it was just one of those things. My fault more than yours, Kirk, if it was anyone's."

"It's darn nice of you to take the blame," Kirk said mischievously.

"I'm not taking the blame!" Mac said hastily. "It's just ... just one of those things," he finished lamely.

With elaborate patience, Isabelle Fleming asked, "What is one of those things?"

"The plates have been mislaid." Mac's face turned crimson.

I almost gasped aloud. In my preoccupation with more dire things I had never thought to ask why the picture was being retaken. If I had thought about it, I should have imagined that the lighting had been wrong or that a model had been badly posed. Such an incredible occurrence as the plates having been lost would never have entered my head. For no reason that I could name the uneasiness that Julie had succeeded in quelling arose within me again.

Mrs. Fleming seemed to have decided to make the best of it. With one sweeping glance she looked over all the models who had drawn a little closer so as not to miss a word.

"I see you're ready," she said. "I'll go and dress."

Mac, with Julie assisting, escorted Erika MacCormick's aunt to her dressing room. I went to Kirk.

"How in heaven's name," I asked him, "could you mislay those plates?"

Kirk grinned a shamefaced grin. "Some dopey things have happened at

Photo Arts, but in all the years this one wins. Mac claims he left them on the darkroom shelf before he went home. They're probably some place right under our noses, but we couldn't take a chance. The picture's due in the morning. I bet as soon as we finish tonight we'll find those plates. You know."

"That's usually what happens. Poor Mac! All this extra expense ... the models and ..." I looked around the studio. "I thought Julie said there were five models, besides Mrs. Fleming."

"Yeah, five," Kirk said. "I'd like to know where the hell the fifth one is!" He glanced at his watch. "Mrs. Fleming will be raising roofs if we don't get under way."

"Who's missing?"

"A woman named Madge Lawrence. Why?"

"Is she ... usually late?"

Kirk frowned. "No, she's very conscientious. I've never known her to be five minutes late, let alone a half-hour as she is now."

Julie came swinging briskly into the studio. "Oh, Kirk, Mac wants to see you."

"Pardon, Haila. Business," Kirk said.

Julie passed me without as much as a glance in my direction. I followed her to the dining room table where she was checking last minute details.

"Julie," I said, "one of the models is missing."

"Yes," she answered impatiently, "Madge Lawrence. I've been trying to locate her, but the Models Bureau is closed and Madge doesn't seem to have a phone."

"Perhaps, Julie, something happened to Madge Lawrence."

Her head jerked up sharply; there was anger in her eyes. "Haila! Stop being silly! I told you there isn't going to ... I swear everything's all right! Sorry to disappoint you. ..." She halted abruptly. Then she put her hand on my arm and said softly, "Haila, forgive me but, please, go home. Go home, Haila!"

She moved to the other end of the table. She was right; I should go home. Since she was so confident that nothing was wrong it was foolish and presumptuous of me to concern myself. And certainly there was no indication of any impending evil here. Mac and Kirk were being their usual jubilant selves all over the place, the models were acting the way all the models I had ever known acted. The mere thought that there might be a murder on the premises was preposterous. One dignified but harmless dowager, one sometime matinee idol, two good-looking young men who wouldn't be so uncharming as to kill and a peroxided Goldilocks. And a shy, disarming set-builder named Harry. Home, Haila.

I was buckling my coat when Mac and Kirk converged upon me and began a critical survey of my face and its environs.

"Is this the right end, Mac?" Kirk asked.

"Well, that's a nose, isn't it?"

"Yeah, I'm afraid it is. But we could shoot from the back of her head."

"Does her head have a back, Kirk?"

"What is this?" I yelped.

"We're using you instead of Madge. We can't wait any longer."

"Oh, no!" Julie had convinced me that this was no place for me.

"We're in a jam, Haila. Help us out." Mac was serious.

I said, groping for an excuse, "But look at me! My sweater and skirt would scarcely do for a formal dinner party!"

"Pose stripped!" Kirk said. "They can change the copy. 'Mrs. Isabelle Fleming, of New York, Aiken and Newport, was not embarrassed when her unadorned sister popped in unexpectedly, for her guests couldn't take their eyes off her complete set of Cottrell Silver…' "

Mac snapped short his chuckle. "Don't, Kirk, we haven't time. I'll find something for you to wear, Haila."

He found me something to wear. When he held it out toward me, even Kirk was doubtful.

"A portiere!" he said. "No, Mac, she'll look like a door."

"Not if she stands still and doesn't swing."

"Mac," I insisted, "it *is* a portiere!"

"You can drape it around your shoulders some way, Haila," Mac pleaded. "We'll pose you so just your head, some beautiful bare shoulder and an inch of velvet will show. The first dressing room to the right. For a pal, Haila."

With no good thoughts for Photo Arts or any of its inhabitants, I stood in front of a full-length mirror and pulled my sweater off over my head. Then, wriggling out of my slip straps, I started draping. The effect I finally achieved was something that reminded me of a dress my grandmother had once taken back to exchange for a pair of water wings.

Ashamed to walk unescorted into the studio, I sank into a chair before the mirror. Was this I, and if it were, what was I doing here? As I stared at my weird reflection, my mind went racing back to the time of Julie's entrance into my apartment and then came slowly forward.

If only I knew what Julie knew. If only I could be as sure as Julie that her experience in the darkroom had no ominous meaning.

But here I was in Photo Arts, about to substitute for a missing model. And if, by any chance, Madge Lawrence had been the intended victim that afternoon and here I was in her place …

There were limits to what I'd go through for my pal, Mac.

I heard Kirk Findlay in the studio shouting at the top of his voice. "Hey, Haila! C'mon!"

## Chapter Three

THE ROAR OF HILARITY that greeted my entrance into the studio shocked, for the moment, all thoughts of sudden death from my mind. Everybody was assembled about the dining room table, and everybody, including Mrs. Isabelle Fleming, was delighted with the sight of me. As for me, I was perfectly willing to look like something a thoughtless wave had washed up if it could provoke such universal happiness.

I noticed then that I had been wrong; the mirth was not unanimous. Julie Taylor was not amused.

"Everyone's ready, Mac," she said. Her tone was brisk and businesslike, her eyes were unsmiling. "Do you want the same positions we had this afternoon?"

"Yeah. Places, please, folks."

The group began to move. Robert Yorke seated himself in the chair at Mrs. Fleming's right, Lee Kenyon in the one at her left. May Ralston bounced into the place beside Kenyon and Jim Snyder moved to the foot of the table. I dropped into the one vacant chair. And for the first time I really looked at the dining table.

Mrs. Isabelle Fleming might be billed as the star of this picture, but Cottrell Silverware was in a fine position to steal it from her. The table was literally crammed with it. At each place seven pieces gleamed, and the flower bowl in the center was unmistakably Cottrell. Spread around it in profusion were all the odd pieces in the Cottrell cast; a salad fork, two serving spoons, a gravy ladle and, in front of Mrs. Fleming, an elaborately scrolled carving set. My stomach quailed at the mere thought of the menu that would require all that silver. The Cottrell company was making Isabelle Fleming a more exhibitionistic than discriminating hostess.

Mac was checking the camera, Kirk the lights. Julie, sliding around the table behind our chairs, put last-minute touches on the flowers and silver. Harry, unnecessarily, was testing the braces on the set.

"Are we eating?" I asked.

"No," Mac said. "It's that moment before you start. You're all sitting there admiring the silverware. One of you has remarked on its beauty and your hostess is astounding you by explaining that it is very, very economical, too. See?"

"I get it."

"You're all looking at her." We looked, and Mrs. Fleming smiled graciously at us, the perfect hostess. "Lee, drop your left hand a bit. There, that's it. A little more smile, Haila. And Jim, you'll have to duck your head some. Fine. No, wait a minute. May! Swing your head toward Mrs. Fleming more." He laughed at May's dirty look. "I know it's away from the camera. Maybe we can get you to Hollywood the next time we use you."

"Lights okay?" Kirk asked.

"Fine." Mac looked at us over the camera, squinting his eyes. "All right, now. Pretend you aren't having your picture taken."

"Pretend you're people," Kirk added.

I held my pose while the camera clicked. The moment that Mac emerged from behind it I began tinkering with the million pins that were holding me together. I could be out of this thing and this place in a jiffy.

"We'll shoot again in ten minutes. Remember your positions."

"Shoot again!" I said. "Was that just for fun?"

Mac smiled at me with great tolerance. "Color's come in since you went out, Haila. You know, color?"

"I've heard."

"We do a test negative in black and white before we do it in color. It says so in a book I have. I'll lend it to you sometime." He was removing the plate from the camera, handing it to Kirk. "After Kirk develops this black and white, we check it and then shoot again for keeps. Hurry them, will you, buddy? I want to do some toning down on these flowers."

Kirk scooted for the darkroom, and the models, with one accord, got up from the table and moved carefully out of the set. Mac busied himself at the table, Julie and Harry Duerr at the desk. Mrs. Isabelle Fleming, without a word to anyone, started for her dressing room. Robert Yorke was in front of a wall mirror, rearranging his tie. In the far corner the two tall young men were having a smoke with May Ralston. That, I decided, seemed to be the most harmless group. I drifted over to it.

"Cigarette?" Jim Snyder asked me.

"Thanks, I need one. There aren't any pockets in this drapery."

Lee Kenyon flicked his lighter on for me and while I was getting my tobacco burning I could see May Ralston sizing me up.

"You're on the stage, huh?" she finally said.

"Now and then," I admitted.

"You think I could get on?"

"Ain't you on?" Lee Kenyon kidded.

"I used to do solo stuff. Until one night my father was at the same banquet. But the stage don't really interest me. I'm interested strictly in Hollywood."

Kenyon opened his mouth and then closed it quickly as Mrs. Fleming, returning from her dressing room, approached us. She passed without stopping. Lee Kenyon half turned to her.

"Lovely evening, Mrs. Fleming."

His tone startled me. I had never heard so much rank impudence in four ordinary, innocent words. He sidestepped as he spoke so that he could look directly into the woman's eyes, and there was scorn in his gaze, and laughing derision. I waited tremulously for Isabelle Fleming's reaction.

She said evenly, without glancing at him, "Yes, isn't it?"

"And how is your charming niece?"

"Better now, I'm sure."

Her words drifted back to us from the other side of the room where she stopped beside Julie at her desk. She hadn't so much as paused throughout the conversation; she hadn't wasted a glance in his direction.

"What the devil, Lee!" Jim Snyder exploded. "I suppose you think that was funny!"

"It amused me."

"What have you got against her?" May asked with interest. "Just because she's rich?"

"I'll tell you," Snyder said maliciously. "He turned this job down flat when he first heard about it. Then, when he found that Isabelle Fleming was posing for the picture, he jumped at it. But his social climbing didn't work out very well this afternoon and now he's sore."

"I ignored her this afternoon," Kenyon said loftily.

"Yeah, you missed your chance."

Kenyon smiled pityingly at the other man. "Compared to you as a social climber, I'm still on all fours. You and your golf! You don't like golf, you like country clubs. You've never earned an honest cent in your life."

"Dancing in that dive of yours is honest money, I suppose!"

May's interest was revived. "You dance, huh? What do you do? I mean, what type? Rumba?

Snyder laughed. "No. He taps while the girls change for their next number."

"Yeah? Where at?"

Again it was Snyder who answered. "At the Barrel Room. The Barrel Room, located on Greenwich Village's swanky Sullivan Street!"

Kenyon was smiling now, but his voice was unpleasant and his eyes had narrowed. "My biographer! At the moment I dance at a Village hot spot. But at some moment soon I'll be doing things you never thought possible at

Carnegie Hall. Then, later, I'll consider an engagement at the Rainbow Room. It's inevitable. Just like Jim's working himself up to being a caddy."

Jim's face flushed red with quick anger, but before he could reply I excused myself from the charming group and retreated to my dressing room. It hadn't been such a harmless little circle as I had imagined. I would be safer, I decided, and happier by myself.

In my dressing room the minutes lagged by on slow ticks. I added more pins and more prayers to my portiere and tried to amuse myself by leafing through a models catalogue. It was while I was studying a whole page of Madge Lawrence pictures, Madge in evening gown, in riding habit and in smart tailored suit, that I heard Julie calling places from the studio.

A few minutes later the camera had clicked again and the picture was really over and done with. Everyone heaved a sigh of relief, but mine topped them all. It was the first time I had felt that this assembled company could actually disperse without any of it getting hurt. With one movement the models rose from the table.

Julie was shouting above the clamor of people making for their dressing rooms.

"I'll have your money ready for you by the time you're dressed, everybody! Haila!" I went over to her. "Haila, will you sign a release? The others signed theirs this afternoon."

"Sure." I followed her to the desk.

She gave a little self-conscious laugh as she opened a drawer. "I wouldn't be surprised if you'd like to sue us when you see this picture in the *American* or the *Cosmo*," she said conversationally. "In that rig, I mean."

"I wouldn't be surprised, either. So I'd better sign away that chance."

I took the pen she offered me and scratched my signature on the dotted line. When I raised my head, Mac was standing at my side.

"Thanks, Haila, for everything."

"Don't, Mac. In a minute you'll have me thinking I really did something for you."

"You did. I wish I could do something for you."

I looked at him standing there, his hands thrust deep into his slacks pockets, the old MacCormick grin plastered all over his face, and then I looked at Julie. She was studiously ignoring us both, fussing ineffectually with the papers on her desk. I wondered if she could be thinking about the description of Mac that she had given me today. "You wouldn't know him anymore" was what she had said.

I said wickedly, still with an eye on Julie Taylor, "You can, Mac. You can turn me one of those cartwheels you used to do all over town."

"Haila, I've aged since then! I'm an adult now."

"Please, Mac! Just a few for my nostalgia."

The Graylock Building seemed to shiver on its foundation as the ever-obliging Mac MacCormick's seventh cartwheel landed him in the corridor outside the studio door. I turned back to Julie.

"Julie, I don't think Mac has changed so much. In fact, he turns a happier cartwheel than ever."

She raised her eyes to mine and then dropped them quickly. I could see the pinkish flush that suffused her face creep up toward the widow's peak that her brown hair made on her smoothly curved forehead.

"I've got to count money, Haila. The wolves will be back any minute now."

She was already piling bills in little stacks on the desktop, ostentatiously oblivious of anything else. Shrugging helplessly, I left her.

I was halfway into my dressing room before I noticed the woman bent over a suitcase as she unsnapped its catch. She was tall and very slender with thick murky black hair and eyes that contrasted startlingly with the milky whiteness of her skin. Madge Lawrence's exoticism was even more pronounced in person that it had been in her pictures.

"Excuse me," I said, "I ..."

She straightened up, pulling an exquisite evening gown of filmy black chiffon out of the suitcase. She draped it carefully over a chair back.

"Come in," she said. "I'll be ready in a second." With one hand she was pulling off the incredibly small hunter green hat she wore, the other worked at the long line of buttons on her hunter green jacket. Her voice was deep and slightly husky. "Are they ready to shoot yet?"

"They've finished the picture," I said.

She frowned, and the little lines that appeared on her face changed it instantly from striking to strange.

"They've finished it! But how could they without me?"

"I took your place." I gestured awkwardly at my drapery. "We fixed up a sort of costume."

"I see."

"I'm awfully sorry. They waited for you ..."

"I ... I understood that the call was for ten o'clock."

"No, nine."

Her even white teeth caught at her lip and for a moment she looked angry. Then she picked up the chiffon gown and began to repack it. I stood staring at her, fascinated for some unknown reason, until she turned with a cold questioning look toward me. I backed up into a corner and changed hurriedly into my sweater. Scooping up my hat and purse, I mumbled goodnight to Miss Lawrence and ran out.

It was just as I passed the darkroom door that I heard Mac's voice. I don't know why I stopped, my feet glued to that spot on the floor and my ears buzzing with an effort to hear. The words that I had caught were ordinary enough. But there was something in Mac's tone, a sharp, ominous tenseness, that held me there.

"Kirk!" I heard him say. "Look! Here in the wastebasket!"

Quick footsteps crossed the darkroom floor, then Kirk's voice, sharp, like Mac's, and shocked, too.

"What the hell! Our plates! The pictures we took this afternoon."

"Yes." The one word was spoken grimly. "No wonder we couldn't find them."

There was a clinking sound of broken glass, then Kirk's incredulous voice. "They've been smashed to pieces!"

"They couldn't have fallen off that shelf ..."

"Listen, Mac, those plates weren't broken accidentally, then hidden here. They were smashed deliberately with a hammer. That's the only way you can do a job like this ... they're in smithereens!"

"Yeah, I've dropped plates accidentally and they didn't break ..."

I didn't wait to hear anymore. I had to find Julie; she was wrong! The plates had not been mislaid, they had been deliberately smashed. Why? The answer to that word screamed its warning.

Julie was at the dining table, just starting to pack the silverware in a plush lined case. I tried to keep my voice low and steady.

"Julie," I said, "the plates ... the pictures you took this afternoon. They weren't lost. They were deliberately smashed to bits!"

She looked up at me and it shocked me more that her eyes were calm than if they had been wild and full of the terror I was feeling.

Slowly, she said, "I know."

"You know!"

"I saw the pieces in the wastebasket in the darkroom when I came in tonight. I don't know who did it. Nor why."

I put my hand out and grasped her shoulder. I shook her hard. Anything to get Julie Taylor out of this trance, to make her see what was happening around us.

"Julie, don't you see what this means! It means you were right about this afternoon. That person in the darkroom broke the plates so that tonight you all would be here in the studio again. We've got to tell them now, Kirk and Mac. To warn them!"

"Haila, don't be silly ..."

"I'll tell them myself, I'll ..."

Too swiftly for me to realize what was happening she had shrugged her shoulder out of my grip and her hand shot out to catch my wrist. The nails bit into my skin like jagged teeth. But her voice was cold and steady.

"You won't say a word about this afternoon. You won't mention it to anyone. I won't let you."

Her hand tightened as she spoke. Two little curved lines on either side of her mouth gave her face an almost ugly look. Her eyes glittered as she stared at me with an unspoken threat.

I wrenched my arm free with a sudden jerk. There were bright red dents where she had clenched it.

I said, "I'm going to tell them. Now!"

"Haila!" Her command was flat and sullen. "All right, you win. Listen, Haila!" She raised her head defiantly. "I smashed those plates."

"You ... you smashed them ..."

"Yes. Now you know. Now, let me alone. Forget about it."

She turned again to the silver. Viciously she continued storing it away. Then suddenly she dropped a fork upon the table. With a smothered exclamation she rushed from the studio.

I was too shocked, too bewildered, to think any more, to even try to reason. Absently, I began putting silver spoons in their grooves, then a fork or two and a butter knife.

Then I stopped. I was tired. None of this was my business. Why wasn't I home being a good and happy wife, toiling and moiling over a hot stove? Why wasn't I trying out new recipes, taking spots out of neckties, making myself beautiful for my husband. ...

"Julie!"

It was Kirk's voice, shouting wildly. He flashed across the studio doorway, running down the corridor. I heard a door slam, then another, then Mac's voice, shouting too. I saw the streak of May's golden head as she raced down the hall.

They were standing there outside a dressing room door, Mac and Kirk and May, and others, and they were bending over the limp little form huddled on the floor.

I saw Mac push Kirk aside and raise Julie's head. After a moment her eyelids fluttered and then, slowly, she looked around the circle of anxious faces, from one to the other. She turned her head toward the door and a whimpering sound broke from her lips.

Kirk kicked open the door.

Mrs. Isabelle Fleming sat before her makeup table, her eyes focused into the mirror at a point above her head. Her mouth was slightly open in a grimace. Her hands were twisted strangely at her throat.

I saw all that in the glass. The eyes, the mouth, the hands.

Then I saw that Isabelle Fleming was sitting there, erect and somehow dignified, with the Cottrell Silver carving knife sticking like a long wicked finger out of the back of her neck.

## Chapter Four

THE STUDIO HAD GROWN dismally cold by two o'clock when we had arranged ourselves, upon request, to face the two detectives who sat at Julie's old desk.

For the first time in many hours there was silence on the thirty-seventh floor of the Graylock Building. The huge skyscraper had returned to its nightly slumber, to be groomed in its sleep by the battalion of scrubwomen whose pride in their eighty-seven-story charge had suddenly been increased by the murder of Mrs. Isabelle Fleming, society millionairess. Only the sound of occasional footsteps and the opening and closing of elevator doors broke through the sepulchral quiet.

That quiet rang more deafeningly and ominously in our ears than all the clanging uproar that had such a little while ago abruptly ceased.

Before there had been an endless parade of men; the place had teemed and bristled with them. The procession had started with the officers from the first prowl car to reach the scene and the detectives from the homicide squad. Then came the special investigators from the district attorney's office, technicians from the laboratories, the medical examiner and his assistants, photographers and, finally, the police stenographers, those vultures whose darting pencils gobbled up the words that would later be flung back in our faces.

Before there had been noise. Sirens wailing in the streets below. Footsteps that shuffled and ran and stamped. Telephones shrieking the instant that their receivers had been dropped back into their cradles. Voices, both strange and familiar, barking and whispering and droning. Questions and answers, many more of the first than of the second.

There had been movement, some businesslike and quick, some almost hysterical. The medical examiner bending over Isabelle Fleming with grim certainty. Cameras swallowing up her rigid form. White-clad men carrying a white-covered body away. Fingerprint men pressing our hands on squares of paper. The Cottrell Silver carving knife being carefully, almost tenderly wrapped and carted off. And drooping, frightened people reenacting what had happened. Where they had been and when. What they had seen and heard. Murder-shocked people trying frantically to remember trivial things that were now important because Isabelle Fleming was dead and because one of us had killed her.

All that had been confused and urgent; now it was methodically quiet. It should have been a relief to us, a respite. It should have been an interlude in which we might pull ourselves together, a chance to stop feeling and start thinking clearly, so that each of us could prove his innocence and go home to bed. It should have been all of that.

It wasn't.

It was as though what had gone before had been a prologue, merely a buildup, for what was now to come. Perhaps the cold efficiency with which the two detectives were figuratively rolling up their sleeves made us sense that. Perhaps the tenseness of our own tired bodies. Or it might have been just the deadly quiet of the studio.

Then there was still another thing that in my mind foreboded trouble. Julie had not yet told the police of what had happened to her that afternoon in the darkroom. And I, cognizant of her experience, was an accessory to the crime of withholding evidence. I comforted myself with the reasoning that it was up to Julie to do the talking. But if she continued to refuse, eventually I would have to take it upon myself.

The two men at the desk remained motionless, their heads bent over piles of notes, scribbled ones that they had made, stenographers' notes already typed.

One detective, a Lieutenant Wyatt, was short and heavy, with India-ink black eyes and close cropped black hair. He was a cop who had obviously worked his way up from a beat and was fighting every minute to keep on working up. There could be little doubt in his mind that some day soon he would be New York's Commissioner of Police. His assistant, Lockhart, was pink and plump. His rufous scalp shown through the wispy thinness of his blond hair and his mild blue eyes peered out of gold-rimmed bifocals.

Lieutenant Wyatt leaned forward and spoke, so suddenly that had we not all been steeled by endless waiting we would have leaped at the mere sound of his voice.

"The facts!" he announced, tapping rhythmically on the desk with a pencil. "Isabelle Fleming was stabbed to death with a silver carving knife. It entered her body through the back of her neck and severed her spinal cord. She died instantly and apparently without a sound. That was approximately at twenty minutes after ten.

"The knife has been identified as the one which lay on the table over there for a picture you took. It was on that table while you shot ..." he paused to consult his notes, "the test negative, and it was there when you took the final picture. Therefore, between that final shot and Miss Julie Taylor's discovery of the body, which seems to have been only a few minutes after the murder, that knife was removed from the table, carried out of this studio and into the victim's dressing room where it was shoved through her neck.

"Each of you has denied, of course, that you either carried or used that knife. No one saw anyone else carry or use it. You say that there was nobody in this place before, during or immediately following the murder except those present now. Obviously then, one of you here did carry that knife and did use it." He referred again to his notes. "Ralph MacCormick, Kirk Findlay, Julie Taylor, Harry Duerr, Lee Kenyon, James Snyder, May Ralston, Haila Troy, Robert Yorke and Madge Lawrence. Ten of you. And one of you took the knife and killed Isabelle Fleming with it. One out of ten. This shouldn't be a hard case to solve. Should it, Lockhart?"

"No. But it will be," said his assistant.

"Well, we'll do our best. So all of you can stop worrying right now. All but one of you, that is. And that one's worries will soon be over." He smiled encouragingly at us all. "All right, now we'll get back to business. When that knife was used as a weapon, it was behind a closed door that barred all spectators. But when it was removed from that table it was in the middle of this large room, and Miss Taylor was sitting at this desk where Lockhart and I are now. It seems that it would be more of a task for our killer to have got hold of the knife than to have used it. So we'll work on that track for a while.

"Unfortunately, Miss Taylor can't help us much. She can alibi only one person: Haila Troy. She watched Mrs. Troy walk away from the table and saw her leave the room. And Mrs. Troy did *not* take the knife away with her."

I hoped my sigh of relief wasn't as audible as it sounded to me. Good old Julie Taylor! I cast her a grateful glance but she wasn't looking at me. Her eyes were fixed steadily on the detective's face.

Wyatt was going on. "So then. Miss Taylor saw others of you come in and go out of the studio. She was busy at her desk; she didn't pay any special attention to what you did. She didn't see any of you touch the knife; on the other hand she isn't able to swear that any of the people she saw in this room did *not* take the knife. So we'll give each of you a chance to prove for yourself that you didn't take it. That's being fair, isn't it, Lockhart?"

"More than fair," Lockhart said stoutly.

"You let me know if I do anything unfair."

"Sure. After all, this murderer is an American citizen."

"All right, we'll begin."

He drew a deep breath; we let ours out. Not one of us had budged during his speech. Wyatt looked at us for a long quiet minute, then, tapping his pencil again, went on.

"Mr. Kenyon!"

Lee jumped to his feet. "Yes?"

"You can sit down. We'll keep this informal." Wyatt waited until Lee, with a foolish grin, had reseated himself. "Mr. Kenyon, you were the last to leave the table after the final shot."

"Yes."

"The other models had gone to their dressing rooms. They say. Findlay had taken the plates into the darkroom. MacCormick was still at the camera, his back to the table. Mrs. Troy was at this desk with Miss Taylor, signing a release. You could have taken the knife then, Kenyon. No one would have seen you do it, if you were careful."

Lee Kenyon's perfect teeth gleamed as he smiled. I had seen that smile before in magazines. He said, "Yes, I suppose I could have taken it. Easily. But I didn't."

"Why?"

"Why!" His surprise was genuine. "I didn't want it. I didn't need it. I wasn't going to kill anybody! What reason did I have to kill Mrs. Fleming?"

"We're not going into motive just yet," Wyatt said. He turned to his assistant. "Put a little star after Kenyon's name, Lockhart. He could have taken the knife."

Lee was on his feet again, filled with acid protests, but Wyatt waved him aside and turned his attention to Robert Yorke.

"Now, Mr. Yorke, you came back into the studio after the final shot. And you went back to the table."

Yorke leaned forward in his chair. His attitude was one of interest rather than strain.

"Yes, I did. I ... I had forgotten my cigarette case. I came back for it."

"You'd left it on the table?" A note of eagerness had crept into the detective's voice.

"No, not on the table. In fact, I hadn't left it there at all. I found it later in my dress suit."

"Then you made that trip to the table for nothing?"

"Yes. It turned out that I had. Stupid of me." Yorke smiled with charming frankness and gestured meaninglessly.

"A star for Mr. Yorke, Lockhart."

"He's got one."

The smile and the charm dropped from Yorke at once. "I tell you I didn't take that knife! I can prove it to you!"

"Not by Miss Taylor, you can't. She has testified that she barely glanced at you while you were in here."

"I don't need Miss Taylor to prove it."

"Go ahead, do it in your own way, Mr. Yorke. We want everybody but one of you to prove he didn't take it."

The actor turned to May Ralston. "As I was leaving the studio I passed Miss Ralston. She was just coming in. Miss Ralston, tell them the truth. Was I in possession of that knife?"

May smirked. "Well, you weren't wearing it in your lapel. But he might have had it tucked in his pants of course."

"Miss Ralston!" Yorke shouted. Then, quickly, he lowered his voice and smiled a gentle reproof. "Miss Ralston, I'm being suspected of murder, you know."

"Who isn't! Look, if I saw you with it, I'd say so. It'd prove I didn't take the thing."

Wyatt drawled, "Can you prove it any other way, Miss Ralston?"

"No. Give me one of your old stars."

Kirk laughed. "You can give me four," he said.

Wyatt turned to him sharply. "Go on, Findlay," he invited. "Explain that remark."

Kirk said pleasantly, "Sure. Right after the final shot, I was with Mac at the camera, as you've said. He handed me the plates and I took them into the darkroom and …"

Mac spoke for the first time. "And Kirk didn't come back into the studio. And he didn't go near the table when he left. So no matter what he says, he couldn't have taken that knife. And as for me …"

"It isn't your turn, MacCormick," Wyatt said. "It's Miss Lawrence's turn."

The phone buzzed before he had finished speaking and Lockhart flipped the receiver to his ear. He grunted twice into the mouthpiece and then whispered to Wyatt. Lockhart then relayed the message that Wyatt had muttered back.

"Hold tight," he said. "We'll let you know when. And keep your big feet off Mr. MacCormick's pretty desk out there, you ain't at headquarters."

The receiver clicked and Wyatt returned to us. "All right, Miss Lawrence. No, wait a minute. We'll take Mr. Duerr next, I think."

Harry Duerr jumped. "What … what did I do after the final shot, you mean?" The policeman's impersonal nod made Harry lose some of his self-consciousness. "Well, it's my job to strike the set. I went into the storage room to arrange the shelves so I would have room for the window draperies when I took them down. We bought the drapes for this picture and …"

"How long did you stay in the storage room?"

"I was still there when … when Mrs. Fleming's body was discovered. I was there all the time."

"And can you prove it?"

"Well …" Harry looked doubtfully around. "No, I can't. Nobody came in while I was there."

"Too bad," Wyatt said. "Now, Miss Lawrence, what about you?"

Madge Lawrence's black eyes burned like coals in her white face, but she answered calmly. "What is it you want to know?"

"I want you to give me an alibi. The knife, remember?"

"I didn't even see it tonight. I wasn't in the studio at all. The picture had been taken by the time I got here."

"Why were you late?"

"There was a mistake somewhere. I had understood that my appointment was for ten o'clock."

"What gave you that idea?"

"When Miss Leonard … Miss Leonard at the Models Bureau … called me, she said the job was for ten o'clock."

"But this Miss Leonard told all the other models nine o'clock."

For just a moment the burning eyes blazed into flame. "There was a mistake. I've told you that. Perhaps it was mine; perhaps someone else's."

The detective decided to let that go. "When you arrived here, what did you do, Miss Lawrence?"

"I went directly to my dressing room."

"You didn't go into the studio? You're sure?"

"Yes. I didn't go there until after … after the police had arrived."

"All right. When you went through the reception room was it empty?"

"No. Mr. Snyder was there."

Wyatt shifted his short body so that he faced Jim Snyder. Jim immediately straightened in his chair, like a schoolboy who knows he is about to be called on and hopes the question is an easy one.

"Tell us about yourself, Snyder."

"Me? Well, sure, I was in the reception room. Why not? I was all over the place. I didn't have to change my clothes because I was going to a formal party afterwards. So I just meandered about. In and out of the studio, the reception room … well, just all around."

"Why didn't you go to your party instead of meandering all around?"

"I was waiting for my money. Besides, it was early; I had time to kill."

"And that knife?"

"Sure, I could have taken it. But I didn't."

Wyatt nodded at his assistant who laboriously drew an asterisk on the paper before him. Jim leaned back, relieved that his ordeal, despite its conclusion, was ended. Wyatt, however, had a minor surprise in store for him.

"Snyder, while you were meandering about ..."

"Listen!" Jim burst out in exasperation. "I admitted that it was possible for me to have taken that knife! Isn't that all you want?"

"Snyder, while you were meandering around did you see or hear anything you haven't told us about?"

"I've already told Lockhart everything I saw! And a stenographer took it all down. You've got it right there in front of you!"

"After Miss Lawrence left the reception room, how long did you stay there?"

"I don't know ... a few minutes, maybe. I was looking at the cartoons in the *New Yorker*."

"When who came in?"

"Who came in?"

"Yes," Wyatt said with elaborate patience, "who opened the door, the outside door, and walked in?"

"Nobody."

"Might you have been so interested in those cartoons that you didn't notice?"

"No. All the models were in their dressing rooms or in the studio. ..."

"I don't mean the models. I mean someone who wasn't involved in the picture."

"Listen. Except for Madge Lawrence nobody came in the reception room while I was there. I was only there a few minutes, then I went back and talked to Kenyon."

Wyatt heaved a great sigh and turned wearily to Lockhart.

"That's why this case isn't going to be a cinch, Lockhart. Our people aren't cooperating."

"It isn't that they're just not cooperating," Lockhart said mildly. "They're just lying."

Jim Snyder started toward Lockhart threateningly. "Listen, flatfoot, nobody's going to call me a liar. ..."

Mac was in front of him. "Don't, Jim. It's their job, they have to ..."

"They don't have to get tough!"

Wyatt silenced him with a single look. "Get Mrs. MacCormick in here, Lockhart."

Mac said in surprise, "Is she here? Mr. Wyatt, may I see her alone for a few minutes?"

"She's been informed of her aunt's death. We cops aren't the brutes Snyder thinks."

"Yes, but ..."

A blue-coated arm swung open one of the big double doors and in the opening stood Erika MacCormick. Her lovely citron-colored hair fell in a long sleek bob over her mink-coated shoulders, her opaque eyes moved slowly over our collective faces. She tried to smile and the delicate rather thin lips trembled in the effort. Kirk was one side of her, Mac on the other in a moment. They brought her over to our semicircle and sat her between them. No policeman was going to get tough with Erika.

"Mrs. MacCormick," Wyatt began, "you …"

Erika interrupted him in her low, almost drawling voice. It was the kind of voice that Jeff could rave about. In fact, Erika was the kind of girl Jeff could go on and on about, and too frequently did. "Please," she said, "let's not have the preliminaries. I'm not a child. My aunt has been murdered here tonight. I fully understand that now and so … so please go on from there. You needn't handle me with gloves."

"Thank you," Wyatt said. "Mrs. MacCormick, you are Isabelle Fleming's sole heir?"

Both Kirk and Mac leaned forward to protest at his insinuation, but Erika laid a hand on each of their arms and answered the question quietly.

"Yes. There are no other relatives."

"You've read the will?"

"No. But my aunt made me very conscious of the fact that I was to be her heir. Conscious of the responsibility and all that."

"I see." Wyatt paused and the silence gathered momentum. "Mrs. Mac-Cormick, how did you spend the evening?"

"Must I go in for complete details?"

"No. Where were you at ten o'clock?"

Erika said, "You know, of course."

"Of course. Police routine."

"Then you tell me."

"At ten o'clock you were here."

"Yes," Erika said. "I was."

Her answer had been calm but she might have touched off a high explosive for the effect those words had. Erika MacCormick had been here! Erika, coming in unobtrusively, leaving again, speaking to no one. I glanced at Mac. He was staring at his wife with disbelief. That expression changed slowly to concern and then to something that was almost fear.

Wyatt took over the situation before any of our reactions had time to crystallize into words. "Why did you come here?"

"To collect my husband."

"But you didn't see him?"

"No. He was still busy with the picture. So I left."

"MacCormick," Wyatt said, turning, "did you know that your wife was coming for you?"

Mac hesitated. "Well ... No, I didn't."

"In the tone of one stating a simple fact," Wyatt said, "Mrs. MacCormick was not on friendly terms with her aunt."

Erika's eyebrows arched with delicate surprise. "But of course I was! Why do you say that?"

"You knew your aunt was here tonight?"

"Certainly."

"Yet you left without seeing her, without even attempting to see her?"

"Oh, that!" Erika smiled a little at the detective's maneuvering. "I had seen Aunt Isabelle only the other day. Friday. There was no reason for me to see or speak to her again tonight. We were aunt and niece. Just that; no more."

"Then you were not on friendly terms with her," Wyatt insisted.

Mac started up again, and again Erika restrained him.

"It might keep you from wasting a great deal of time and suspicion, Mr. Wyatt," she added deliberately, "to know that I never left the reception room all the while I was here."

"Will you prove it, Mrs. MacCormick? Just for the records."

"How should I go about it? I've had so little experience in proving my honesty. I've never had to before."

"A witness would help."

Her eyes swept calmly over the circle of faces, over Madge Lawrence's sullen mask, over May Ralston's belligerent pout. They skipped past me and Robert Yorke and Lee Kenyon and came to a stop at Jim Snyder.

"Jim Snyder," she said with a nod at him, "was with me all the time. You'll be my witness, won't you, Jim?"

Snyder shifted uncomfortably under the barrage of stares that was turned on him. A dull red crawled up his neck. But he didn't open his mouth.

Wyatt was saying, "There you have it, Lockhart. No cooperation."

"Yeah, the golf player he swung and he missed."

"Maybe he misunderstood."

"And maybe his mother never told him the one about honesty and the best policy."

"Don't blame his mother, Lockhart. Be fair. All right, Snyder, what about it?"

Erika looked puzzled. "This is ... it's all over my head."

"She came in late," Lockhart said.

Wyatt explained. "Snyder testified that he saw no one but Miss Lawrence in the reception room. We tried to make him say he saw you there, but he wouldn't. Checking on your entrance with the elevator boy we were fairly sure that he had. All right, Snyder, why?"

Jim Snyder said furiously, "Why didn't you ask me if I'd seen her, instead of trying to trap me! That was a filthy trick!"

"Were you with her all the time she was here?"

"Yes."

"Then why didn't you say so? That would alibi her better than a lie."

"I wasn't trying to alibi her. I'd … I'd simply forgot."

Lee Kenyon chuckled. "Don't be too hard on my little friend, Officer. He's not very bright."

"Go to Hades," Jim Snyder said.

"Careful of them epigrams, buddy," Lockhart grinned.

Wyatt watched Jim for a moment longer, then returned to Erika. "After you left, did you come back to the reception room again?"

"No."

"That checks with the elevator boy. All right. Now, where did you go then?"

"To a little bar on Forty-ninth Street. I meant to call my husband from there and tell him to pick me up. But I met some friends and forgot about it."

"You forgot all those hours?"

"They were extremely interesting friends. And very nice. I'm sure they'll be nice enough to alibi me."

Wyatt sighed. "Well, in spite of all Snyder's efforts, we can't seem to involve you in this affair."

Erika turned to Kirk and held out her hand. He fished a cigarette from his pack for her. Mac had a match burning by the time she got the cigarette to her lips. Relief seemed to settle over all three of them. Wyatt immediately blew it away.

"MacCormick!"

"Yes, sir?"

"After your wife, you stood next to gain by the death of Isabelle Fleming."

Mac said, "When a man's wife inherits a million dollars, I suppose you might say …"

"A million? You know that is the amount?"

"I know it's a lot of money. A million is as high as my imagination goes. It might be five or fifty million."

"It's approximately eight," Erika said.

"A nice round number," said Lockhart.

Wyatt looked at Mac sharply. "How's business?" Mac's reaction to his question caused him to say, "I can find out some place else, if you'd rather."

There was a long pause before Mac said, "Business is lousy. I'm … I'm broke."

Our surprise was very real, but there was no doubt that Wyatt's was feigned when he exclaimed, "You'd never know it! You couldn't possibly have spent much more money on this place you've got here."

Mac smiled ruefully. "That's what broke me."

"You take quite a few pictures, don't you?"

"Not quite enough."

"This business means a lot to you?"

"Just about everything."

"And you need some money pretty badly then, to pay bills and tide you over the rough spots?"

Mac knew well enough what his interrogator was getting at.

"No, Mr. Wyatt, you're wrong. The murder of Isabelle Fleming doesn't get me the money I need. It … it finishes me up for good."

"What do you mean?"

"I had a talk with Isabelle Fleming after we had taken the picture this afternoon. She promised to lend me thirty thousand dollars."

"She promised you thirty thousand dollars," Wyatt repeated slowly. It wasn't clear whether he believed Mac or thought that he had done some quick thinking.

"Yes. To keep this studio going it will take that. Thirty thousand, not eight million. I would have had that money tomorrow, when I need it. It would be months, I suppose, before I'd have access to eight millions."

Lockhart piped up, "Eight million in the offing, that's pretty good security."

"Yes," Wyatt nodded, "Mrs. Fleming's money makes you a safe investment. So that doesn't help much."

"A guy suspected of murder," Mac said, "isn't a very safe investment."

"Who's suspecting you of murder?" Lockhart's pinkish eyebrows took a leap in mock surprise.

"Pardon the interruption," Mac murmured.

"Now, about that loan," Wyatt continued, "it is a good point. In your favor. If you were promised the money it wouldn't have been necessary for you to do away with Isabelle Fleming."

"It wouldn't be good business," Mac said.

"No. So all you have to do is prove she promised you the money. Go ahead."

Mac shook his head. "I can't."

"C'mon, try! If you don't, it'll look to Lockhart as if you made the story up. To avert suspicion, as he says."

"I don't think I can. We were alone, no witnesses and nothing in writing. I was to see her tomorrow to arrange the details and get the money."

"Then you can't prove it," Wyatt said.

"No."

"Of course you can prove it, Mac!" Julie crossed to Mac's side and then swerved to face Wyatt. There were two bright spots of color highlighting her cheeks. "Of course he can! Or rather, I can do it for him!"

"That would be being a very good little secretary," Wyatt said tersely.

"When I got here tonight ... I was late ... Mac was all excited and happy. The first time in a long while." Her words were tumbling over each other. "He said to me, 'Julie, everything's going to be all right! Aunt Isabelle's going to finance us. We're set now!' He said, 'I'll give you a raise, I might even give you your back pay!' There! Doesn't that prove it? Those were his very words! Well, *doesn't* it prove what he's told you!"

Wyatt was watching Julie with a quizzical smile. He liked her; you could see that. But he wasn't to be taken in by sweet young earnestness. He looked at Erika.

"Did you know that your aunt had promised your husband a loan?"

"No, I couldn't have known. I didn't see either of them after those arrangements had been made."

"Did you know your husband was going to approach her for a loan?"

"No."

"Isn't it strange that he wouldn't have told you?"

"He doesn't bother me with business."

Wyatt persisted. "But it *is* strange, isn't it, that he shouldn't have informed you that his business was about to be saved?"

"No," Erika said, with a suggestion of a smile, "it isn't strange."

The dialogue was interrupted by the blue-uniformed man who came into the studio then and handed a filing card to Wyatt. He looked at it a long time then handed it to Lockhart. Lockhart looked and passed it back. The card was placed conspicuously before them on the desk. Wyatt jerked up his head and looked at Kirk.

"Findlay," he asked, "did MacCormick tell you about this loan, too?"

"Before or after?"

"After."

A lightning-like flash of uncertainty trembled in Kirk's eyes. To anyone unfamiliar with his whizzing reaction it might have passed unnoticed. There was only the breath of a pause before he answered.

"Sure he told me. The minute he got back to the studio. Thirty thousand tomorrow. I whooped with joy; it was damn good news!"

"Because of your back salary?"

Kirk, determined not to let the policeman ruffle him, grinned. "Mr..
MacCormick's and my relationship is not mercenary. We consider photography an art form; we're fellow devotees. All I ask is an occasional twenty-
five cent piece for bread and honey. And occasionally, I get it."

Wyatt scowled at his flippancy. He said nastily, "How do you pay your
rent?"

"I don't," Kirk snapped. He had lost patience. "I live in a tree. One of the
trees at Radio City."

Wyatt ran his eyes over Kirk's good-looking tweeds. He smiled a thin
smile.

"And your clothes?" he asked.

Kirk was getting mad. "I made them out of the bark. The Rockefellers
are furious, but helpless. They can't climb."

"You should write, Mr. Findlay."

"You should be a detective, Mr. Wyatt."

The detective stopped smiling.

Julie leaned across the desk toward him.

"But hasn't Mac's story been proven?" she pleaded. "You've heard both
Kirk and me. That's two of us, Mr. Wyatt. And Mac."

"Yes, that's two of you," Wyatt said noncommittally, dismissing the whole
subject. He picked up the filing card that had been placed before him. With a
thoughtful frown he studied it. Still holding the slip of paper in front of his
face, but raising his eyes to look over it, he said, "I have here a report from
the police laboratories, the report on the carving knife which was used to
murder Isabelle Fleming. The handle was carefully wiped off after the knife
had been plunged into her back. There were no fingerprints on it."

He lowered the card and looked slowly around the room at each of us in
turn. No surprise was registered on any of the faces that he peered into. All
of us were aware by that time that this had been no impassioned crime, that
it had been thoughtfully and cleverly worked out. We had already too much
respect for our murderer's intelligence to expect him to leave his signature
in the form of such damning evidence as fingerprints.

"However," Wyatt went on, "there is a part of that knife which was not
cleaned off. Only a small part, about an inch and a half long, of the blade,
between the hilt and the part of the blade that penetrated into the body. That
part was left unwiped. And on that part there were prints." He swung around
quickly to look at Julie. "Miss Taylor, your prints."

Julie said, "But I ... I handled the knife, I've told you that. I unpacked it
and put it on the table. Just before the picture tonight I polished it. I polished
all the silver. Unless every bit of the knife had been wiped off my prints
would surely be somewhere on it. It doesn't mean ..."

"Yes, Miss Taylor. We know that. It would look a great deal stranger, frankly, if none of your prints had been on it."

"Oh," Julie breathed, "then you don't think that I ..."

Wyatt interrupted her quickly. "Did anyone help you polish the silver?"

"No, I did it all myself."

"And after you had finished, did you notice anyone touching any of it?"

"No," Julie said.

"None of the models? While they all sat at the table, no one put a finger on any piece of silver?"

"I don't think so; at least, I didn't see anyone. We'd asked them to be careful not to touch it. It had all been arranged very carefully just where we wanted it."

"Then, to the best of your knowledge, not one person handled that carving knife between the time you put it on the table and the murderer removed it."

"I ... I can't swear to that," Julie faltered. "I wasn't watching all the time."

"To the best of your knowledge, I said!" Wyatt repeated. "Did anyone ..."

"No," Julie said.

"Then how do you account for this?" Wyatt slid the card across the desk top toward her. "Besides your prints on that one and a half inch of unwiped blade, are the fingerprints of one other person. That person is Ralph MacCormick."

## Chapter Five

MAC SAT STARING DUMBLY at his hands, while the echo of the detective's words clattered in the big quiet studio. Then the silence was exploded as Julie's fist hit the desk with a resounding bang.

"It doesn't matter about the fingerprints!" Each word was a bullet fired in Mac's defense. "It doesn't matter at all, I tell you! Mac didn't ..."

"Sit down a minute," Miss Taylor."

"No! You've got to listen to me ..."

"Later, Miss Taylor."

"But I can show you ..."

"Sit down, Julie," Erika said in her quiet voice. Julie sank sullenly back in her chair.

"Now," Wyatt said. "MacCormick, have you any idea how ..."

Mac looked up quickly. "Yes. I know why my prints are on the knife. I remember when I put them there."

"Yes."

"After we had taken the test shot, I stayed at the table for a minute or two … to rearrange some flowers. I didn't need the test negative to see that they were wrong. I moved the flower bowl up toward the head of the table; to do it I had to move the knife, too. I touched some other things as well. My fingerprints should be on the flower bowl and the salad fork."

"I see." Once more Wyatt's glance swept over the room. "Perhaps someone saw MacCormick handle that knife at the time he claims he did."

After a slight pause Harry Duerr said hesitantly, "Yes, I did. I …"

"Where were you?"

"When I was at the desk with Julie I noticed a crack that might cause a light leak, so I went behind the set to check …"

Wyatt snapped him up instantly. *"Behind* the set! And yet you saw MacCormick touch the knife?"

"No, I didn't actually see him, but … well, I heard him tell Kirk that he was going … going to tone down the flowers a bit, I think he said. Then I heard him moving things on the table. Silverware. He must have touched the knife. I mean …"

"You mean you can tell the difference between a carving knife and a fork being moved by ear. Huh-uh, Duerr, it's no good. Now, if you saw MacCormick leave the set …" Wyatt suspended his question for Harry's answer.

"No, I didn't," Harry said miserably. It would be a long time, you could see, before he came out of his shell again to offer any help.

Mac spoke suddenly in a strangely loud voice. "Look, Mr.. Wyatt. You're assuming, of course, that the murderer wiped his own fingerprints off the knife handle after he had committed the murder."

"Of course."

"Then if I had done it, wouldn't I have known that more of my prints would be on the blade? Wouldn't I have completely obliterated all of them while I was at it? Don't you give me credit for that much intelligence?"

"Yes," Wyatt said, "I do. But on the other hand …"

"On the other hand, what!" Mac's voice was unsteady.

"First only you and your wife stood to have profited by Isabelle Fleming's death. Your wife has an alibi; you have none. You admit yourself that you need money. Badly. You say Mrs. Fleming had promised it to you, but your only proof of that is the word of your two pals who would both cut off their right arms for you. So there's your motive; financial gain. More than that even. Escape from financial ruin."

"All right, there's my motive," Mac said, his lips tightening. "Go on."

"It was you who arranged for Isabelle Fleming to pose for this picture."

Mac said wearily, "I did it to get an advertising agency contract. Not so that I could murder her."

"You might have meant to kill her this afternoon. You might have tried then." It was my imagination, of course, and my far from snow-white conscience that made me think Wyatt's beady eyes were boring into mine as he said that. I didn't dare to look at Julie. I held my breath during the pause he took there nevertheless, and didn't let it out until he had gone on. "At any rate, Mrs. Fleming left this studio alive and well this afternoon. It was you who decided to retake the picture tonight."

"Because," Mac said desperately, "we couldn't find the plates."

"And it was you who found them right after tonight's picture had been taken. Found them smashed."

"Yes. But it wasn't I who …"

"Who smashed them? I'm not saying you did. I'm only saying you had an opportunity to do it. Then, tonight, after the final shot had been taken, you sent the models to their dressing rooms …"

"He didn't send them!" Kirk objected.

"All right, he didn't send them. But he remained in the studio after they had left it. And it was he who gave the plates to you, Findlay, and told you to take them to the darkroom. That left him alone at the set. He could have picked up the knife from the table …"

"He *didn't* pick up the knife!" It was Julie, on her feet again, triumph screaming through her voice. "Now will you let me tell you!"

"Yes, Miss Taylor. Now I know you were at this desk. You couldn't tell me before whether anyone had touched the knife or not. But now I suppose …"

"Yes, now I can," Julie defied him. "And this won't rest on the word of Kirk or me. Haila Troy can tell you this." She turned to me. "Haila, tell Lieutenant Wyatt why Mac couldn't have taken the knife."

With one accord, they wheeled on me. I found myself flustered and trembling. I could save Mac, Julie said. And I didn't know how. This was so important that I wasn't just nervous; I was frightened. Wyatt took pity on me.

"Tell us, Mrs. Troy." His voice was gentle, but there was a challenge in it all the same.

"Well, let's see." This was for Mac; I went cautiously along. "After that final shot, Julie asked me to sign a release and I followed her over to that desk. I did see Mac give the plates to Kirk and I saw Kirk start out with them. Mac was doing things to the camera. Then I bent over to sign my name. When I looked up again, Mac was beside me."

"But for several seconds you didn't see him?"

"Yes …"

"And in those seconds he could have taken the knife?"

"... I suppose so."

"But he didn't!" Julie interrupted. "I would have seen him."

"You asked Mrs. Troy to tell this story. Why don't you let her?" Wyatt nodded curtly to me.

"I wouldn't have noticed if he'd taken it then," I said. And suddenly I knew what Julie meant. Of course Mac didn't take the knife. I felt my voice unconsciously rise in elation. "He didn't take it!" I said.

"You could tell he didn't have it when he stood beside you?" Wyatt asked smiling.

"She's got X-ray eyes," Lockhart offered.

Wyatt's beam broadened. "Is that it, Mrs. Troy? You could see he didn't have it concealed in his shirt or in his trousers somehow?"

"No. I know because ..." I hesitated. I could feel what was coming the moment I spoke; Wyatt would ridicule me, the rest would laugh. I drew a deep breath and plunged in. "I know because Mac turned a series of cart-wheels from the desk clear out through the door. And you can't very well turn cartwheels with an eight-inch knife concealed on your person."

There was a hideous silence that was broken by May Ralston's snicker and Robert Yorke's deep chuckling sound. I said lamely, trying to sneak past that spot, "He didn't come back into the room after that. At least, not while I was here."

"Those cartwheels, Mrs. Troy. They interest me. Why did he turn cart-wheels?"

"Oh, for God's sake!" Kirk shouted. "Because he can't turn somersaults! What on earth's so unusual about a man turning cartwheels!"

"Nothing," Lockhart concealed. "Everybody does nowadays. Nobody but acrobats walk out of rooms anymore."

Julie said loudly, "I'll tell you why he did them! He was feeling wonder-ful; he was in sky-high spirits because of Mrs. Fleming's loan."

Wyatt scowled at her. "Miss Taylor, you should be a lawyer." He turned sharply to Mac. "Do you always turn cartwheels when you want to show that you aren't carrying a concealed weapon?"

"Look, Wyatt, I know it sounds silly ..."

"It is silly!"

"Yes. But Haila ... well, she understands. We've always done crazy things. We got to kidding around and she asked me to turn some cartwheels. And I did. It was supposed to be funny."

"Don't accuse us of not laughing," Lockhart said.

"Mr.. Wyatt!" It was Erika, speaking in her soft, arresting tone. "Please take my word for this. My husband is something of a little boy. He does things like that. Often I don't understand them either, but I'm not surprised by them. I rather think you're the first person who ever has been. Mac can only be explained by one word. That word is ... Mac."

Wyatt contemplated Erika for a long, quiet minute.

"All right. MacCormick couldn't have taken the knife because he turned cartwheels."

A subdued sort of pandemonium broke loose. You could have heard Mac's sigh of relief ten blocks away. For a second he looked as if he might turn some more of those things. The models relaxed as one person. Snyder and Kenyon lit cigarettes. May Ralston powdered her nose. Kirk was grinning; he seemed to have completely forgotten that, although Mac was safe, Isabelle Fleming was still dead. Julie flopped into her chair exhausted but victorious. She was Portia after the trial scene. Wyatt turned to mutter something to his assistant. His mumblings went unheeded by the others in the room.

This was the moment I had been waiting for, the chance to call Jeff. He had probably been unable to break through the barricade of police outside Photo Arts; he was probably at home worrying his head off about me.

I slipped out of the studio and into Julie's reception room. The officer there allowed that it would be within the law for me to phone my husband. I dialed our number and listened to the long insistent buzzes go unanswered. Frowning, I hung up.

"Let him have his fun, lady. He don't get a chance like this every night."

"He isn't having fun!" I snapped, with more assurance than I felt. I wasn't at all convinced. Jeff might have landed a job; he might be out celebrating. Or he might not have got a job. In that case, he'd be celebrating that.

The people in the studio could have been occupants of Madame Tussaud's. Not one of them had changed his position enough during my absence to be noted by the human eye.

"This," I muttered to myself, "is where I went out."

As if cued by my entrance, Wyatt jerked himself upright. His knuckles rapped on the desk top.

"The pictures. Not the test negative, the final shot, I mean. I'd like to have a look at them."

"The final shot hasn't been printed yet," Kirk said. "But you can see the negatives, the color plates. I'll get them."

He was on his way out.

Mac called after him, "They're in the drying room, Kirk."

Julie opened her eyes to ask suspiciously, "Why? Why do you want to see them?"

Wyatt smiled at her. He seemed to be liking Julie Taylor again. There was admiration in his smile, but no answer. It was obvious that there was to be a suspension of all actions until Kirk returned with the plates.

We hadn't long to wait. In a few minutes Kirk appeared in the doorway. He stopped there. His face was a study in bewilderment. His hands were empty.

"The negatives," he said slowly, "are missing."

Mac said impatiently, "In the drying room, Kirk. Didn't you look in the drying room?"

"Yes, I looked there. I looked in both the darkrooms, too. The test negative is there, if you want that. But not the final shot."

"But they must be ..." Mac started to rise.

The palm of Wyatt's hand slammed down on the desk. "What kind of a place is this! Do you ever really take any pictures? Or don't you bother? This afternoon's were missing, that's why you retook tonight. And now ..."

"I carried them into the darkroom," Kirk insisted.

"And now it can't be found." Wyatt's chair flew backwards as he bounced to his feet. "Just what does that camera of yours see that we shouldn't!"

My eyes jumped to Julie's face. Twice in one day that had happened. Both times that Isabelle Fleming had been photographed the negatives had got as far as the darkroom, and no further. It had been Julie who had destroyed the first set, by her own admittance. Had she destroyed the second plates as well? I couldn't keep quiet any longer. I had to tell Wyatt what happened to Julie in the darkroom that afternoon. I had to tell him that it was Julie who had broken the first set of plates.

She was looking at me, hard. She knew my thoughts. She made no movement, said nothing. But her face, her whole body, telegraphed a frantic message. "No, Haila, don't! Please, please, don't!"

Had one of the detectives caught a glimpse of her at that moment Julie would have had to explain that expression on her face if it had taken a rack, hot irons and sundry other dainties of the Spanish Inquisition to drag it out of her.

I don't know why I sat there silently while Wyatt barked questions about the two sets of mysteriously disappearing negatives. I don't know why, when he turned to me, I mumbled that I knew nothing. Perhaps Julie had hypnotized me into giving her a few hours grace, a chance to work for Mac's complete vindication. Or perhaps it was because I was rooting so hard for Mac myself that made me withhold evidence, a dangerous business at best.

Mac and Kirk were collaborating on a duet, a story of their darkroom procedure. Mac had taken the plates out of the camera after he had shot the final picture ... Kirk had gone into the darkroom with them and begun the developing … four or five minutes later Mac had cartwheeled in on him and together they had finished the job … Kirk had come back into the studio then … Mac had taken the negatives into the drying room …

Wyatt broke in. "Then you didn't actually see MacCormick take them in and leave them there?"

"No, but I had gone back to the studio because Mac said he would."

"I put them there," Mac said harshly. "I swear to God I did. Wyatt, let me take a look around the place, they must be somewhere here."

"They'll be looked for," Wyatt said. "But Lockhart and I will do the looking. There is something in those negatives that we're not supposed to see, that no one's supposed to see. It'll be better if Lockhart and I find them."

Lockhart dragged himself to his feet and followed his superior out of the room. Not one of us moved. There was stillness on both sides of the closed studio doors as we waited for the detectives' return. For it was dramatically obvious that they had been right.

Those negatives of this afternoon had been broken, those of this evening hidden or destroyed because they would reveal some evidence damaging to someone. And that someone had taken care that such evidence would not come to light. Inane images flashed across my mind, products of a benumbed brain. A lurid hand reaching stealthily to slide a carving knife across the table; the knife already hidden up a black dinner coat sleeve, the handle alone protruding; a face turning away from Isabelle Fleming with hate and murder rampant on it.

The studio doors swung open. We straightened in our chairs like a schoolroom of naughty children surprised by a hawk-nosed teacher. Like Kirk, Wyatt stopped in the doorway, but unlike Kirk, his hands were not empty.

"Where did you find them?" Kirk gasped.

Wyatt crossed the room to Mac. "Which one is this?" he said, holding up a negative.

"That's the test shot. The one we made first."

"And this?"

"That's the final shot."

"All right. We'll take a look at the test negative first. Gather around, everybody." He held the glossy black sheet up to the light as we crowded close behind him. It was clear, sharp negative in black and white; we could distinguish easily each model, each piece of china and silverware. "See anything unusual?"

The thing he lifted next was a color transparency of the final picture. It was not so distinct as the other had been. We had to press closer to him, straining our eyes. The sound Julie made at last was almost a sob.

"Yes, Miss Taylor. What is it?"

"The knife," Julie said softly. "It's gone."

"That's right. The knife, it's gone."

Mac snatched the plate from Wyatt's hand. "It couldn't be gone! It's got to be there!" He studied the picture, then slowly handed it back to the detective. "Yes, it's gone. It wasn't there when I took the picture. That means ..."

"Your cartwheel alibi is shot to hell," Wyatt said.

Erika spoke. "I don't ... I don't understand."

"It's very simple. The knife was not taken after the final shot, as everyone supposed it had been. The murderer picked it up after the test shot, hid it some place until the chance to kill Mrs. Fleming with it came. There's only one reason why this plate should have disappeared. Because once it had been seen, it would knock the stuffing out of MacCormick's alibi." He wheeled on Mac. "But you didn't hide it. You still say you didn't hide it?"

"No, I didn't."

"You didn't know, I suppose, what this would do to your alibi?"

"I didn't know. I thought the knife was on the table when I took the final shot. I didn't notice that it was gone."

"Can you prove that you couldn't have taken it between the shooting of the test shot and final one?"

"What were you turning then?" Lockhart asked.

"What did you do after the test shot?"

"Oh, God, I don't remember!"

Julie cried, "Of course he can't remember! How could he? I don't know what I did that far back, not after all these hours of questions and questions!" She was dangerously near the breaking point.

"You'll remember, Miss Taylor," Wyatt said grimly. With great serenity he eased himself back into his chair, tilting it slightly, making himself completely comfortable, as though he were settling himself for a double feature instead of a third degree. "Oh, yes, Miss Taylor, you'll remember. All of you will. Let's start remembering now. All right. Suppose, Miss Ralston, you begin ..."

May Ralston groaned. "I've got a nine o'clock job tomorrow morning, this morning. I'll look eighty ..."

"Suppose, Miss Ralston," Wyatt repeated quietly, "you begin."

May Ralston began and, almost two hours later, I finished. And it had all wound up to nothing. People had left the studio, returned to it and left again. They had been near the table, they had seen others near it, but no person had seen another take the knife.

When Wyatt stood up at last there was a sag to even his shoulders. "We'll call it a day," he said gruffly. "Go home and go to bed. I guess I don't have to caution you not to leave town, hold yourselves in readiness for any questioning we may want to make. Don't try any funny stuff."

"Please check your addresses with me," Lockhart ordered.

We lined up in front of Lockhart at the desk. May Ralston squeaked her information and dived out of the studio. The others gave theirs in tired, monotonous voices. Madge Lawrence, as cold and aloof as she had been at the beginning of the evening, ignored Snyder, Kenyon and Yorke in their attempt to be chivalrous, and stood a little apart until everybody else had reported to Lockhart before she checked in.

Wyatt moved away from the desk toward Mac. "MacCormick," he started to say.

Erika's hand shot out to grasp her husband's arm. "He may leave, mayn't he? You're not going to hold Mac?"

Julie, on his other side, echoed her. "You can't do that! You haven't anything…"

Wyatt looked straight at Julie. "I have something," he told her sternly. "The over-eagerness of you pals of his to alibi him. For everything. From the loan he was supposed to get to turning cartwheels out of the studio. It doesn't quite ring true. It's not much, but it's something."

"Don't get discouraged," Mac said, "it's a beginning."

"A good one," Wyatt said. "They may not be shielding you, but they're afraid of something being turned up. They know more than I've heard about tonight."

"Goodnight, children," Lockhart said. "Sleep tight."

## Chapter Six

THE RAIN MUST HAVE DRIZZLED to a stop hours before we were finally paroled from Photo Arts, for the streets and sidewalks were bone dry when I stepped out of the Graylock Building at last.

It was that moment just before dawn, that one moment when New York catches its breath in preparation for taking up its career of being the world's busiest metropolis. Usually it was a moment that made me forgive Gotham for all its urban sins; noises, smells, heat, cold, pushing crowds. Usually I wanted to stay with it until it was over. But not this time. This time I wanted to get home in such a hurry that I said to heck with the budget and when a cab tentatively slowed down I nodded to the driver.

I had been among the first to leave the studio. I had sneaked out to avoid any possible talk with Mac and Erika. Or Kirk and Julie. Or that other charming couple, Wyatt and Lockhart. I wanted to be alone for a while, alone with Jeff, that is. I wanted to tell him all about everything, to let him think for a moment or two, and then to reassure me that MacCormick was not a murderer. I needed to be told that. In fact, I could have used someone who would tell me that Isabelle Fleming was not even dead; that she was sleeping safely in her sumptuous bedroom in her sumptuous house on Fifth Avenue, instead of all stretched out in the autopsy room of the medical examiner. What I needed was escape. A novel by Wodehouse. An Andy Hardy picture. Or my husband.

"Haila! Just a second!"

Julie hopped into the cab after me, slid the glass window between the driver and us closed, and perched herself on the little seat that faced me.

"Can I take you home, Julie?"

"No. No, I'm not going home yet."

"You should."

"I have things to do. Haila, thanks for not saying anything about what I told you this evening. About the darkroom, I mean."

"I should have told Wyatt all about it. I wasn't being a very good citizen."

"You were being an awfully good friend to ..." Julie hesitated.

"To Mac?"

"To all of us. And, Haila, will you please go on not saying anything?"

"I can't, Julie. You know I can't."

"Just for a little while?" she pleaded.

"But why?"

"Oh, Haila ... just ... just promise!"

"If you'd only tell me!" She shook her head and her eyes filled with tears. "If you won't tell the police about it, Julie, I'll have to."

"Tomorrow?"

"Yes, tomorrow."

Her fingers found my arm and clutched it. "You don't think that Mac ... that Mac did it, do you?"

I couldn't answer her. I couldn't bring myself to say stoutly the "no" she wanted to hear. And yet I couldn't crush the hope in her face by saying that I did. I didn't know.

"Oh, God!" Julie said. It was a little prayer. She jumped out of the cab and slammed the door. I watched her run back into the Graylock Building.

"Seventy East Ninety-third, driver."

The cab had pulled to the corner and was waiting for the light to change when I spied Jeff. Emerging from a Childs, he stopped in the middle of the sidewalk, raised his head, and stared up toward the thirty-seventh floor of the Graylock Building. I could see his lips move as he put the Troy Curse on all and sundry who were keeping him from being up in Photo Arts. He was about to sit on the curb to take up and continue his vigil when I saved the price of a cleaning bill by shouting at him.

With Jeff close beside me and his arm around my shoulders, I let everything go and permitted myself the pleasure of a minor nervous breakdown. Jeff held me closer and murmured the right things in my ear and at Fifty-seventh Street I had recovered sufficiently to blow my nose and reach for my compact. At Seventieth I was a well woman.

"I'm sorry, Jeff," I said. "And thank you for not throwing me out of the cab."

"There's a fine for littering the streets."

Leaning back against his shoulder I turned my head to inspect him. He was still the same; he hadn't lost his hair since I had seen him last; he hadn't broken out in a rash; his nice nose hadn't been demolished in a street fight and badly set by a tipsy acquaintance. He was all right; not much, perhaps, when you compared him to Einstein or Tyrone Power, but he was all I had; my husband.

"How long had you been waiting, Jeff?"

"I got there about twelve. The dumb cops wouldn't let me in."

"Why didn't you tell them you were my husband?"

"I did. They congratulated me. Haila, are you suspected of murdering Mrs. Fleming?"

"I don't think so. The detectives didn't seem very enthusiastic about my chances."

"Are you too tired to give me the sordid details?"

"I'm tired, Jeff, but I've got to talk about it. You know."

"I know. Go ahead."

We were crossing Seventy-eighth Street when I started my account of the evening's happenings with Julie's arrival at the apartment. And when I finished with her visit to my taxi, just before I saw Jeff, we were sitting on the studio couch in our living room. An empty coffee pot stood on the serving table and the ashtrays were overflowing. Jeff had hardly spoken during my entire story and now he was thoughtfully squashing out a full-length cigarette that he was sorry he had lit.

"What do you think, Jeff?" I asked.

"I think that unless the cops know more than you people told them, they're not going to find out who killed Isabelle Fleming."

"Jeff, you could handle this case better than Wyatt!"

Jeff laughed. "Your husband can lick Mrs.. Wyatt's husband, can't he?"

"I'm serious!"

"Thanks. You could play *Candida* better than Katharine Cornell."

"Thanks. Listen, Jeff, you solved that theater murder. It was you who found out who was made up to kill."

"Luck."

"No!"

"One case doesn't make me a detective. Wyatt has probably solved dozens."

"But in this murder ... you know something about photography and Wyatt doesn't. And you know the people and he ..."

"Sweetheart! Contrary to public opinion the police of New York City are not a bunch of illiterates who flunked out of grade school."

"They didn't flunk out of Dartmouth! Like you did!"

"I wish you'd stop boasting about me. Besides, I didn't exactly flunk out. The dean was kind enough to explain to me that by the time I graduated, I would be too old and feeble to get a job as a civil engineer."

"You could handle this case better than Wyatt," I said doggedly.

"Haila, look. Murder doesn't pay," Jeff said patiently. "I'm a married man. I've got a family ..."

"A family! Oh, Jeff, why haven't you told me!"

"I thought you'd put two and two together when you saw me knitting little things. The point is I didn't have a job when I married you ..."

"It wasn't your fault. You were swept away by my beauty."

"Don't be flippant."

"Jeff, you're embarrassing me!"

"And you ain't getting any uglier. And I still don't have a job. Maybe if your eyes crossed I'd get connected with a salary. I could use one. At the moment my bank account is a cool ninety dollars."

"There's my seventy-five. And I'll get a part soon. I've a chance for two or three."

"The day you start working and I'm not, I move to the nearest YMCA. You aren't going to support me."

"You're so old fashioned, Jeff."

"Um-hum. I think the automobile is a device of the devil and inside plumbing is a fad. I believe in bloodletting, garters, mother love and a husband supporting his wife. Even if the husband is me and the wife is you. I'm not fooling around with any more murder."

"But, Jeff ..."

"I know. You married me for better or worse, but it's got to get better. Let the cops handle the crime and I'll keep on looking for a position that suits my limited talents."

"Your talents aren't limited."

"Everybody's jealous. That's why they won't give me a job."

"You've been out of a job for a month. And two weeks of that we spent on our honeymoon."

"I remember." We let a silent moment slip by while we had fun remembering. Then Jeff asked, "Where were we?"

"Hmm?"

"On our honeymoon. Where was it we were?"

"I wouldn't know. I seem to recall something about a boat."

"So do I. It could've been Staten Island."

"Cuba, maybe, Jeff. There were a lot of Cubans hanging around."

"What did they want?"

"They wanted us to teach them the rumba."

Jeff laughed and pulled me to him. "This will probably be my last minute alone with you. From now on I won't be able to get near you for cops."

"Oh, dear! I'll be questioned some more, won't I?"

"Sure, and shadowed. They won't let you out of their sight. You aren't any different from the others."

"Jeff, if you worked on the case, it would all be over sooner. We could be alone at last sooner."

"Haila, don't tempt me! God knows I'd like to go around pretending I'm a detective, chasing murderers. It's a wonderful way to die. But I'd be a very mediocre sleuth and I'm going to be a wow in the publishing business."

"Publishing! I thought Mac had inspired you to go into photography. I thought you were planning on propositioning John Scott and Anton Bruhle and ..."

"That was last Friday. I'm not interested in photography any more. I pawned my cameras. Where do you think the ninety bucks came from?"

"Well, tell me about the publishing business then."

He derricked his feet up on the coffee table and leaned back comfortably." I was splitting a beer with a friend of mine in the Biltmore bar when he introduced me to a friend of his. We fell to discussing books and finally this fellow confessed he was in the publishing business. He said I had some interesting and original ideas. You know me after I've had half a beer."

"So he offered you a job?"

"We're seeing each other at his office at ten this morning. I guess he wants to size me up in the daylight. But, frankly, I think it's in the bag. He called my pal later in the evening and said so."

"Jeff, that's wonderful!"

"Sure, books! After I've been in that advertising department a month everybody in America will be wearing glasses. My motto is: a book in every library!"

"I'm glad, Jeff, but ... do you have to start right away?"

"That's what I gather."

"I wish you could solve Mrs. Fleming's murder first."

"First! From what you told me that case will take years to solve!"

"It might take Wyatt years, but ..."

"But I could do it of an afternoon! Haila, Haila!" Jeff laughed, then turned serious. "Darling, they're not going to keep that job for me, they're in a hurry. I got a lucky break and I have to take advantage of it."

"You're right, I guess," I said grudgingly.

The phone rang and Jeff went into the bedroom to answer it. He was right, of course. He had to have a job. And from the books I'd been reading lately the publishing business could use him. One more book about a doctor by a doctor and I was going to need a doctor. If I could find one who wasn't all tied up writing a book. But then, on the other hand, it had to be proved that MacCormick didn't kill Erika's aunt. Mac could use Jeff.

And at the moment Mac was more important than the book business. Or even the minor matter of Jeff's earning a living. But it wasn't for me to decide. After all, I was only a one-month-old wife. I hadn't the experience of the ladies who write for magazines. And they said to let your man lead his own life, not to destroy his identity.

I glanced up and saw Jeff standing in the bedroom doorway. He was worried. "Jeff," I asked, "who was it?"

"Mac MacCormick."

"Mac! I was just thinking about ..."

"Why didn't you tell me that the police are trying to pin it on him?"

"I thought I made that clear, Jeff!"

"You made it clear that Wyatt thinks Mac had a motive and that he had the opportunity. But from your story so did everybody else."

"Mac's the only one with a motive. And he doesn't have that if you believe that Mrs. Fleming promised to finance him. Which I, personally, do believe. But unfortunately Wyatt doesn't."

"Erika had a motive."

"Jim Snyder alibied her. Why did Mac call you, Jeff?"

"He wants me to help him. By finding the real killer."

"Are you going to?"

Jeff sat down in a chair across the room. He put his elbows on his knees and his head in his hands.

"Jeff," I said, "are you?"

"I wish I was sure I could."

"You mean you think Mac's guilty?"

"No, Mac wouldn't murder. I mean I might make things worse for him with my fine Italian hand."

"This is no time for modesty."

"I'm being honest, not modest. Listen, you and Mac and the rest of you, you're upset and you imagine that Wyatt is trying to pin the murder on Mac. Cops just pin murders in the movies. Wyatt isn't up for reelection. He's got a steady job."

"It isn't that Wyatt is trying to frame Mac. I don't think that! In trying to solve the murder Wyatt has developed a good case against him. But it's wrong, he's making a mistake. He might *prove* Mac did it, and still be wrong."

"Haila, innocent people aren't ..."

"It could happen! Just once and if that once is Mac ..."

I didn't finish. The little clock on the mantel tinkled out nine o'clock. Jeff would have to hurry to get cleaned up in time for his appointment with the publishing man.

"Haila, when Julie fainted, you know, when she saw the body ..."

"Yes?"

"How long did it take her to come out of it?"

"A minute or so, I guess. Why? Jeff, you aren't going to prove Julie's the murderer!"

His smile was grim. "I get it. I'm supposed to pick out somebody none of us like and ..."

"No! But ..."

Jeff bounced out of his chair with the finesse of a high-class Jumping Jack. "I'm going up to the studio and see Mac and the boys."

"Me, too!"

"Huh-uh, Haila. You do me a favor and get some sleep. I promise to phone you at noon and tell you where I am so we can get together."

"Well, all right ..." Jeff scooped up his topcoat and hat and started for the door. "Hey!" I shouted after him. "What about your appointment with the publishing man?"

"If he calls, tell him I have to see a man about a murder. And Haila ..."

"Yes, darling?"

"You're beautiful."

"Oh, Jeff, thanks ..."

"You're so beautiful I hope I don't prove that you killed Mrs. Isabelle Fleming. So long, sweetheart."

## Chapter Seven

THE GIANT CLOCK in the Graylock Building's lobby was warning the late lunchers of its white-collared family that it was two on the dot when I rushed past it and squeezed into an elevator. Jeff, deciding that I could use another hour of sleep, hadn't telephoned me until one. Then I had taken time out for a shower, an extra-special makeup job and a hearty breakfast. Experience had taught me that if I intended to camp on Jeff's heels until he got the slayer of Isabelle Fleming, or vice versa, there would be little opportunity to keep my nose unshiny, let alone care for the entire body beautiful by bathing, eating or sleeping. So I risked a complete overhauling and refueling, in spite of the certain knowledge that minutes lost might mean a husband likewise.

One of Wyatt's little men had been laying for me on the other side of our street. I had invited him to share my taxi with me and save the city some money, but he had turned up his big nose at my advances and pretended that we were two other people. However, when I twisted around in the elevator to face the doors, he was already stationing himself in strategic position in the Graylock lobby from where he could watch all the elevators. He would be waiting for me.

Julie's cool green reception room was empty, her desk closed, but voices drifted through the doors from the studio. One of the voices was Jeff's. I stopped to listen. Jeff, Mac, Kirk, Harry Duerr and Lieutenant Detective Wyatt. Then the dry tones of Lockhart. A stag party for me to break up. I took a deep breath and plunged in.

They were all grouped around Wyatt, who had taken up his old post at Julie's desk. He had sat in that chair so much in the last twenty-four hours that he was beginning to look as if he belonged there. I half expected to see a picture of his wife and kiddies rising out of the litter of papers that covered the desk.

"I had hopes," he was saying to the circle of faces about him, "that a good night's sleep might refresh some of your memories. Apparently, it didn't. None of you saw anyone else take the knife off the table and, of course, none of you took it yourself. That's still your story?"

Mac and Kirk and Harry shook their heads absently and in unison.

"And you, Mrs. Troy?"

I jumped. He had given no sign until then that he had seen or heard me enter.

"No," I said, "I …"

"No. That's what I thought. Lockhart and I have been doing some visiting this morning. Nobody's able to remember anything they couldn't remember last night. And the net result is still that any one of the models or your people could have picked up the knife between the test and the final shot. Nobody has been able to get himself eliminated. There seems to have been an awful lot of milling around."

"There was," I said. "And I milled my share. I'm afraid I had opportunities to take the knife. But, frankly, I missed them."

Wyatt nodded wearily. "That's what everyone says. But one of them, at least one of them, is lying."

"I figure," Jeff propounded as he crossed the room to my side, "that a person who murders does not find it difficult to stoop to fibbing."

Wyatt turned to Mac and Kirk, neither of whom looked as if they'd closed their eyes since I had seen them last. "Your pal Troy is a student of human nature."

"Do you find that comes in handy in your detective work, Mr. Troy?" Lockhart asked.

"It must be fascinating, Mr. Troy," Wyatt went on, "to dabble in crime."

It looked as if Jeff were set for some tough sledding. He grinned at me. "The boys are peeved. They're afraid I'll dabble around and upset some of their theories."

"Mr. Wyatt," I asked, "have you seen Julie Taylor?"

He frowned. "No. She wasn't home this morning. And MacCormick and his colleagues won't tell me where she is."

"We don't know!" Kirk said.

"Call her again, will you, Harry?" Mac requested.

Harry went to the phone and dialed the number. There was no answer.I knew then, since the detectives hadn't talked to Julie, that they didn't know yet of her darkroom experience. I couldn't withhold that evidence any longer, despite her pleas. Murder wasn't the sort of thing you took in your own hands. Julie was wrong; I was convinced of that.

I told Wyatt the story, as quickly and as completely as I could, and waited for him to lash me into a pulp for my reticence. He surprised me. Perhaps he considered the news too important to waste time reprimanding me. His eyes were on Mac.

"MacCormick!" he snapped. "You seem surprised by this development."

"I am!" Mac's mouth was still open.

"You two, Findlay and Duerr. Did you know about this?"

"No ... huh-uh," Harry said, shaking his head deliberately.

"I'm still in a fog." Kirk turned to me and there were spaces between each word. "You mean to say, Haila, that Julie Taylor thought there was a killer in the darkroom with her and she didn't tell us!"

"And that Julie smashed our plates that afternoon?" Mac was even more incredulous.

I said helplessly, "That's what she told me."

"But why!" Kirk yelled.

"Shut up," Wyatt growled. Then he smiled pleasantly. "Shut up for just a moment, please do. MacCormick, what time did you finish this picture you took yesterday afternoon?"

"A little after four, I think."

"And what happened then?"

"Well, the models went immediately to their dressing rooms. Mrs. Fleming left as soon as the picture was taken. She was tired and her car was waiting, so she didn't bother to change her clothes."

"And you ... what about you?"

"I fooled around with the cameras. Took the plates out, helped Harry put some lights away. Then Kirk asked me ..."

"Kirk can tell me about himself."

"All right. Julie said she had a headache and she went home. So I took care of paying the models and having them sign their releases. Then I cleaned up a bit and left."

"Time?"

"About five."

"Where did you go?"

"I went to Mrs. Fleming's house. I had a business appointment with her, remember?"

"Why didn't you talk to her before she left?"

"Because she was tired. She asked me to come to her house."

"And when you left the studio ... who was here?"

"Nobody. Everyone had gone by then."

"And the plates? Where were they?"

"I'd taken them into the darkroom and put them on a shelf."

Wyatt pounced on him. "So you were alone here for some time."

"Yes! Just me and the plates!" Wyatt was getting Mac down.

The detective turned to Kirk. "What time did you leave?"

"About quarter of five."

"Did MacCormick send you away?"

"So he could be alone with the plates? No, buddy. I asked Mac if I could go. I had some things to do and as a favor to me he said we wouldn't develop the pictures until that night."

"All right," Wyatt snapped. "Duerr, what about you?"

"I left right after Kirk. I took a camera along and as soon as I had a bite to eat, I went over to Times Square. I wanted to get some shots of the big electric signs and ..."

"What time did you get back?"

"Pretty late. I got interested over in Times Square. Julie Taylor and Mac and Kirk were all here when I arrived."

Wyatt swung back to Mac. "You went directly to Mrs. Fleming's?"

"Yes. I stayed there until six o'clock. She promised to take stock in Photo Arts and advance me the money immediately. I was to see her again today."

"Sure," Wyatt said. "And when did you come back here?"

"I was going to meet Kirk here at seven. So I stopped at our apartment. It had started to rain and I wanted to change into a slicker. I had a sandwich and got here a little after seven."

"Your wife was at home?"

"No."

"Where was she?"

"I don't know. Having dinner with someone, probably."

"And when you got here …?"

"Kirk was already here. We went into the darkroom together to develop the plates. We couldn't find them. We hunted for almost an hour."

"And," Wyatt said significantly, "you were the last person to leave in the afternoon."

Kirk leaped to his feet. "Listen! I've just remembered! When I got to the studio the door was open!"

"Open?"

"Unlocked! Don't you get it? Someone could have come in here and ruined those plates while Mac and I were out!"

Wyatt smiled. "An alibi for your friend."

"Well, damn it, it is! It's a possibility."

"MacCormick, did you lock the door when you left?"

Mac shook his head. "I don't remember. I've been known to forget to lock it. Julie's found it open a couple of times and given me hell."

Harry Duerr asked shyly, "If Mac did lock it, how about a skeleton key?"

"A good old skeleton key," Lockhart said.

"Well," Wyatt said, "until we prove different, somebody else could have come in and spoiled those plates." It was obviously a concession on Wyatt's part; he didn't believe a word of it. "Findlay, when you got here … go ahead."

"I only got here a couple of minutes ahead of Mac. I stretched out on the old sofa and smoked a cigarette. Then Mac came and we discovered that the plates were missing."

"That the way it was, MacCormick?"

"Yes, we looked everywhere for them but …"

"But in the waste can!" Lockhart said.

"Would you have looked there?" Mac demanded.

"Yeah," Lockhart said. "But then, I'm that type."

"I bet you collect old love letters," Jeff said.

"And then," Wyatt continued, "when you couldn't find them you decided to retake the picture. That night."

"We had to. The pictures had been promised for this morning. Kirk telephoned Powers and the Models Bureau. They got the models for us again. We called all over town and finally got Julie at Haila's. She arrived in about half an hour, just before Harry. Kirk and I had nearly everything set and Julie and Harry helped us finish. The models started arriving and ... and you know the rest."

"Not quite all the rest," Wyatt said dryly. "Mrs.. Troy, when you found that those plates had been ruined, you ran to Julie Taylor and told her."

"Yes. Because in my mind, such as it is, the implication was that the reason they had been ruined was to give the murderer a chance to try again. I wanted Julie to tell Kirk and Mac so that they could do something."

"And then Julie told you that she had smashed them herself," Wyatt mused. "Now, why would she say a ridiculous thing like that? Unless it were true."

"And if it were true," Jeff said, "why would she admit it to Haila?"

"Lockhart," Wyatt ordered, "call her up again."

Lockhart dialed, listened and hung up. "Still no answer.

Wyatt went back into his brown study. "Little Julie Taylor. A nice kid. Lockhart, let's you and me go look for her. She could answer a lot of questions for us."

"I'll go look for her myself," Lockhart said. "With pleasure."

"You've got a wife, Lockhart."

"She couldn't come with me. She has to watch the kids."

"C'mon, Romeo, on our way."

Jeff stepped forward and stopped them. "Mr. Wyatt, about the evening plates, you know, the murder picture ..."

"Yeah?"

"Where did you and Lockhart find them?"

"Why?" The detective didn't like anybody to ask *him* questions.

"I've got some I want to hide. Pictures of me eating with my elbows on the table."

"They found them in the waste basket," Mac said. "The same one we found the afternoon plates in. Mr. X seems to have a penchant for waste baskets."

"See," Wyatt said, "anything you want to know, ask MacCormick. He's a pal of yours; he'll probably tell you who killed his wife's aunt. If you're unfair enough to ask him. C'mon, Lockhart."

Now it was my turn to mess up their exit. "Mr. Wyatt, that little man of yours who is following me ... is he necessary?"

"Don't you like him?"

"It's nothing personal. His blue serge suit clashes with my ensemble."

"Oh. Well, that isn't the reason I'm going to call him off. I need him more other places."

"Then my wife isn't a suspect anymore?" Jeff asked.

"I know you'll keep an eye on her for us, Troy. And I know that you'll tell us anything you find out about this case."

"Sure, I will."

"Sure, you will. I bet!"

After the outside door slammed behind the two detectives, there was a marked easing of tension in the studio. Mac allowed himself the luxury of stretching out on the horsehair sofa. But in a second he was back on his feet. "Those guys give me the shakes!"

"Relax, kid," Jeff said. He looked at his watch. "Yorke ought to be here soon." Jeff responded to my puzzled frown. "I want to talk to the people. You know, a bit of fireside chatting. Yorke's the only one we could reach by phone. Julie must've taken all the rest of them on a picnic."

"Julie!" Kirk exploded. "Julie Taylor. I don't get it. All that darkroom business! Why the devil didn't she tell us, Mac?"

"I don't get it either. And Julie didn't smash those plates. They were still whole when I put them on the shelf, long after Julie had gone."

"She had a key," Jeff said. "She might have come back and done it. It might have been Julie who left the door open, if you didn't, Mac."

"You don't believe that, Jeff?" Kirk asked.

"No. Not a word of it." He walked around the room looking at the ceiling. "Were you expecting Julie this morning?"

"Not especially. Not after the night we all had. But …"

"But you did think she'd turn up?"

"Well, yes."

"I don't know where else she'd go," Kirk said. "She wouldn't pick this morning to visit the Hayden Planetarium."

"No," Jeff agreed. "Today's Men Only Day up at the Planetarium. Let's call her again."

Kirk took his turn at the phone. It was no go. Worried, he slapped the receiver down.

"She'll pop in any minute," Jeff said cheerfully. But none of us was convinced. With the exception of him, we all sat around and wondered about Julie. He seemed to be doing some independent worrying.

Finally Harry asked, "Mac, could I start tearing down the set?"

"No. It has to stay up. Wyatt's orders."

"I'd like to be doing something."

"I don't know what it would be, Harry. Tomorrow we'll take that whiskey picture. Why don't you go home for the rest of the day?"

Harry shook his head. "I'll stick around."

Jeff sat on the edge of the desk. "Mac, tell me something about these models you used last night. Start with the Lawrence woman."

"Madge. She's hardly spoken a hundred words in the dozen times we've used her. I don't seem to know a thing about her, do you, Kirk?"

"Nope. I used to think the cat had her tongue. Until one day I called her a name and she stuck it out at me."

"And that's all you know?"

"Practically. I don't imagine she models for the money that's in it. She seems to have all she needs of that stuff. Her clothes are terrific. Walking edition of *Vogue* sort of thing. On the other hand she doesn't seem to be modeling for fun; she certainly doesn't act as if she likes it. I don't know why she poses."

"And what about the other girl, May Ralston?"

"A blonde," Kirk said. "You'll have to see her to believe her."

"And this Jim Snyder?"

"A professional amateur golfer. Makes his living being entertained during tournaments. When hospitality is slack, he poses."

"And Lee Kenyon?"

"I can help you there," Mac volunteered. "He's a dancer. Erika discovered him tapping to Beethoven and trucking to Mozart in some obscure nightclub. She thought he was wonderful, tried to boost him into the big time by having him meet the right people and seeing that he had the right clothes; that sort of thing. She finally did get him a Fifty-second Street engagement, but he flopped. And Erika lost interest in him. An artist had come along who could paint tastes and odors." Mac's grin was followed by a helpless shrug. "Erika's like that. She has to have a protégé; someone that she can root for."

"But none of those people could possibly have had a motive," Kirk said. His eyes suddenly narrowed. "Or could they?"

"I'll dabble around," Jeff said, "and ..." He broke off abruptly. His voice had a new enthusiasm in it. "Mr. Robert Yorke, I believe!"

"Huh?" Kirk grunted.

Jeff's nod turned us all toward the doorway. Robert Yorke stood there awaiting our attention for his entrance. It was easy to imagine how female hearts had pitter-pattered when he stepped onto a stage. Despite the tiny lines that were beginning to form around his eyes, he belonged, even now, in Hollywood. Perhaps his was one of those voices that just didn't record. I could see how that might be; it was a trifle thin.

Yorke smiled and bowed ever so slightly, but ever so suavely, before he moved toward us. He came easily, jauntily, his hand outstretched. A matinee idol without a matinee.

"How do you do, Mrs. Troy?" He took my hand and lingered over it. He made me feel like a girl again. "And this must be your husband," he said, turning to Jeff. "How are you? Glad to know you." His manner had changed from romantic to I'm-just-one-of-the-boys as if he had flipped a dial from one radio station to another.

"I'm glad to know you, too, Yorke." Jeff was pumping his hand, smiling. You couldn't help liking this actor, although you knew that he had planned it that way; that that was his business.

"Hello, Yorke." Mac stood up, glancing at his watch. "I've got to call Erika. I'll use the phone in the reception room. Be right back." He disappeared through the swinging doors.

Yorke smiled a refusal of Jeff's proffered cigarettes and drew an expensive gold case from his pocket. I was standing close enough to notice that his cigarettes were one of those cheaper brands, the ones they named after race horses.

"Yorke," Jeff said, "Mac has asked me to try and help out the police on this murder …"

"Oh, yes. You're a detective, aren't you? I've heard about you from an actress friend of mine. You're very good, I understand."

Jeff's grin was a masterpiece of deprecation. "Then you don't mind if I ask a few questions?"

"I'd be delighted."

Jeff questioned; Yorke answered. Jeff ferreted and rooted; Yorke did his best to be helpful. Nothing came to light that I had not already known and told Jeff. He finally gave up on events immediately preceding and following the crime.

"Had you ever met Mrs. Fleming before last night?" he asked.

"No, I can't say I had. Of course, I knew of her. In fact, I've been aware that there was a Mrs. Sanford Fleming ever since that scandal about Sanford and that woman."

"What woman?" The defeated look vanished from Jeff's face.

"Don't you remember? No, probably not. It was years ago. I imagine you were still more interested in marbles than front pages of newspapers at that time."

"How long ago was it?"

"So long ago that I don't even remember the details of the case. Fourteen or fifteen years ago, I'd say. Shortly after Sanford Fleming died."

"*After* he died!"

"Yes, it was a law suit that Isabelle Fleming brought into court. I remember it as being a rather sordid business, but that is all I do remember. Actually. I have a notoriously bad memory." He laughed in quiet amusement. "In fact, speaking of my memory reminds me that I've forgotten an appointment I have at three. So if you'll excuse me ..."

"Just a second," Jeff said.

"I'm sorry. I really must rush away. I'll just stop and see if MacCormick happens to have anything for me. Nice seeing you all and good luck, Troy." Then he was gone. Robert Yorke also knew how to make an exit.

"If you want to talk to him some more, Jeff, I'll ..."

"Don't bother, Kirk. I'll see him again."

Harry Duerr stepped out of the corner by the windows. He had been so quiet that I had completely forgotten that he was still around.

"I think I'll go home if Mac really won't need me any more today," he said. "Or if you don't, Mr. Troy."

"It's all right with me."

"If there's anything I can do ..."

"I don't think so."

At the doors he stopped and turned back to us again.

"Look, Mr. Troy," he said hesitantly, "I've only been up here at Photo Arts a couple of months; perhaps I shouldn't try to stick my nose in this thing. But ..."

"Yes?" Jeff said encouragingly.

"Well, what I want to say is this: you don't have to know Mac MacCormick a couple of months to know that he's incapable of murder. I don't care how much evidence or motive or anything else piles up against him, I know he didn't kill Mrs. Fleming. I'd like to help you prove he didn't, if it needs proving. I'd like to feel that I'd done something ..." He paused again. His clear gray eyes had darkened in their earnestness. He relaxed suddenly and smiled. "The point is I'd probably be no damn good at all. But if you could use me in any way ... at any time ... well, I'd appreciate it."

He turned quickly and went out. There was a little silence as the doors closed behind him.

Then Kirk said stoutly, almost defensively, "Harry's a nice guy. He'd do anything for Mac. He means it."

"You're a nice guy, too, Kirk," Jeff said. "You'd do anything for Mac. And you did."

"What?" Jeff's innuendo was too much for even Kirk.

"Those negatives. You should have found a better place to hide them."

Kirk's mouth fell open. "You ... you knew about that?"

"Sure," Jeff grinned.

"Listen, Jeff ..."

"Wait, see if I'm right. Wyatt sent you out to the darkroom to get him those negatives last night. You went in and got them. You looked at them. And then you saw that when that final shot had been taken the knife was no longer on the table. You knew that knocked Mac's cartwheel alibi all to hell. So you tried to get rid of them quick. Only you didn't quite make the grade."

"I didn't have much time," Kirk said miserably. "I couldn't smash them. I would have had to use a blunt instrument on the damn things and it would have made too much noise. So I just … just hid them. I thought I'd get a chance to really get rid of them later, but I didn't."

"Tough," Jeff said.

"Look, Jeff, don't tell Mac. He's sore at Julie and Harry and me now for trying to help him. He says if makes him look more suspicious."

"It might."

"But I shouldn't have flubbed those negatives," Kirk said. "Not that Mac needs that kind of help!" he added emphatically. "He didn't kill Isabelle Fleming. Why would he? She promised him that money, I know damn well she did!"

Kirk hadn't been that positive last night when Wyatt had questioned him about the loan; I remembered the brief hesitation before he answered Wyatt. But there was neither doubt nor hesitation in his statement now.

"I believe it, Kirk," Jeff said. "But a word of advice from an incompetent friend, son. It's being a good pal, but it's also illegal to destroy evidence."

"I wish I had swallowed the damn things. How did you know I hid them, Jeff?"

"Because you told Wyatt you couldn't find them. That you'd looked and they were gone. If you really had looked for them, the first place you would have searched would have been that waste basket. That's where you found the afternoon's missing plates. And instinctively, you would have taken another gander there and found them. And just as instinctively, you thought of hiding them there."

"Damn my instinct!" Kirk said ruefully. "I didn't think …" He covered up quickly as the doors at the end of the studio swung open.

With a preoccupied expression, Mac crossed the room to the desk and hastily jotted a note on a sheet of paper.

"We're using Yorke in that whiskey ad tomorrow. That fishing picture. I've been talking to him; he'll be here at five. Ask Julie to get some tackle and boots and, you know, all the usual stuff."

"Julie …" Kirk began doubtfully.

Mac looked up. "Yes. Maybe you'd better do it yourself, Kirk. Try Spauldings. I think Julie rents those things from them."

"Right." Kirk grinned suddenly. "I hope Julie shows up soon. I'll make one hell of a stylist."

Jeff said, "Did you get hold of Erika, Mac?"

"Yes. She's coming over here to pick me up. We have to go to the Fleming house. Funeral arrangements and things. She'll be here soon."

"I hope," Jeff said, and we all silently seconded that hope, "that she has Julie with her."

## Chapter Eight

THE OCTOBER SUN had already swung across Manhattan and was attacking Photo Arts through its western windows when Erika arrived. The somberness of her severe black suit made her flash like chromium against a velvet drop. Erika was never meant to mourn.

She barely acknowledged Kirk's presence, nodded briefly in my direction and only half accepted Jeff's words of sympathy. Then slipping her arm through Mac's, she murmured that they must be going.

"Erika!"

Mac let the door he was holding open for her pivot back into position, as she turned to face Jeff. She cocked her smooth blond head to one side.

"Yes?"

"There's something you might help us with, Erika. One answer to one question."

Erika's puzzled eyes made Mac explain. "Jeff's going to ... help solve this case."

"Help solve this case," Erika repeated. "It's thoughtful of you, darling, to put it so impersonally." She went to Jeff and said evenly, "Naturally, I'm very anxious to have the person who killed my aunt punished. Electrocuted, in fact. And if there's anything I can do, Jeff, well, here I am."

"Do you remember a lawsuit, Erika," Jeff asked, "that your aunt brought to court? It was about fifteen years ago."

A fleeting shadow crossed her face. She hesitated. "Yes, I vaguely remember it. But certainly it can have nothing to do with ..."

"It mightn't," Jeff agreed.

It was Mac's eyes that were puzzled now as he looked down at his wife. "I never heard about a lawsuit, Erika."

Erika's smile was a grimacing one. "You weren't supposed to, Mac. Aunt Isabelle spent a great deal of money keeping that skeleton in its closet. And I think it would be thoughtless of us to drag it out now that she is dead."

Mac said, very quietly, "If Jeff thinks it might help ..."

Erika raised her head in swift protest. "Of course, Mac!"

"Tell us about it, Erika," Jeff said.

"My uncle left some money, quite a lot of it, to … to a woman. The rest, of course, went to Aunt Isabelle. But Auntie contested it. She went to court. She was able to prove that the will was made under duress by coercion. And the will was declared invalid." Erika shrugged gracefully. "That's all there is; is that what you wanted?"

Jeff was frowning thoughtfully. "How much did Sanford Fleming leave to this woman?"

"I don't know exactly, not very much though. I mean, not very much in comparison to the entire estate. Somewhere between fifty and sixty thousand dollars, I believe."

Jeff's frown had deepened. "But that could only have been a fraction of Sanford Fleming's estate."

"Yes, that's what I said." Erika was getting impatient.

"But when that will was declared invalid it meant your uncle died intestate. And when a man dies intestate in New York State, his widow receives only one-third of his estate."

"Exactly," Erika said.

Jeff exploded. "But, my God, Erika! Do you mean that Isabelle Fleming sacrificed millions to get back thousands?"

"It wasn't the money she was contesting. It was the fact that her husband had left something to another woman … had remembered another other woman in his will. That was the reason she took it to court."

Jeff whistled softly. "Your aunt must have hated that woman an awful lot. In fact, several million dollars worth of hate."

Erika shrugged again. "She wasn't fond of her. But I don't believe she would have done it if she had realized the mess it would cause. She loathed scandal; I think that might have been why she contested it in the first place, to put a stop to any scandal that might arise out of the bequest. It worked just the other way, of course. The papers were full of it, all of them jammed with the story. Aunt Isabelle spent a little fortune quieting them down, buying up the more lurid editions, that sort of thing. And that made it worse, too. But all of that was when I was a child; by the time I went away to school it had been forgotten."

"This woman," Jeff asked, "where is she now?"

"I've no idea."

"Do you remember her name?"

"Lewis. Amanda Lewis. I haven't heard of her since the case. Her name was never mentioned in the family after that. She may be dead."

"What did she look like?"

"Jeff, that was fourteen years ago!" Erika said. "I was only a child. And I never saw her; I wasn't taken to court."

"Her picture in the papers?"

"No, Jeff! If I saw it, I don't remember. Jeff, this thing mustn't be dragged out again. I'm holding my breath as it is for fear the newspapers will start rehashing it. It can't have anything to do with what happened last night. And Aunt Isabelle … she'd hate it so."

Before Jeff could answer, the door swung in, nearly knocking Mac off his feet.

"Oh, I *am* sorry!" said May Ralston. Soft baby curls dripped down her forehead from an off-the-face number of forget-me-not blue. Two more ringlets peeped coquettishly out from each side to nestle on her cheeks. Her eyes were wide and blue and provocative. To look from her to Erika made you realize that there are blondes and blondes.

Erika didn't smile with the rest of us at the expression on Mac's face as he rubbed his wounded derriere. "Mac, we've really got to go," she said. "There's so much to attend to." Her glance at May as she passed her was a reprimand for May's flamboyant taste in hats and cosmetics.

Mac said, "Can I do something for you, May?"

"My hatbox. I left it here last night."

"Kirk'll take care of you."

"I'm in an awful hurry."

Mac waved at us. "I'll keep in touch with you, Jeff. So long." He chased after his wife.

"Hello, May," Kirk said. "You know Haila. And this is Jeff. Jeff Troy."

May walked directly to Jeff and stuck out her red-nailed fingers. Hiya, Jeff, how are you?"

"I'm fine, May," he said, taking her hand too enthusiastically. "How are you?"

"That murder gave me a hangover." She slowly withdrew her hand and perched herself on the edge of the desk, her legs expertly crossed. All of a sudden she wasn't in a hurry. I accepted that as a nice compliment to my husband and blew away the chip that was forming on my shoulder.

"You look swell in a hangover, May," Kirk said.

"Do I? Thanks. Do you think so, too, Jeff?" The look she gave Jeff made me hold my breath, close my eyes and count ten. If when I opened them again, Jeff wasn't walking out the door with May, I'd mail the invitations to our Golden Anniversary; our marriage would survive. I opened my eyes. I still had a husband; he was laughing at her. "Mind if I ask you some questions, May?"

May's face lit up and her skirt moved another inch away from her knee. "Are you a reporter?"

Kirk said quickly, "Yes, he is."

"Honest! What paper, Jeff?"

"The *Daily Worker.* I do Cholly Knickerbocker stuff."

"Do you use pictures in your column?"

"Sometimes," Jeff said. "For instance, I'd use the picture of a girl who danced with Joe Stalin."

"I've danced with Lucius Beebe. Does that count?"

"Just five. Ten for Stalin."

"Aw, you're kidding me! I know who Stalin is. He's somebody in Europe or some place. I bet you aren't even a reporter!"

"He's a detective," Kirk said.

"Are you!"

"I'll say!" Jeff admitted.

May challenged him. "Let's see your badge."

"I can't. I don't have anything on under it. May, do you know anything that you forgot to tell the police … that slipped your mind?" Jeff was flattering her. May hesitated. "Do you, May?"

"Well, I don't want to get into any trouble …"

"You won't," Jeff assured her.

"I'll trust you. If you don't let it go any farther." May looked around the room before she spoke again. "I'm not related to Mrs. Fleming. In any way."

"Who said you were?"

"Nobody yet! But if they find out, they will. They'll say … they'll connect me with the murder!"

"If they find out what, May?" Jeff asked.

"My middle name is Fleming! May Fleming Ralston!"

"Hmm," Jeff said significantly.

"But, honest, I'm not related in any way. I asked my mother. To make sure I wasn't connected with the murder. She says the Fleming stands for May Fleming. She used to be my mother's partner in a vaudeville act. My mother named me after her for sentimental reasons. She was married to my father when my mother met him."

"Hmm," Jeff said.

"You don't believe me, do you?" May's high heels clicked as they hit the floor. "I knew you wouldn't! I'm going! I'm not going to stay here and be convicted of murder just because my middle name's a coincidence! Where's my hatbox?"

"In your dressing room, I guess," Kirk said.

"Thank you!"

May Fleming Ralston stormed out. The angry popping of her heels along the hall was terminated by a slamming door.

"Jeff," I said, "you shouldn't have frightened her."

"The only thing May's frightened of is that she won't be suspected. She wants her picture in the paper. Kirk, let's get busy on the phone and see if we can't locate Kenyon and Snyder. And Madge Lawrence."

"And Julie Taylor," Kirk said. He swung the dial and held the receiver to his ear for a long time before he slapped it down. "Jeff, I'm going to Julie's. I'm going ..."

"What good will that do, Kirk?"

"I don't know, but ..."

"Take it easy. Maybe Julie's on her way back here with Wyatt and Lockhart." Jeff proceeded to dial a couple of numbers without success. "Nobody's at home today. Look, Kirk, if I can't see these people in person, I'd like to at least look at their pictures. Snyder, Kenyon and Lawrence. They're the ones I haven't been able to get any line on."

In about five minutes Jeff and Kirk were ensconced at the desk behind a stack of models catalogues. Not a word nor a glance was being wasted on me. I curled up on the old horsehair sofa in the corner. The activities of the last twenty-four hours had been tiring enough, and the crisis that my marriage had just undergone had completely exhausted me. In spite of all efforts to keep awake and listen to the questions that Jeff was firing at Kirk, my eyelids began to droop. The last thing that I remember was Jeff pulling the heavy drapes across the big windows, covering me with my coat and kissing me on the forehead.

A sharp, metallic click awakened me. The studio was cold and completely dark. Outside, in the main hall, I could hear an elevator door slide back and forth. But here in the studio there was nothing at all; no sound, no movement. And yet that clicking noise that woke me had been ... perhaps it was the outside door snapping behind Kirk and Jeff; perhaps that elevator had stopped to take them down.

I sat up and groped for my shoes, trying to remember where the light switch was. I found both shoes at last, slipped into them and sat waiting a moment, hoping that my eyes would grow accustomed to the darkness. There wasn't a glimmer of light to even outline the forms of things. I reached out my hand; on one side of me there was nothing, on the other only the coarseness of the sofa's back.

The clicking sound that I had heard before came again now. Four or five times in quick succession.

"Jeff?" I called. "Jeff! Kirk!"

My only answer was a movement close by the blacked-out windows. There was someone in the room with me. Not Jeff, not Kirk. Someone who wasn't too enthusiastic about my knowing of his presence. Or of his identity.

But I was never one for being reticent. Meeting new people had always been my pleasure. "Hey!" I said charmingly, "Hey!" And I stepped in the general direction of the corner opposite me.

I felt, as well as heard, the swift brushing sound as he sped past me. A sudden gush of cold air told me that the studio doors had swung open and closed. Jeff and Kirk might still be in one of the other rooms. I shouted at the top of my voice. The only response I got was my echo.

With both hands extended in front of me I ran to where I knew the doors must be. My hands connected with smooth hard wood that gave under the pressure. I felt for the corridor light switch and snapped it on. There was no one in the long length of hall. Quickly I thrust open the reception room door, flashed on the white-shaded lamp there. One glance showed that it, too, was empty.

There was nobody in the big main hall, either. The elevators were at its far end; he couldn't possibly have reached and boarded one of them in those few brief moments. He must, then, be still inside, in the darkroom or one of the dressing rooms maybe.

I was turning back into Photo Arts when I noticed it. Halfway down the hall a door was settling with snaillike slowness into its frame. The door to a stairway. It was through that, then, he had gone.

I rushed to it and pushed it open; I was on the broad staircase landing. There was no one in sight. I stood still, straining my ears for footsteps. The big door wheezed closed behind me, but there was no other sound. You can't work up much speed on your tiptoes, I realized; if I hurried I might still be able to introduce myself to my bashful little playmate.

I had taken three quick steps down when a very nasty notion stopped me in my tracks. Perhaps no tiptoeing was going on. Perhaps my buddy was waiting for me around the next turn of the stairs. I wasn't in a hurry anymore. I'd take my time and figure this thing out.

If he wanted to do me bodily harm ... to put it mildly ... why hadn't he let me have it in the studio? Simple. It was too dark. You can't aim a gun by ear. So he had tricked me into following him into the fire stairs which, except in case of fire, are sure to be deserted. And at the moment there was no fire going on.

I suddenly lost all desire to meet any more people. I pivoted and went back up those three steps, across the landing to the door. I pressed both hands against it. It didn't budge. But of course it wouldn't; the darn door opened in. I grabbed the knob and pulled. Still it didn't budge. The door had locked itself behind me.

But there were other doors, up and down. If he had gone up, I wanted to go down. However, if he had gone down ... I had to be right. The sensible way to make a decision of this sort is to flip a coin. But you can't flip a coin when your hands are shaking so you can't hold a coin. I went up.

I pulled, pushed, beat and kicked at the door on the next landing. It wouldn't open. Then I understood. *All* the fire doors were locked; every one of those eighty-seven doors on the eighty-seven floors of the whole Graylock Building was locked. It was after five-thirty; at five-thirty the fire doors automatically locked. Not from the building side; laws prevented that. But from my side there wouldn't be an open door except at the bottom and at the pinnacled top. Nice work. I had locked myself on an eighty-seven flight staircase with ... with, perhaps, the murderer of Mrs. Isabelle Fleming.

He had lured me into the staircase. He had expected me to go down, to rush headlong down the steps after him. He would be waiting for me some place below. But he must have heard me come up; by now he would be creeping up to this floor. Suddenly this floor didn't appeal to me any longer.

I ran up and up, stumbling and floundering as I went. Once I halted to listen. The stillness scared more daylights out of me than any noise possibly could have. I climbed some more, fighting for my breath. Darn the cigarettes that I had smoked, darn every single one of them. But maybe cigarettes didn't hurt you, didn't cut your wind. Joe DiMaggio smoked them and so did Bucky Walters. Perhaps it was the altitude that was getting me.

And then I couldn't go up anymore. Every muscle in my body went on a sit-down strike. I collapsed on the cold cement stairs. Let the murderer catch up to me. Any end was better than this. I listened intently. Nothing. No sound at all. Maybe my murderer was a cigar smoker and it would take him a long while to arrive. I could wait. I had time.

The spots cleared away from before my eyes. My breathing calmed down to a mere gasping. The excruciating pain of complete exhaustion seeped out of my legs and left them numb.

There was still no sound of approaching footsteps. Where could that murderer be? I would give him five more minutes. If he hadn't shown up by then, it was no date. I would start fleeing again. It would serve him right for keeping a girl waiting.

My breathing had become as normal as it would ever again be and still no footsteps. A horrible realization came over me. I wasn't being chased! I had come plowing up all these flights for nothing! The murderer must have been as frightened as I. He must have pattered down those steps away from me as fast as his little feet would carry him. By now he was having a soda at Schrafft's. And I ... where was I?

I was midway between two landings. I pulled myself up slowly to the one above me. The numbers on the door were a five and an eight. I was fifty-eight floors from the ground. Fifty-eight flights of steep, hard steps to the bottom and ... twenty-nine to the top.

Once again I had a choice to make; up or down. Up was certainly tougher ... but down was exactly twice as far. I experimented; I went up three and then down three. In my condition I could see no difference. I started up.

Each flight seemed to grow steeper as I trudged up it. My throat was parched and I was wheezing at the seventy-fourth floor. I wondered what time it was. I wondered who was president now. I wondered if the Graylock Building kept a staff of St. Bernards. I hoped my St. Bernard would bring a coke instead of brandy. No, there wouldn't be any St. Bernards. They might be all right for the Alps, but this was a different matter.

I plodded on. At the eightieth floor tears started streaming down my cheeks and I began to pray. But only one prayer came to mind and I soon stopped that.

*"Now I lay me down to sleep ..."*

That wasn't helping my morale.

I staggered on up to the eighty-fourth floor. Three more to go. Only three more flights to go. Thank ... Oh, God, what if that door was locked!

It was by sheer force of character that I prevented myself from slipping over the brink into stark raving madness. I got a grip on myself. I composed myself. And I stumbled frantically up those last three flights.

The door swung wide as I fell against it. I was free. The world was mine!

I tottered over to the elevator and rang the bell.

Out of the polished and shining door of the elevator a face stared into mine. It was Victor McLaglen after he had been trapped in a coal mine over the weekend. I moved and he moved. I raised my hand; he raised his. It wasn't Vic. It was Haila. I was glad to see her anyway. I had never expected to see her again.

The doors slid open and I crawled into the car. The operator looked at me curiously.

"I didn't know there was anyone left on this floor," he said. "How'd you get up here?"

"I walked," I said.

He laughed heartily.

## Chapter Nine

IN FRONT OF 70 East Ninety-third Street I thought of the four flights of steps that led to our apartment and I quailed. I quailed all over the place. If there had been a pup tent handy, I would have pitched it on the sidewalk and resided there indefinitely. That dingy little basement apartment on Charles Street that I had hated so my first year in New York seemed like heaven to me now. No, not heaven, either. Heaven was approached by those alleged golden stairs.

Gritting my teeth, I started to climb. Valiant might be the word for Carrie. The word for Haila was "Up."

After my escape from the Graylock Building I'd made a halfhearted attempt to locate Jeff and Kirk. From a drug store across the street I'd called Photo Arts; there had been no answer. The only place for me to go then was home. Home was where the Absorbine Jr. was. If my visitor at the studio had been forced to go up, as I had, instead of down, I thought ruefully, he could be easily apprehended by the police now. They would merely have to search for ten blistered toes, two fallen arches and a pair of pernicious charley horses and they would get their man.

I had been soaking my body and soul in an almost boiling bath for I had no idea how long, when I heard Jeff in the living room.

"Haila, where are you?"

"In the bathtub, Jeff."

"What for?"

"What for! I'm entertaining Eleanor Holm and Johnny Weismuller!"

"Shall I mix you a drink?"

"Please! Who's with you?"

"Just Billy Rose and Lupe Velez. Hurry up!"

To give myself a lift I initiated a wedding present I had given myself; a turquoise satin tailored negligee. I hobbled into the living room and met Jeff at the studio couch, where he handed me my drink.

"You look wonderful, Haila."

"It's a nice negligee."

"I mean you. Personally. You look radiant ... healthy!"

"I've been exercising," I said weakly. "Jeff, I've just had the most horrible experience that has ever been lived through by a human being!"

"Cannibals? I told you to stay off Sixth Avenue."

"Listen, Jeff!"

And I launched into an account of my life since I had seen him. Not until

77

it was obvious that Jeff was feeling sorry for the wreck that once had been his wife did I let up on the harrowing details.

"It's a wonder you're alive," Jeff marveled.

"Who says I'm alive!"

"Lie down."

"Why?"

"I'm going to give you a Swedish massage."

"No!"

"C'mon, it'll be a counterirritant. That guy who chased you was a Swede. Swedes always make a clicking noise in the dark."

Jeff rolled me over on my stomach and went to work, bruising me briskly from top to bottom. "You didn't get a glimpse of that person, Haila?"

"Ouch! No. Hey, I don't hurt there!"

"A masseur deserves to have some fun. That clicking noise ... what did it sound like?"

"It sounded like a clicking noise! Let me up!"

"Roll over, stomach up. I'll iron out your charley horses."

"You leave my charley horses alone!" I pushed him away and sat up, reaching for my drink.

"Feel better now, don't you darling?"

"Aw, shut up. Darling."

"You're lucky you married a fellow who knows massaging like I do. From Alpha to Omega."

"You took a course in it at Dartmouth!"

"No. Wellesley. Haila, didn't you even get a chance to tear a button off that person's coat when he passed you? Can't you give me any sort of a clue?"

"Sorry, Jeff."

"That clicking noise! What on earth was it? Can't you describe it?"

"No, it was just ... you know ... just ..."

"Did it sound like somebody tapping a pencil against their teeth?"

"It might have been a coin against a window ... or ... Jeff, I really don't know! It clicked!"

Jeff lit a cigarette for me, then one for himself. He didn't speak. I watched him finish his drink. Then I asked, "Jeff, you aren't discouraged, are you?"

He grinned at me. "I should be, I guess. I'm not doing so well, am I? I haven't even proved yet that Mac didn't kill Mrs. Fleming, let alone prove who did."

"You've only been working on the case about ten hours, darling."

"If only I could get hold of a clue ..." Our buzzer interrupted Jeff and he pressed the button that released the downstairs door. "I can't even get a motive for anybody but Mac. And Erika, of course. Why, I haven't even been able to get in touch with three of the characters in this gay little comedy!"

"Which three, Jeff?"

"Snyder, Kenyon and Lawrence. Kirk and I, when we left you to take a snooze, went calling. Snyder and Kenyon weren't home and Madge Lawrence doesn't seem to have a home."

Jeff answered the knock on the door. It was Wyatt. He smiled wryly at the sight of Jeff. "I hoped I'd find your wife alone."

"My wife's never alone. Come in and sit down, Mr.. Wyatt."

"Thanks." He inspected all four of our chairs, chose the least comfortable one and dumped himself wearily into it.

"Haila," Jeff said, "I think you should tell Mr. Wyatt about what just happened to you."

"All right." And I did. He, too, was intrigued by the clicking noise, but I could be of no more help to him about it than I was to Jeff.

"If I were given to jumping to conclusions," Wyatt said, "I'd conclude that this was the murderer returning to the scene of the crime. To correct some error he made."

"Listen, Wyatt," Jeff said, "whoever it was certainly wasn't connected with the studio. None of them, not even Erika, would have sneaked around in the dark. Any one of them could surely have found a chance before six o'clock tonight to do whatever they wanted to do."

"Maybe," Wyatt grunted.

"Jeff," I asked, "did you and Kirk lock the door when you left?"

"Yes, but ..."

Wyatt interrupted him. "Forget about that door. It can't help us a bit. There are keys for it all over town. I've never run up against such a gang of key-losers. In the last six months, MacCormick says, he's had at least a dozen new ones made. Anybody that made a point of it could have got hold of one. I'll check on what everybody was doing and where they were doing it between five and six this afternoon. We'll see what comes of that. Mrs. Troy?"

"Yes?"

"I want you to tell me about your friend, Julie Taylor."

"Julie! Is she all right?"

"I haven't talked to her yet. Tell me what you know about her."

"Well, Julie's almost twenty-seven. She came to New York ... let's see, in 1936. We lived in the same girls' club on Fifty-seventh Street that year. That's where I met her. Photo Arts was her first and only job in New York."

"Six years," Wyatt said, "on the same job with lousy pay."

"Sometimes no pay."

"Hmm. I wonder why."

I shrugged. Let him find out for himself that Julie would have starved at the North Pole to be near Kirk. She had never even confessed that to me, so I wasn't going to pass it along for a stranger to kick around.

"Would you know, Troy?" Wyatt asked. Jeff shook his head. "All right, Mrs. Troy, go on about Miss Taylor."

"Julie came from Cleveland ..."

"43654 Lakewood Avenue."

"Yes. Her mother and a sister live there. Her father's been dead for some years. She goes back there twice a year; Christmas and summer vacation."

"And her friends?"

"She has millions of friends in New York. She ..."

"It's the ones out of New York I'm interested in."

"Well, there's an aunt in Boston ..."

"423 Prince Street. All right, go on."

"Her roommate from Ohio State lives in Trenton now. I don't know her address."

"1126 Washington Avenue."

I said impatiently, "You know as much about it as I do. Why are you asking me?"

"I want to know more."

"You should ask Julie then," I insisted.

"I can't. Miss Taylor has disappeared."

"She's disappeared!" I echoed.

Visions of Julie disappearing overwhelmed me; Julie, a black bag tossed over her head, being carted off by kidnappers; Julie being lured into a passing automobile and driven, screaming and protesting, out of the city; even visions of Julie, in her tweed coat and little brown hat as I had seen her last, standing in plain view one moment, vanishing into thin air the next, like some trick moving picture.

"Miss Taylor has left town," Wyatt said curtly.

"Oh, no! No, Julie wouldn't do that! Why, that's running out on Mac and Kirk and all of us. She wouldn't do anything like that." I added, with all the confidence that I could muster, "You don't know Julie Taylor."

"Miss Taylor left town this morning at half-past five."

"But, why? Why would she? She hasn't anything to be afraid of; she didn't kill Mrs. Fleming."

Wyatt smiled. "No matter who I named you'd say they didn't murder Mrs. Fleming. You're a great believer in the goodness of human nature, aren't you Mrs. Troy? I think that's just fine. And I wish you were right.

Then there wouldn't have to be any policemen. Or preachers."

"How do you know Julie left town?" Jeff asked.

"We cops are clever. You see if you can't be clever, too."

"She must have gone to Cleveland, then," I said, "to her mother's."

"She left fourteen hours ago. And she isn't there yet."

"How do you know she isn't?"

"You aren't a detective, Mrs. Troy, so I'll tell you. Cleveland police. And by the same means, we know she isn't with her aunt in Boston, her old roommate in Trenton, or with another sister in East Orange that you forgot to mention. So where did she go, Mr. and Mrs. Troy?"

"Look, Mr. Wyatt," I said, "Julie didn't go visiting."

"Nor hiding?"

"No! If she left town it wasn't on her own power. She was taken, forced to go, dragged!"

Wyatt said patiently, "She left town all by herself. She wasn't dragged away. I'll admit she might have been forced ..."

"Oh, you do!"

"... forced by circumstances. And when we know those circumstances, we'll know who killed Isabelle Fleming."

"You've got to find her, Mr. Wyatt!"

"That's what I've been intimating."

"No, I mean you've got to find her for her own sake. I don't care what you say, Julie never ran out on us. She must be in trouble, or in danger."

"I hope not," Wyatt said, "I like little Julie Taylor."

There was something frighteningly ominous in his voice. He thanked me, nodded good-bye and started for the door. Jeff followed him to the landing.

Instinctively, I went to the telephone and dialed Julie's number. I couldn't believe that she had even gone at all. I heard the sound of the connection being made, then the long buzzes as her telephone rang. I almost whooped for joy when I heard one buzz snapped short and her receiver lifted. But the voice that answered Julie's telephone wasn't Julie's. It was a man's voice, soft and flat and vaguely familiar.

I said, "Who ... who is it?"

"Detective Lieutenant Lockhart speaking. Yes?"

I hung up. That much of it, at least, was true. Julie had gone. Lockhart was probably searching her apartment.

"Jeff," I said, as he came back in and closed the door behind him, "Julie wouldn't leave New York voluntarily! She wouldn't desert Mac and Kirk and the rest of us. Something has happened to her!"

"You get dressed quick. We'll go down to Julie's and snoop around."

"Lockhart's there now. I just called."

"He won't see us."

Our cab was rolling down Park Avenue when, in one last effort to get my mind off Julie, I said, "Jeff, where does Lee Kenyon live?"

"He and Snyder share an apartment, or did share an apartment, on Eighth Avenue. Over a barber shop."

"Did share?"

"The superintendent told us that Kenyon had moved out this morning. He didn't know where."

"If you want to see Kenyon, he dances at the Barrel Room."

"That dive on Sullivan Street?"

"Yes. Let's go, if there's nothing we can do about Julie."

"We'll see. But I'd better go alone."

"No."

"They drink and smoke in the Barrel Room, Haila. It's nasty."

"And they have scantily dressed girls. That's why you're not going alone, darling."

The taxi swung around the ramp that surrounds Grand Central. My thoughts went back to Julie again.

"Haila," Jeff said, "isn't it strange for a model not to be listed in the phone book? Madge Lawrence, I mean."

"Not if she hasn't a phone. Oh, I see what you mean! Of course, Madge has a phone. A model has to have one."

"Why wouldn't Madge have hers listed?"

"It does seem strange."

"Kirk telephoned Miss Leonard at the Models Bureau and asked for Madge's address. But Miss Leonard wouldn't give. Said it wasn't permitted."

"Well, maybe it isn't."

"But when I called her a few minutes later and asked for some other model's address ... one we picked at random out of the catalogue ... it was permitted then. Do you suppose that Madge and Miss Leonard are joint proprietors of a marijuana den?"

The cab stopped a few blocks below Gramercy Park on Irving Place in front of Julie's house. It was one of those quaint old apartment buildings left over from the nineties. Its elevator, an elaborate gilded cage, should have been turned out to pasture with Man o' War. Fred, the operator, was an old pal of mine and he grinned wildly when he spied us.

"Miss Taylor's disappeared!" he shouted. Any worry he might have felt for Julie's safety was smothered under his excitement.

"Were you here when she left?" Jeff asked.

"You bet! She come in about five and went right back out about twenty minutes later."

"Did she have a suitcase?"

"Sure, a big one. It had green stripes. Airplane luggage, they call it," he added knowingly.

"Did you speak to her?"

"Sure. I said, 'Going some place, Miss Taylor?' and she just shook her head. She didn't look like she wanted to talk so I didn't say anymore."

"Did she take a cab?"

"Wait a minute!" Fred dashed out of the lobby to the sidewalk, put two fingers in his mouth and whistled shrilly. A cab pulled up in front of the door. A moment later we were being formally introduced to the driver.

"Kenny, I want you to meet two friends of Miss Taylor's."

Kenny grunted.

"Tell them, Kenny," Fred went on, "about Miss Taylor this morning."

"What about her?" Kenny was blasé.

"What about her!" Fred turned to us in exasperation. "He was the last one to see her alive and now he says, 'What about her?' "

"Listen, Kid Pop-Off!" Kenny said savagely, "you got confidential word that Miss Taylor is dead?"

"Why, no, I …"

"Then keep your mouth shut! I took Miss Taylor to the Pennsy Station. I left her out in front of it. I offered to carry her bag but she wouldn't let me. I seen her walk into Pennsy Station, get it! That's all! So don't you go makin' any cracks about me bein' the last one to see her alive!"

Kenny turned on his heel and strode out.

Fred shook his head sadly. "I got a theory that Kenny is secretly in love with Miss Taylor. He lets her run up a bill in his cab. That's love, if you ask me."

"Everybody likes Julie," Jeff said.

"Sure they do. She makes people feel good. You know what? Every year for two years now she took me up to the Yankee Stadium opening day. She got more friends in this here building … even Miss Frost. Why, Miss Frost is her best friend, I guess. And everybody else here hates Miss Frost. And she hates them. She won't talk to nobody but Miss Taylor."

"Where's Miss Frost's apartment?"

"Right across the hall from Miss Taylor's. She's been living there since nobody knows."

"Will you take us up to see her?"

"She won't talk to you."

"We'll talk to her."

Fred gave us a doubtful look. "Get in," he said, "you're the boss."

Jeff had been knocking stubbornly for a full three minutes before Miss Frost's door was finally flung open, so vigorously that we were almost drawn into the room by the suction it created.

"Come in and hurry up!" Miss Frost commanded. "Before the turtles get out!"

We scrambled in and she slammed the door behind us with a resounding bang.

"Turtles?" Jeff inquired politely.

"Yes, turtles!" Miss Frost snapped, not unturtlelike herself. She was a stocky little woman of perhaps forty-five, with salt-and-pepper colored hair, a severe nose and a remarkably determined chin. Her eyes, however, were a soft brown that was completely out of keeping with the rest of her face. She squinted them noticeably when she spoke, as if she were aware of their softness and ashamed of it.

"I hope none of them got out," Jeff said, looking around the room. There wasn't a turtle in sight.

"Sit down, since you're here! I hate people standing around!" I eased myself gingerly on the edge of a davenport and Jeff was about to flop into a plump old Morris chair when Miss Frost shouted, "No, young man!" Jeff leaped into the air. "Do you want to squash Philadelphia?"

Jeff examined the chair. "But I … I don't see Philadelphia, Miss Frost."

"No?" She rushed out of the room, whamming the door behind her. A moment later she was back. Again the door banged, this time with such force that it promptly bounced open a couple of inches.

"They're all in the bathroom, all of them! Sit down!"

"How many do you have, Miss Frost?" Jeff asked, glancing cautiously into the chair before seating himself.

"Are you making conversation, young man, or are you really interested in turtles?"

"I'm very fond of turtles."

Miss Frost glared at Jeff. "I hate them," she said.

"You … you hate them?" Jeff echoed.

"I hate them. That's what I said. And I especially loathe my eleven."

"Then why …"

"Relatives. Relatives send them to me! Have for years. It started with the Boston Exposition in 1910. Every time someone goes to an exposition or a fair or a whatnot, I get a turtle! The first three were a coincidence. Now my relatives have the notion that I'm collecting them. The idiots!"

"Why don't you sell them, Miss Frost?" Jeff asked. "To Campbell's or Heinz's?"

"One doesn't sell one's gifts, young man!" Miss Frost said regally.

A large turtle entered from the bathroom.

"Is that Philadelphia?" I asked.

"No. San Francisco. And now, young man, what do you want?"

"We're friends of Julie Taylor's and ..."

"Does that give you the privilege of breaking into my apartment at nine o'clock at night!"

"We're sorry. But we hoped that you might be able to tell us ..." Jeff stopped. He was staring at the doorway. A trio of terrapins was entering in single file.

"Pittsburgh, Detroit, New York! I can't tell you anything, young man."

"Julie didn't tell you where she was going by any chance?"

"I didn't even know that she had left until I found the note under my door this morning."

"What note? May I see it, please?"

"You may not! St. Louis ate it."

"What did it say?"

"Practically nothing. She merely asked me to tell our cleaning woman, one that we share on Thursdays, that she would be out of town and not to bother with her apartment."

"But she didn't say where ..."

"No!"

"Nor for how long?"

"No! Here comes Paris!"

"Paris, France?" There was admiration in Jeff's tone.

"Naturally!"

"You'd never know it. He looks as American as the others." He hurried on as Miss Frost beetled her brows in our direction. "Today's Tuesday. Your cleaning woman comes on Thursday. So Julie expected to be gone that long at least. And she wouldn't leave a note of that sort if she were being forced out of town at the point of a gun," he added to me.

"It's going on ten o'clock," Miss Frost said.

There was no mistaking the invitation in her voice. We thanked Miss Frost and left her alone with her eleven international turtles.


## Chapter Ten


SULLIVAN STREET was ablaze with burning boxes, crates, paper cartons, and all the assorted inflammables that New York's gamins nightly uncover to satisfy their appetites for juvenile incendiarism. One eye on their fires, the other on a sharp lookout for the policeman, they tended to their business with the seriousness of battleship stokers. Jeff and I threaded our way through the red glow of the bonfires toward a neon sign that spelled out all the letters of the Barrel Room except one of the O's.

Under the glass cases that lined each side of the garishly colored entrance were photographs of the Village's Hottest Nite Spot's current attractions. Various gals in various stages of dishabille smiling coyly over their bared shoulders. A dusky young lady with a long bob and big black eyes billed as "The Polka Girl." A trio of sleek young men with shiny trumpets known as "The Three Swinging Fools." And Lee Kenyon in a Paul Draper pose, complete to white tie and tails, under the conventional heading, "Tapper Extraordinaire."

The steep staircase was painted a midnight blue and splashed with silver stars, out of whose centers gleamed more pictures of more luscious lovelies in less and less attire.

The wailing of a four-piece band met us at the bottom steps. Evidently one of the three swingsters doubled in drums and another had a friend who played a piano. The Polka Girl was taking her cue as we entered, and the accompaniment quieted to a throb as her strangely unmusical voice raised itself in a dare to all the unescorted males in the surrounding gloom. She gave; she raffled off her soul.

"Don't be misled," Jeff whispered. "She goes straight home after the show and writes a long letter to her brother whom she's putting through a Midwestern theological seminary."

A voice asked if we would like a table. I was about to inquire if there were any tables when my eyes succeeded in piercing the darkness enough to see that there were; lots of them. I took Jeff's hand and we followed the squat little Italian to a distant corner. I plunked myself down where I hoped a chair would be. We ordered rye highballs.

By the time our drinks appeared, Lee Kenyon was in the midst of his number. It was certainly tapping extraordinaire. It was Nijinski, Bill Robinson and the Radio City Rockettes all rolled up into Lee Kenyon, and not quite jelling. It was Modern Art, arresting but confusing. To his friends, Lee Kenyon was probably a genius; to his colleagues, a screwball.

The Polka Girl had had only a pinpoint of light upon her; Lee Kenyon had a large white spot. But even that couldn't quite keep up with Lee. Often it lost him entirely and went sweeping frantically around the room to locate him. During one of its more far-flung jaunts, Jeff nudged me so hard that I nearly fell off my chair.

"What, Jeff?"

He half rose and peered across the room in the opposite direction from Lee's leaping figure. I tried to see what had so acutely attracted his attention.

Light colored circles that were table tops, dark forms that were people, white blotches that were faces. A scurrying waiter showing even less regard for Lee's artistry than some of the patrons. Nothing, certainly, to provoke Jeff's attack on me.

"Jeff, what is it!"

"Over there. To the left of the band. Third table from the … What the devil!"

The wandering spotlight was abruptly quenched in its chase after Lee. The place was in total darkness. A few hesitant notes continued to come from the horns, a few tapping steps from Kenyon, then even they stopped. Cued by the blackout, the inevitable female wisecrack rose to get its inevitable laugh. "Hey, keep your hands off me!" Giggles and laughter and more attempts at humor grew into a hubbub, and then into confusion. Near me, a familiar voice exploded in a curse. It was followed by the tinkling of a breaking glass and the crash of overturned chairs. Then a moment's unexpected silence as the whole room quieted simultaneously.

"Jeff!"

There was no answer. I reached out; felt nothing. I groped around the table and my hand came against the back of Jeff's chair. It was empty.

"Jeff!" I called again.

Someone mockingly took up my cry and in a moment the whole place was hilariously shouting for Jeff. The band started playing, not quite together. Above it I heard that familiar voice again, this time in a groan. There was the heavy thudding sound of a body falling.

The lights flashed on.

The place was fully illuminated now, not by the spot nor by the ingeniously hidden wall fixtures, but by naked electric bulbs on the ceiling. The glare made me close my eyes, not, however, before ascertaining that Jeff had completely disappeared from view. When I managed to open my eyes again, I saw him.

He was sitting on the floor at the edge of the dancing space. His hands were cupped about his chin and he was moving it experimentally. I sidestepped through the tables to him, getting there just in time to help a couple of gentlemen and a waiter help him to his feet.

"What happened, buddy?" one of the men asked.

Jeff brushed us all aside and bolted for the stairs. I met him on his way back down. Still rubbing his jaw and ignoring my questions, he headed for our table and beckoned a waiter.

"A double rye," he said. "Straight."

The ceiling bulbs had been extinguished and the Barrel Room was once again plunged into its seductive twilight. The band was playing smoothly in an attempt to assure the clients that everything was fine again.

"Jeff, what did happen!"

"I got hit."

"By what?"

He wagged his jaw. "A croquet mallet."

"I don't imagine this dive is frequented by croquet players."

"All right, by a fist then," Jeff grudgingly conceded.

"Who punched you? And why?"

"Because he didn't want me to hold on to him until the lights came back on and I could see who he was."

The waiter reappeared, slid a highball glass half filled with rye across the table and followed it with a glass of water and a check. They didn't trust you at the Barrel Room.

"Look," Jeff said, reaching in his pocket. "What happened?"

"What happened?" The waiter's face was blank.

"You know, a few minutes ago."

"Oh!" Comprehension brightened his face like the aurora borealis. "The lights went out."

Jeff controlled himself nobly. "I see. I wondered why it got so dark. Well, what made the lights go out?"

"Just the spotlight went out. That's all."

"Where's that spotlight connected?"

He shrugged. "I'm just a waiter," he said and moved off.

Jeff glared after him. It must be some place over there."

I looked in the direction Jeff had indicated. At a table against the far wall, sitting alone, was Erika MacCormick.

"Jeff!" I exclaimed. "Look!"

"Yes, didn't you know?"

"What's she doing here? And alone!"

"Nice quiet place to mourn. C'mon."

Erika watched our approach with smiling indifference. Her waiter lifted two empty old fashioned glasses from the table and set a full one before her. She raised it to her lips and fluttered long, gold-tipped lashes at Jeff.

"Are you hurt, Jeff?" She was amused.

"A headache. And you'll have one, too, if you keep on drinking old fashioneds."

"It's only my second."

"Third," Jeff corrected pleasantly.

"No." She glanced sharply at him and frowned at his smile. "Oh, yes, my mistake. Third."

"Second," Jeff said. "Who had the other one?"

"Let's not play games." She turned to me. "This isn't a very nice place to bring a husband, Haila. I'm surprised."

Jeff said, "You wouldn't bring yours here, would you, Erika? Or did you?"

Erika smiled too sweetly. "Mac's working. I was just about to call him and ask him to pick me up here. I wanted to see Lee's new routine."

"Oh, yes. He's a protégé of yours."

"I don't like that word. I thought Lee had talent and I tried to help him."

"Do you still think he has talent?"

"Not as much as I once did. And it's impossible to help him."

"You've stopped trying?"

"Months ago. He won't listen to advice. He's a very arrogant young man."

"I see." The conversation lapsed until Erika, with a sudden move, reached for her wrap. Jeff said quickly, "Erika, I wish you'd remember a little more about Amanda Lewis."

"I wish you'd forget about Amanda Lewis."

If Erika thought that dismissed the subject, she was mistaken. Jeff went on, "Your Uncle Sanford must have been a gay old dog."

"As I remember him, he was a grim-faced tycoon. Dynamic."

"Sure, that's it! Edward Arnold."

"Not quite. There was nothing Diamond Jim Brady about Uncle Sanford. He was all business. I never heard him laugh."

"If he didn't laugh around the house, he must have had his secret laughing place. Those were the days ..."

"Don't be silly, Jeff!" Erika snapped.

"Those were the days," Jeff continued, "of real democracy, when capital and labor got along. Millionaires and working girls. That is, girls working for Ziegfeld. Amanda Lewis ... let's see. If she was a luscious show girl in the roaring twenties, she'd probably be about thirty-five now. Faded and bitter. Probably eating her heart out hating Isabelle Fleming for taking away her just deserts by contesting Sanford's will ..."

"What are you getting at, Jeff!"

"That Amanda Lewis had a motive for murdering your aunt."

Erika said in disgust, "She hasn't been heard of in years."

"And she certainly wasn't at Photo Arts on Monday night," I added.

"That we know of," Jeff said.

"Stop dreaming," Erika suggested.

But Jeff persisted. "Think of Amanda as she must be today. Platinum and blowzy from drinking gin in her bad luck. Fat and tough and filled with hate. The ex-Ziegfeld beauty who once had a penthouse on ... where did the boys have their penthouses in the twenties?"

Erika laughed sarcastically. "I hate to spoil your fun, but Uncle Sanford wasn't one of the boys."

"No?"

"No. And it happens that Amanda Lewis wasn't a showgirl."

"No?" Jeff asked again.

"Amanda Lewis was the first Mrs. Sanford Fleming."

"She was ... what!"

"His first wife. Aunt Isabelle was his second. Didn't you know that, Jeff?" Erika's smile was sugary.

"A divorce?"

"Really, Jeff, I'd rather not discuss it."

"But why, Erika?"

"Frankly, I don't approve of your meddling in this case."

"But this morning you said ..."

"That was this morning."

The conversation took another nosedive. Jeff looked around the room. He motioned to a pasty-faced young man who was tinkering with a spotlight, arranging gelatins.

"Hey!" Jeff said.

"Me?" The young man came to our table.

"Did your spot break down?"

"Naw. It's all right. The plug just came out." He pointed to a floor plug between Erika and the empty chair beside her.

"Oh," Jeff said. The boy went back about his business. Jeff was smiling at Erika again. "The floor plug just came out."

Erika stood up, drawing her sable coat around her shoulders. "I think it was ridiculous of Mac to bring you into this. You're going to do him more harm than good. And I shall tell him so!" The flash of her eyes seemed to light up her golden lashes.

"Now, Erika ..."

"If he won't call you off ... well, at least, you won't get any help from me. If Mac needs a detective, we'll hire a real one, a good one. I'm not interested in answering your silly, prying questions that have nothing to do with the murder. Good-by, Haila. When you've succeeded in convincing your husband that he shouldn't play cop, call me. Until then ..."

Her words drifted off, but there was no necessity for her finishing them. We watched her slip through the now-jammed room. Every eye in the place watched, too, as she disappeared up the stairs.

"Jeff," I said. "All that devastating innuendo ... were you inferring that there was someone with Erika?"

"There was. Someone who saw me before I saw him. I just caught a glimpse of dark blue shoulder as he ducked behind the table."

"To pull out the light plug!"

"Sure. And then make an exit without being seen. I almost stopped him. But not quite."

"You've no idea who it was, Jeff?"

He rubbed his jaw. "It could have been Joe Louis. Let's go back and visit Lee Kenyon."

"But he was dancing when you saw Erika, he ..."

Jeff was already asking a waiter where he could find Kenyon. We were led through an end of the kitchen and down a dirty corridor filled with shivering chorus girls awaiting their cue. Raising both hands high above his head, Jeff plunged through them.

"My God, a gentleman!" the only brunette said in a genuinely awed voice.

"How'd he get in the Barrel?" one of the seven blondes cracked.

Lee Kenyon was sitting before a mirror painting a bewitching little mustache on his upper lip. He was clad magnificently in a white and gold costume, a replica of the one Massine wears as the mad Peruvian in *Gaieté Parisienne*.

The dancer seemed pleased to see me and to meet Jeff, even before we made some flattering, if slightly insincere, remarks about his act. He pointed to the red nick on Jeff's chin. "You weren't the chap who was clipped out there in the dark?"

"Yeah. You didn't see, by any chance, who did the clipping?"

"No, I got all tangled up myself when the lights went out. I didn't know that anybody had been hit until afterwards when one of the waiters told me. Sit down, won't you?" He dragged out an old piano bench that was the sole furniture in the little beaverboard room. "Would you like me to send for some drinks?"

"Not for me, thanks," I said.

"Jeff?"

"We can only stay a minute. Kirk Findlay and I stopped in to see you this afternoon. Between five and six." He said it with great casualness, but he watched Lee closely.

"I was checking into my new abode just about then," Lee answered. "The Sherry-Netherland."

Jeff whistled. "Nice going."

"I hope you'll all call on me there." He smiled. "It's much safer, I assure you, than the Barrel Room. Incidentally, what are you doing down here? Slumming?"

There was bitterness in Kenyon's voice. I said lightly, "This isn't slumming for us, Lee. This is the Sert Room compared to where Jeff usually takes me."

Jeff laughed. "I don't approve of nightclubs. They discourage breathing. And that will eventually undermine national health. Look, Kenyon, Mac Mac-Cormick has asked me to play detective and make a nuisance of myself generally."

"Oh, so that's why you called on me." He looked intently at Jeff for a moment. "Go right ahead, I don't mind. It's decent of you to put me on my guard so that I don't incriminate myself." His smile was decidedly thin.

"I'm not having much luck incriminating. Incidentally, I don't suppose you know where Madge Lawrence lives, do you?"

"I never saw the woman until yesterday."

"Did you ever see Mrs. Fleming before yesterday?"

Kenyon turned quickly to look in the mirror. Wetting his little finger he removed some stray powder from an eyebrow. "You think I did, don't you?"

"I heard that your attitude toward her was … familiar. Contemptuously familiar, to be exact."

Kenyon smiled kindly at me to show that he knew where Jeff had got his information. "I was kidding. I never saw her except in the papers. All I was trying to do was get a rise out of Snyder. He's a social climber and he was bending his knee before her."

"Snyder seems like a nice guy," Jeff said.

Kenyon started. "Have you talked to him? Did you see him this afternoon?"

"No, it's Haila who says he's a nice guy. He wasn't home either between five and six. You didn't move because you two don't get along together, did you?"

"No. We're old friends, such old friends that we get on each other's nerves, ride each other at every opportunity and take advantage of all those pleasures of old friendship."

Jeff's eyes roved around the room and stopped in a corner. "Beautiful luggage you've got there." He nodded toward an expensive-looking leather bag.

"Thank you."

"Wonderful clothes, too." Jeff flipped his head toward the racks where a tweed suit and evening clothes hung. "I admire your taste. New, aren't they?"

Lee nodded. He was no longer glad to see us. His guard was plainly up. "I got sick of looking like a Bowery bum."

Jeff sighed. "I wish I had a rich uncle who passed away."

"What do you mean?"

"Nothing. Well, new luggage, new clothes. The Sherry-Netherland ..."
Kenyon grinned with boyish frankness. "I'll only be there until they send
me a bill."

"I get it. The fancy clothes and luggage are credit-getters?"

"Exactly. I'll admit it's an unoriginal idea but I think I can make it work.
Up to a certain point. I'm taking a vacation from my usual squalor."

The door burst open to admit Jim Snyder. He was more than a little tight
and in wonderful spirits. He was so glad to see me that he was a bit embarrassed when I admitted in my introduction that Jeff was my husband.

"What are you two doing in this dive?"

"Getting clanked on the chin," Jeff answered. "Did you just arrive?"

"Me? Yeah. What happened?"

Jim roared at Jeff's story and thought he deserved what he got for bring-
ing a delicate flower like me to such a place. Kenyon was bored by his
alcoholic gallantry.

"Sit down, Muscles," he said.

"Well, we'll be going," Jeff said.

Kenyon stuck out his hand. "I'm glad that you liked my dancing."

"I did, very much. That routine, the new one ..."

"New one? I didn't do any new routine tonight."

"You didn't?" Jeff raised his eyebrows.

"I wouldn't waste any new stuff on this dive. What gave you that idea?"

"Erika MacCormick mentioned it to me."

"Erika? Was she here?"

"Yes."

"I didn't realize," Kenyon said, "that she even knew I was dancing in this
hellhole. God knows I haven't advertised it. Of course, Jim has. He gets a
malicious pleasure out of my misfortune."

"I just saw Gregory outside," Jim said. "He says you're quitting this
Saturday."

"Gregory is correct. God bless Gregory."

"What in hell are you going to live on? First you give up posing, and now
this!"

"And now all this," Jeff said, "and the Sherry-Netherland, too!"

"The Sherry-Netherland!" Jim gaped.

Kenyon smiled placidly. "You haven't been home yet, Jim? Well, I moved
out on you, old man. Thanks for stopping in, you Troys." He shook hands
with both of us and opened the door. "You leaving, too, Jim?"

"No, I'm not!"

Jeff and I did. We had already spent more money than we should have,
and when Jeff suggested a taxi I put my foot down, although the pains shot

clear up to my hip. We walked east to Wanamakers and then boarded a Lexington Avenue local.

A figure was huddled on our outside steps. It was Kirk. His tousled head was propped against the door and he was sound asleep.

## Chapter Eleven

UNDER THE WARM yellow light of our living room lamps, I saw that Kirk's eyes were bloodshot, his face lined with fatigue, and the rest of him so completely caved in that his light tan suit seemed too large for him. My Girl Scout background came rushing to the fore.

"Kirk! When did you sleep last?"

He laughed at my concern. "Just a few minutes ago."

"I mean in a bed?"

"What's a bed?"

"And when did you eat last?"

"Look, I came to see you because …"

"That can wait a second. Jeff, you give him artificial respiration while I fiddle around with some eggs."

Jeff and Kirk followed me into the kitchen, but in spite of their efforts to help, I finally got toast, scrambled eggs and coffee under way.

"It's … it's about Julie," Kirk said.

"Kirk, have they found her?"

"No, Haila. I haven't either."

"You've been looking for her?"

"Sure." His face was screwed up into a sort of smile. "The New York police can't find Julie, but me, I think I might. So I traipse all over town talking to people Julie knew. To see if any of them have any ideas about where she might have gone. No soap."

"Did you talk to the turtle woman?" Jeff asked.

"Miss Frost? Yeah, she was on my list."

"Did she let you in?"

Kirk nodded. "We're bosom friends. Miss Frost has been up to the studio several times … meeting Julie. They had tickets for a series of concerts."

I plunked food down in front of Kirk and poured coffee for all three of us.

"Thanks, Haila." He stared at the eggs without making a move to touch them. "I can't believe that Julie …" He stopped.

"What, Kirk?"

"Ran away. You know how it is with Julie and Mac and me. She wouldn't run out on Mac when he was in trouble any more than he'd run out on one of us."

"Kirk," I said, "you're afraid that Julie is ... that she's been forced to leave, that she's in danger."

"Yes." For a moment no one spoke.

"Eat your eggs," Jeff said. Kirk picked up his fork and made a listless pass at the yellow mound before him. "Kirk, Wyatt believes, in fact, he knows that Julie left town of her own free will and volition."

Kirk refused to accept that. "She might have been tricked into going." He put down his fork. "I'm sorry, Haila, I can't eat. Listen, Jeff, if Julie knew too much ... if she realized who the person in the darkroom with her was ... he might have got her out of town. He could have done it any number of ways."

"Name one, Kirk."

"Well, if Julie thought she could help Mac by meeting someone in St. Louis or Hawaii or any place, she'd pack up her bag and light out. She might even have realized it was a trap and walked into it hoping to bring back the killer. Dead or alive! You know Julie! She's ..." Kirk realized his voice was going soft on him. He took care of that immediately. "Julie's a little dope!" he declared in a loud, challenging tone.

I stirred my coffee thoughtfully. "Kirk's right, Jeff. And another thing; she might have been led to believe that she was going to meet Mac some place. Or Kirk."

"They're nice theories," Jeff said.

Kirk had left his chair and he was moving nervously around our little kitchen. "I wish to God there was something *better* to do than mope around and theorize!"

"There is, pal. You flatten out on the studio couch and catch yourself some shuteye or you'll be among the missing, too. You'll fold up into a vacuum."

"Thanks, Jeff, but I'll go home. These clothes are sticking to me."

"You're sure you'll go home?" I asked.

"I promise, nurse." He turned to Jeff. "What about tomorrow?"

"I'll be at the studio about eleven. Round up Mac and Harry and meet me there, will you?"

"We could make it earlier."

"I've got some things to do before that. I've got an idea to work on. Goodnight, Kirk."

Kirk stood with one hand on the doorknob and looked around our apartment. "A home!" he said. "Imagine having more than one room. And with your own furniture! I've read about people like you, you lucky people."

"Now, Kirk," I said, "you know you wouldn't tie yourself to a lease or any furniture or anything you couldn't pack into one suitcase."

"Wouldn't I, Haila?" Kirk laughed at me. "Goodnight, one and all." Jeff closed the door behind him. "And goodnight to you, Haila."

"Am I going to bed?"

"I want to think, and I can't with you hovering about."

"Oh, Jeff, what a pretty compliment!"

"No," he said, "it's just that I don't want you getting hysterical."

"Hysterical?"

"Yes. When I think my nose starts bleeding."

"Well, stay off the rug. Do your thinking on some newspaper. I'm not sleepy, Jeff, but I'll get ready for bed." I made for the bedroom. "Oh, darling, I hate to bother you with domestic details, but I haven't had time lately to do any laundry. I haven't a thing to wear."

"How charming."

"May I borrow a pair of your pajamas?"

"No." Jeff closed one eye and twirled imaginary mustachios.

"You can't do this to me! I'm a married woman!"

I did find a nightgown after all. Something a romantic old aunt of mine had given me for an engagement present. Looking at myself in the full-length mirror I could understand why auntie had such a large family. After slipping into a negligee, I returned to the living room. Jeff was so deep in thought he had neglected to put his feet up on our new coffee table.

"Jeff ..."

"Huh?"

"Think out loud."

"The Dodgers need an outfielder and a couple of pitchers for next season. God, I can't even find anything about this murder to *think* about. Anything definite, I mean."

"But, darling! There's Julie's disappearance and all that incriminating evidence against Mac and ..."

"Those are things to *worry* about. If I find the murderer, Mac and Julie will be all right. Haila, what do you suppose that person wanted you saw in the studio?"

"Search me! But that's certainly something to think about. And the clicking sound."

"Haila, if only you could describe it, if you ..."

"I can't, Jeff," I said miserably.

"I know, I'm not blaming you. A clicking sound is a clicking sound. The world over. And you were still half asleep."

"Jeff, you should check on people to see what they were doing at the time my visitor was with me at the studio. You should check on Jim Snyder and Madge Lawrence and Robert Yorke …"

"Wyatt will do all that. He can do it much more efficiently than I can. I'm trying to go about this in a different way than Wyatt. There's no point to me just duplicating his maneuvers. Besides, as I said before, so modestly, the police are better at police methods than I am."

"What is your way, Jeff?"

He laughed. "You're not kidding me, are you, sweetheart?"

"Of course not!"

"Well, Wyatt is mainly concerned with the time of the crime. Where were you at ten-twenty? And where were you when the knife was taken? And where were you when the beautiful Mrs. Troy heard the clicking noise? And how does your garden grow?"

"Wyatt wants facts."

"Yes, and when and if he gets enough of them, he'll solve the case. But people aren't giving him facts. Obviously, the killer is lying. And almost certainly, he isn't the only one. Other people are frightened, too. For instance, May Ralston may be lying, not because she committed the murder, but because if she tells the truth about what she was doing at ten-twenty, it will be discovered that she has athlete's foot. Or is a Communist. And these base fabrications of other people protect the murderer and make it tough for Wyatt. So I'm not interested in the time of the crime. I'm interested in before and after the crime. Mostly before, because after the killer is on guard. He's not being himself, not acting naturally. And that brings up another point. May I bring up another point?"

"Go ahead, Jeff, bring up."

"Thanks. Remember I'm talking about premeditated murder. Specifically, the murder of Mrs. Isabelle Fleming. All right. As soon as a person decides to kill, from then through his planning, his deed and even afterwards, he is another person. He has lost his identity. He is consciously behaving as the sort of person who would *not* kill Mrs. Fleming. Therefore, I'm interested in what happened the week, month, year and even decade before last Monday night. Then the killer was acting like a person who was going to kill. He was being himself; a person whose greed or desire for revenge, or whatever the motive turns out to be, was already driving him toward the murder."

"Whether he knew it or not."

"No, Haila, as soon as he *knew* he was going to murder, he became another person, a person who wasn't going to murder. He began to act; play act. If you could pry open a killer's life before he made his decision to kill, you could solve any premeditated crime."

"But, Jeff, you can't ignore the events and behavior of people during and after the crime!"

"I'm not. For instance tonight when we were talking to Kenyon ... he seemed worried about whether I had talked to Snyder. He might've been afraid that Snyder spilled a few beans. Which means that Snyder knows something, probably something about Kenyon and Mrs. Fleming. Perhaps, Kenyon didn't murder her, but his connection with her, if there is one, will uncover someone else's. The murderer's, I hope. Let's go to bed."

"I'm willing."

"I'm not sleepy," Jeff said.

"Is that a threat, darling?"

"Haila, we've been married a month now. It's high time one of us started remembering to open the bedroom window."

"I always remembered before I got married."

"So did I. My, my, life can be beautiful. Did I ever tell you, Haila, that as a creature, you fascinate me?"

By twelve-thirty the next day, Wednesday, Julie's whereabouts were still a mystery. And it was a dismal little group we formed in the big studio, Mac, Kirk and Harry, Jeff and I.

Neither Kirk's spirit nor his appearance had taken any turn for the better since we had seen him the night before. He looked as though he had spent that interim continuing his futile search for Julie Taylor, inane as it was, even to him. He had more beard by this time than I had thought he could raise on an election bet and if his eyes had closed at all during the night, it must have been only for a blink.

Mac didn't look much sprightlier. He might not have spent every minute, as Kirk had, on Julie's track, but I knew there hadn't been any minutes when she hadn't been on his mind.

The two photographers seemed to fill the whole place; they were everywhere. Moving from one chair to another and back again, sprawling on the horsehair sofa, strolling, lolling, fidgeting. Never more than one second in one place.

From a corner Harry Duerr sat watching them, unhappily. You could tell he wanted to help, that he was keeping his eyes and ears open waiting for a chance to do something. His devotion to Mac and Kirk was pathetic.

And Jeff wasn't adding any note of joy to our party. His intense preoccupation prevented us from asking him where he'd been that morning or what he'd done. For the last half hour he had been tinkering, his mind obviously miles away, with the Photo Arts prize Zeiss. The camera lay in fourteen parts on the desk before him. It wasn't until then that I realized the full extent of the boys' anxiety over Julie. Their pride and joy, all fourteen parts of it, in Jeff's inexpert hands brought forth not a single comment. They hadn't even noticed what was happening.

"Jeff," Mac said abruptly. "I'm sorry about Erika."

"Why, Mac?"

"She seems to think that I shouldn't have brought you into this."

"So far she's practically right."

"No, she isn't. I'm not expecting a miracle. Erika told me about last night at the Barrel Room. I'm sure she was alone, Jeff."

"Then who hit me?"

"There's that," Mac admitted miserably.

Jeff went over to the paper cup machine and punched it. He filled a cup with water from the cooler and gulped it down.

Mac went on. "Erika … Erika won't be helping you any, Jeff. She says that I imagined Wyatt was suspicious of me the other night …"

"Imagined, nonsense!" Kirk said. "Wyatt doesn't believe that Mrs. Fleming promised to finance you; he thinks you've got a motive."

Mac's fist suddenly came banging down on the desk. "Why doesn't he arrest me, then!"

"A motive isn't enough," Jeff said. "And another thing, Julie's fadeout has disconcerted him."

"Wyatt hasn't been near me since yesterday at noon. I feel as if he's waiting and watching me. Waiting for me to confess or watching for me to make a mistake. I'm afraid to move. He's got somebody tailing me." Mac smiled grimly. "I gave the so and so a workout last night. I walked from the Battery clear up to Fifty-ninth Street."

"Did you come back to the studio at all after you left yesterday afternoon with Erika?"

"No. Why?"

"Nothing. Erika just mentioned something about it. Mac, I'd like to talk to Madge Lawrence."

"What good will that do?" Kirk said. "She has no motive."

"No one has but me," Mac added. "Look, do we have to pin this thing on someone else to prove I'm innocent!"

Kirk said, "We're not trying to frame anyone, Mac."

Jeff was walking up and down. "Could we call the Models Bureau, Mac? Couldn't you say you have a job for her? I've got to talk to Miss Lawrence."

"Won't Wyatt give you her address?"

"Wyatt isn't giving me anything. I'm flattered. Professional jealousy."

Mac reached for the phone and dialed. "Miss Leonard, please. Photo Arts calling." Then, after a moment, "This is MacCormick, Miss Leonard. Could we have Madge Lawrence this afternoon? Right away, if we can get her. A

Pellton Soap job ... it'll pay twenty dollars. No, we'll furnish the costume. It's a housedress. All right, thanks."

"La Lawrence in a housedress!" Kirk said sadly. "It's like an angel blowing her nose."

Mac slid the phone across the desk. "Miss Leonard promised her at two."

"An hour to wait."

But there was now something to wait for, something definite, and things brightened up a bit. Mac and Kirk and Jeff collaborated on putting the Zeiss together again. Even Harry stopped worrying and came out of his corner to watch.

"Hiya, Harry," Jeff said.

Harry's slow, shy smile appeared for a moment. "Hiya."

Jeff laughed. "You shouldn't use up a whole day's conversation at once like that, Harry."

"Hey, Mac," Kirk said, "remember the time Harry didn't show up for two weeks and it turned out he had been downstairs sending a ten-word telegram."

"Don't let them kid you, Harry," Mac said. "When Erika told me about you, her big point was that we could use a strong, silent type around here. Emphasis on the silent. If you know what I mean, Kirk."

"I'm glib," Kirk confessed. "That's my cross and you'll have to bear it."

"Harry," Jeff said, "how did you meet Erika?"

"My sister went to school with her. In Switzerland."

"Switzerland!" Jeff was impressed.

"Sure," Kirk said, "didn't you know? Harry comes from a long line of economic royalists. He used to wallow in luxury."

"Those days are gone forever, Kirk," Harry said without a trace of regret in his voice. "The Duerrs are working people now."

The phone buzzed sharply and Mac reached for it. The conversation was short and one-sided; the other side. There was defeat in Mac's face as he snapped down the receiver.

"Well, that's that."

"That's what?"

"Madge Lawrence will not be able to pose for us today."

"That's the first time," Kirk said, "that we ever tried to get Madge and couldn't."

"I know." Mac was puzzled, too. "Miss Leonard usually tries to shift Madge's schedule around so she doesn't have to miss anything."

"Sure," Kirk went on, "Leonard's always shoving her down our throats instead of holding her out on us."

"Mac," Jeff said, "What did Miss Leonard say when you asked her about tomorrow or later in the week?"

"Miss Lawrence is booked for the rest of this week … and next."

"Madge is one busy baby."

"She has to be, Jeff, her clothes are a terrific overhead. I know about overheads," Mac said ruefully, looking around the big studio. "They can just as easily lose as make money for you."

Jeff jumped up. "Where is this Models Bureau?"

"East Fifty-seventh Street. 423. Why?"

"We're going up there, Haila and I. I'd invite you all, but …"

Mac shook his head. "Photo Arts is taking a picture this afternoon. Business as usual." He smiled grimly.

"Oh, yeah, you're using Robert Yorke, aren't you? We'll be back. I want to see some more of him. Let's go, Haila. If the pictures in those models catalogues aren't faked, I'm going to have a very pleasant afternoon up there."

"Not if I can help it," I said determinedly.

The reception room of the Models Bureau was a symphony in ebony and crimson and not very soothing to the naked eye. The walls were lined with black-framed cigarette ads, *Saturday Evening Post* covers, fashion drawings … all the more choice pictures for which their girls had been the subject. Through an arch-shaped peephole we could see half a dozen young ladies busy with three times as many telephones, talking, listening and scribbling appointments simultaneously on the models' individual clipboards that hung before them on the wall.

Jeff murmured for a few minutes through the opening to one of the telephone girls. The gist of the matter was that he was Mr. Jeff Troy and should not be kept waiting. He was as surprised as I when, a moment later, we were ushered into Miss Ada Leonard's private office.

No crimson and ebony here. A cubicle that held one black desk meant for business, one Smith-Corona typewriter, four telephones and three straight-backed chairs. It matched Miss Leonard though, a wiry little lady with short gray hair, steel-rimmed bifocals and a briskly efficient manner. She, too, was meant for business.

"I'm Jeff Troy, Miss Leonard, perhaps you've heard of me."

"I'm afraid not."

Jeff worked up a look of shocked surprise. "You haven't! Oh, perhaps you aren't interested in photography?"

"I am. Very much."

"Well, I dabble in photography. Not commercially, of course. Purely artistically. I'd like a model, a woman. Someone rather unusual looking."

"What will you pay?"

"It'll just be part of one day. Would twenty-five dollars be …"

"It would," Miss Leonard said, reaching for a catalogue.

Jeff watched over her shoulder as she flipped through the pages. He kept shaking his head. Then he stopped Miss Leonard and leafed back a few pages.

"There's a striking face."

"That's Madge Lawrence."

"Hmm. Is she good?"

"Very good."

"Could you arrange for her to pose for me?"

"When?"

"At her earliest convenience."

"I'll contact her and let you know."

"But I'd like to see her first. Couldn't I call on her? At her home? If you'll give me her address ..."

"Miss Lawrence is expected here almost any minute. If you care to wait ..."

"I could easily go to see her. Or if I might have her phone number ..."

"She'll be here shortly," Miss Leonard snapped. "Make yourselves comfortable in the reception room."

We waited two hours for Madge Lawrence. Two hours of exposure to so much pulchritude that it would have been a relief to ride on the Bronx Express. Through that one door passed enough of the right kind of faces to launch a million and a half ships. Compared to the girls who paraded into the Models Bureau every day but Sundays and holidays, Helen of Troy couldn't have got a canoe under way.

The first hour I whiled away by pointing out the models that I remembered from my posing days, and others that I knew from their pictures in the magazines. The legs that had sold one brand of silk stockings for the last five years. Another pair that was selling nylon now. The husky young man out of whose mouth, almost every week in the three leading national magazines, came words of wisdom on the automobile and its care.

The second hour Jeff kept score. It was a landslide for the blondes, with corn-color leading, and platinum, ash and taffy following in that order. After the blondes, came the brunettes, raven, brown, chestnut and molasses. The redheads were a surprisingly close third. A mouse-color came in, took one look around her and fled. Obviously a newcomer who would return the next day, probably a taffy.

Jeff had used up his fingers three times and mine twice with his diligent scorekeeping when I nudged him sharply. He tore his eyes away from the figure that had sold a million foundation garments to look at me.

"Don't be jealous," he pleaded, "I'm just trying to decipher the letters on her sorority pin."

I pointed to a blob of yellow curls coming through the door. May Ralston thought she had seen us without being seen. She stopped, turned her back and snapped open her compact. In the mirror I could watch her apply new lips, new cheeks and one new eyebrow. She dropped her case in her bag and came bouncing toward Jeff.

"Damn!" he muttered, "if Madge or Miss Lawrence catches me talking to May the goose is ..."

"Hell-o!" May exclaimed in amazement. "Of all things! You're just the person I wanted to see!"

"Listen, May ..."

"You told the police about my middle name being Fleming, you old meanie!" May pretended to be real mad. "And that old Mr.. Lockhart was at my house again this morning asking me questions!"

"What about?" Jeff's anxious eye was on the door.

"Well, he wanted to know what I was doing about six o'clock last night for one thing!"

"Did he? Now, look, sweetheart ..."

"I asked him who wanted to know. He said Mr. Wyatt. And I said, 'If Mr. Wyatt wants to know, let him come and ask me himself! What does he think, sending one of his assistants up here to see me! I'm just as important in this murder case as anyone else!' "

"That's telling him, May."

Taking her gently but firmly by the arm he led her across the room where he stood whispering earnestly to her for a minute or two. May looked at me curiously. Finally an expression of complete understanding and sympathy came over her face. She patted Jeff's arm tenderly and, with one more glance in my direction, disappeared through a swinging door. Through the little window I could see her taking down and inspecting her pad for future assignments. I walked over to Jeff.

"What did you tell her?" I demanded.

"How you tried to commit suicide the last time I paid some attention to a good-looking girl."

"Jeff, you ..."

"Duck!"

As per Jeff's instructions I crept quickly into a corner and hid behind a newspaper. If Madge Lawrence caught a glimpse of me, all would be lost.

Over the top of the *Herald Tribune's* sports page and a picture of the Columbia football squad, I watched her cross the reception room. She didn't walk; the long thin figure glided, and the sleek black caracul coat streamed out as she went, showing snatches of its Chinese red lining. Her turbaned hat was small and tight, held together in front with a pin in the form of a gold and red bird. Her suede gloves were red, her shoes had high red heels. It made me mentally click my tongue to even contemplate the money that Madge Lawrence put on her back.

With little Miss Leonard bouncing stubbily at her side, she came out of the office a minute later. I ducked my head while she was being introduced to Jeff. They were standing just outside Miss Leonard's door, out of range of my hearing. But I could see Madge's face as she looked up at Jeff, listening intently and then answered. It seemed drawn and strained, as if she were being forced to concentrate fiercely to make intelligible conversation.

Miss Leonard, having done her duty, left Madge alone with Jeff. I edged along the wall bench until I was within earshot of them. Jeff wasn't wasting any time.

"Are you punctual, Miss Lawrence?"

"Always, Mr. Troy. Without exception."

"A friend of mine tells me there was one exception. Monday night."

Her face was suddenly cold. "Are you connected with the police, Mr. Troy?"

"No."

"No, of course not. They don't have to resort to such underhand methods as you have."

"All I want is to talk with you. I haven't been able any other way. You'd be doing Mac MacCormick a favor."

"Why should I do him a favor? The police are satisfied that I know nothing about that business. Why aren't you?"

"Your avoiding the boys at Photo Arts makes me suspicious. Why are you doing it?"

"I'm not interested in discussing my actions with a sensation hunter." She broke off sharply. Miss Leonard had come out of her office, a funny perky little hat squashed down over her wiry hair, an elephantine purse swinging from her hand. Madge crossed quickly to her, linked her arm in Miss Leonard's.

"I rather think Mr. Troy might prefer some other model for this job he has in mind," she told her in a high, distinct voice.

Miss Leonard cast a sharp, almost hostile, glance in Jeff's direction. Her hand closed over Madge's in an understanding pat.

"Of course, my dear," we heard her say as she threw an unmistakable "that's that" nod at Jeff and me and walked with Madge through the outer door.

# Chapter Twelve

NOT UNTIL WE HEARD the clink of closing elevator doors did Jeff and I venture out of the reception room of the Models Bureau. Then we raced down the corridor and shifted nervously from foot to foot while we waited minutes for the next car. It made twelve stops and went down in slow motion. Not too slow, however, for Madge Lawrence and Miss Leonard were still chatting together at the curb outside the building. We watched Miss Leonard raise herself on tiptoe to kiss Madge's cheek. Then Madge, after a few smiling words to the little woman, hailed a taxi and got in.

A second cab pulled into its place. Jeff body-checked a little man with a briefcase while I scrambled in and took possession.

"Follow that cab ahead," Jeff ordered. "And there's five dollars in it for you if you don't lose it."

"I don't know," our driver said doubtfully. "That cabbie came in fourth at Indianapolis about ten years ago."

He must have been right. Madge's man took the corner at Third Avenue as if it were banked. At Fifty-fifth Street the light was yellow and he didn't even slow down to let it redden. He turned west and we roared after him. I knew that now our chase would start. Bracing my feet against the folding seat in front of me, I clung with both hands to the window strap. Our driver threw all his weight on the gas pedal. We swirled around a parked limousine. I could hear the scratching whizz as our fenders lightly scraped. I closed my eyes. It seemed a shame; Jeff and I had only been married one short month.

"What the devil!"

Jeff's exclamation and the scream of the brakes came together. I lurched forward almost into the driver's seat. Jeff didn't make a move to help me aright myself. He was staring open-mouthed out the window.

The pursued cab had drawn to a stop. The driver was twisting his neck to read the meter and Madge Lawrence was paying him off. She had ridden all of two and a half blocks. She turned from the cabbie who was scowling at the change she had dropped in his hand and started walking west. The cabbie shifted gears and rolled contemptuously past her.

Our driver turned to us with a grin. "Still want me to follow it, Buddy?"

"No. Follow the woman," Jeff snapped irritably.

"You said the cab. You said five bucks if I didn't lose the cab. That's what he said, didn't he, Sister?"

"But..."

"I ain't lost it. Be a man of your word, Buddy."

Jeff handed over five one-dollar bills. "I hope you get drunk on it and beat your wife. It'll serve her right for marrying a man so very, very literal. Now, will you follow the lady?"

By that time the lady was at the next corner. She turned it and walked north on Lexington Avenue. We kept about a hundred feet behind her. With her long gliding step and her head held high, Madge marched slowly along. Not looking either to the right or to the left, not glancing behind her. If she knew that she was being followed, she gave no indication of it.

At Fifty-seventh Street she boarded a westbound bus. We crawled along after it in tedious pursuit, across Park and Madison, then back into the numbered avenues, Fifth, Sixth and on westward. Between Eighth and Ninth Jeff said, "Do you suppose that she lives in Jersey? And that she's on her way to a ferry?"

"I've no idea."

At Ninth Madge stepped off the bus. She waited for the traffic light to turn in her favor, then she crossed Fifty-seventh Street and started down Ninth Avenue. The El kept the sun from getting at the pale and dirty little children who were playing on the sidewalks under it. Pushcarts lined the curbs. Small groceries, butcher shops, vegetable stands and cheap dry-goods stores spilled half their wares out onto the sidewalk counters, giving the children practically no room at all in which to enjoy themselves. The air was rampant with the smell of fish that mingled with the sickening sweet odor of decaying fruit.

"Jeff," I said, "do you think she knows we're following her and brought us over into this part of town to lose us?"

"Look!"

Madge had stopped in front of a little butcher shop. After staring into the window for a moment she went in. Here, I thought, is where she means to shake us. But a few minutes later she reappeared, a small brown parcel in her hand, and resumed her march.

I began to think that it would never end. Where was Madge Lawrence leading us? What could she, with all her costly elegance, know of this section of New York? There could be no possible explanation but that she was attempting to get away from us, and yet she was going about it in an odd way. That slow and easy gait of hers wouldn't have outrun anybody in a million years. And amid the tiny urchins and the stooping, beshawled marketers, Madge's tall and vivid figure screamed for attention.

I still don't know how she did it.

One minute she was there on the corner of Ninth Avenue and Fifty-fourth Street, the red bird on her hat almost beckoning to us. She turned the corner without any change of pace at all. We turned it, too, not more than three seconds after she had. And Madge Lawrence was gone.

It was as though she had been jerked up into the very air with wires or dropped through a manhole. It was as sudden and as complete as that. Even our driver who had remained totally disinterested during all our wandering was astounded as he turned to us.

"The lady musta had wings concealed on her person," he said dazedly.

Jeff got out of the cab and investigated. On either side of the street the first four or five buildings were cheap apartments and rooming houses. Limp and grimy curtains covered the windows and battered ashcans lined their front steps. Jeff peered into all of their shallow, shadowy vestibules, but no Madge Lawrence was hiding in any of them. Beyond the fifth building on the south side of the street was a garage. In there Jeff inquired whether a lady with a red bird on her hat had been seen. She had not. He stood in front of the garage and looked across the street. A board fence plastered with signs and so high that it would have been a challenge to a police dog, surrounded a vacant lot.

Completely bewildered and dejected, Jeff finally gave up. He gave the driver our address and climbed back into the cab. Not until we had crossed Columbus Circle did he recover sufficiently to speak.

"She must have gone into one of those rooming houses."

"Obviously," I said helpfully.

"But she wasn't in any of the vestibules or hallways. I looked. Maybe she got into one of the apartments by pretending she was a relief investigator."

"Or she might have formed a friendship while she was on a slumming party."

"Yeah." That was the best Jeff could manage. He was really down.

As we were crossing Central Park at Seventy-second Street he said thoughtfully, "But, you know, Haila, I still don't believe that Madge knew we were tailing her."

"I don't either."

"Unless she saw us when she got in that cab."

"No, Jeff. Madge didn't see us then. I know she didn't. As far as she knew, no one saw her get into that taxi but Miss Leonard."

"What?"

"You heard me. Miss Leonard saw her get into that cab and ..."

"And I've been stewing over that cab business!" Jeff shot forward in the seat. "Driver! Go back to the corner of Ninth and Fifty-fourth! If you get there in ten minutes, I'll ..."

I gripped Jeff's arm.

"... I'll give you credit!" He turned back to me. "And that butcher shop!"

"What about it?" I asked.

I was still unenlightened about it by the time we reached the west side again. The cab stopped before the first building on the left at Fifty-fourth Street. I was afraid to look while Jeff paid off the driver.

He dashed up the steps of the first house. By the time I got to the vestibule he was on his way out. I caught up to him next door. He was running his finger down the list of names above the rusty mail boxes.

"Zebrowski, O'Reilly," he recited, "Tamulis and ..."

He pressed a button.

"What's the name?" I asked.

As the buzzer sounded he removed his hand from the card. The name was Madge Lawrence.

"Madge Lawrence lives here!" I gasped.

"Correct."

"A double life!"

Jeff shook his head. "Just one."

The smell of cooking cauliflower met us on the narrow uncarpeted stairs. A door on the first landing opened. Madge Lawrence stood in it, silhouetted by a dim light from behind. She peered into the darkness, a half-smile on her lips. The smile disappeared instantly as she recognized us. She sagged against the frame of the doorway; all the life seemed to have melted out of her.

"Miss Lawrence ..."

"Yes." Her voice, too, was dead. She turned away from us, into the room. We followed her. Jeff closed the door behind him.

It was the only sort of room a building of its kind could contain. It was small, and the ugly, yellow-flowered wallpaper made it seem even smaller. The one window looked across a dreary airshaft into another window that opened upon a room identical to this one. The furniture was cheap and old and stained. Except for those irremovable stains everything else in the room was clean, scrupulously clean and neat.

Madge stood in the center of it all, her arms hanging limply at her sides, a stony look on her sharp, angular face.

Jeff's eyes moved slowly around the room, flicking across the window, the dresser, the short row of dresses and suits that hung in an open closet. He walked over to that and stood in front of it. He turned suddenly.

"Miss Lawrence," he said gently, "I came here to ask you why you were late at the studio the night that Isabelle Fleming was murdered. But now I think I know."

"Really?"

"Yes. Yes, I think so. Haila described the dress that you brought with you to Photo Arts to wear for the picture. She was very much impressed by it."

He nodded toward the closet. "I don't see it there now. I don't see anything like it. I think perhaps you borrowed that dress and returned it after the picture had been taken that afternoon. Then you had to reborrow it for the retake that evening. And that made you late."

"You're quite right, Mr. Troy. Does it matter?"

"Why wouldn't you tell us that?"

"I don't tell anyone. Even Miss Leonard doesn't know what you know. She thinks I'm a wealthy woman who models to amuse herself. She won't give out my phone number because I've explained that I don't wish business brought into my home. She thinks these clothes I wear are mine. Everyone does! It's better that way. Madge Lawrence has the reputation of being one of the best dressed models in New York, you know. And she borrows nearly all her clothes. As you can see, I'm not nearly as successful a model as I give the impression of being." She glanced around the room and then closed her eyes for a moment. "Fortunately, I have a wealthy friend. It's the only way I permit her to help me … by lending me her clothes. So that I can make fifteen or twenty dollars. And sometimes ten. And sometimes none at all. That isn't disgraceful, is it? To let a friend help one earn an …" she smiled bitterly. "I almost said an honest living."

"I'm sorry we followed you," Jeff said. "I thought you were trying to duck away from me again when you grabbed that cab. I didn't realize until later that you … you were only keeping up appearances for Miss Leonard. That, plus the fact that you went into the butcher shop to buy something and not to give us the slip, was what made me guess that you lived here."

"All right. Now you know all about it. I suppose you'll have to let it be known that Madge Lawrence isn't a rich woman who poses for the fun of posing. That if she's lucky she makes twenty-five dollars a week and half of that must go on her back … for the clothes which she can't borrow from a friend. Tell everybody, I'm sure they'll love it. Especially your flippant friends at Photo Art."

"Mac and Kirk will be very sorry."

Madge looked at him sharply. Then her face softened a little. "Yes. They're two very kind and thoughtful young men. Kindness seems to surprise me; I don't always recognize it."

"Has Mr. Wyatt been to see you?"

She nodded. "I had to give him my address and he's been here. He has been kind, too. I expected him to pass along my secret; it would make an interesting item for a gossip column. But evidently he's kept quiet. Possibly because he knows that I have no connection with Mrs. Fleming nor with her death. Now, please, won't you go?"

"Miss Lawrence, before we go will you tell me about Amanda Lewis?"

"I know nothing about any Amanda Lewis."

Jeff said quietly, "Then I'll have to tell you. She was Sanford Fleming's first wife. She was married to him for only a little more than a year. And then there was a divorce. The 1926 newspapers that I saw this morning hinted that the Fleming family had bought the Lewis family off. Then, shortly after the divorce, Sanford Fleming married Isabelle Tarleton. Amanda Lewis sank out of the picture then for a long time. She didn't come back into it until after Sanford's death ... until after his will had been made public and it was discovered that he had made her a very generous bequest. Unfortunately, Isabelle Fleming contested that will. She proved coercion, rightly or wrongly, I don't know. But Amanda Lewis never got that money. I think that she probably deserved it, don't you?"

"I don't think anything," Madge said. Her face was chiseled hard, like a cameo. "I'm not interested in your story."

"You should be," Jeff said. "There were pictures of Amanda Lewis in the paper I saw. You bear a striking resemblance to her."

Madge turned away from him quickly. She looked out of the ugly little window. But I had caught one glimpse of her face as she swung around.

"Madge!" I said. I couldn't help myself. "You're ... you're Amanda Lewis' daughter. It was your mother who ..."

The straight taut shoulders stiffened even more, and then, all at once, they began to shake spasmodically. She wheeled around to face me. She was laughing.

"Amanda Lewis' daughter! No, Mrs. Troy. There was no daughter. There was no child at all."

"But you ..." I started.

"No, Haila," Jeff said. "Madge is Amanda Lewis."

I said, "But Amanda Lewis ... oh, no! She must be ..."

"Old," Madge said. "She must be very old. That's what you were going to say, isn't it? You thought she'd be an old, old woman, didn't you? An old hag like Isabelle Fleming was? Maybe, older even, for she was the first Mrs. Fleming."

"But you," I said, "you ..."

"I'm a lot older than you think. A lot older than anybody thinks. Except the camera. I don't seem to be able to fool it much. That's why I don't make such a pretty living out of photography anymore. Unfortunately, it's the only thing I can do. And it's going to get worse. In a few years I'll be doing grandmothers, spreading jam on cookies for the little ones, advising daughters-in-law how to hold their husbands. There isn't much money in that. They draw better grandmothers than they can photograph."

I was still bewildered. "You can't ..." I said stupidly, "I don't see ..."

Jeff said, "Madge was only seventeen when she married Sanford Fleming. He was thirty-five. And Isabelle Fleming was ten years older than her husband. She ..."

Madge cut in bitterly. "You see how it works? It's very neat, just a matter of simple arithmetic. And now that you've added it up, will you go please?"

"Not yet," Jeff said. "I've got to know ..."

"Yes. Now you know that I had the motive to kill Isabelle Fleming. You must hear me say it. All right, I'll tell you that, too. I wanted to kill her. I've wanted to for over twenty years. It was because of her that my marriage was broken in the first place. It didn't matter that she was older than Sanford Fleming, or that he was in love with me, married to me. That meant nothing to the Flemings nor to Isabelle Tarleton. Money could do anything and Isabelle had it. Money arranged our divorce. It got Isabelle my husband. And years later it provided witnesses to prove that I had coerced Sanford Fleming into leaving me something in his will. It was Isabelle Fleming and her money that took even that away from me. She put my picture on every front page, slung such mud on my name that I had to get myself another one. She ruined my life. Of course I wanted to kill her. But you'll have to look further for your murderer, Mr. Troy. Because someone beat me to it."

"Did you know that you were to pose with her when you went to Photo Arts that afternoon?"

"Yes." The outburst was over. Madge was tired and spent. Her short answer came in a Voder-like tone.

"But you went anyway?"

"It paid ten dollars."

"And did Mrs. Fleming recognize you?"

Madge shrugged. "I suppose so."

Jeff's hand was on the doorknob. "Thank you, Miss Lawrence," he said simply.

She darted in front of him. "Do you believe me? That I didn't murder Isabelle Fleming?"

Jeff didn't answer.

"I didn't kill her," Madge said between her teeth. "Nobody can prove I did. I never went into the studio until after she had been murdered. I didn't see that knife until it stuck out of her neck."

"Yes, that's what you said ..."

"And it's true! It's true! I had nothing to do with it!" Suddenly her angry excitement was quenched again. "I had nothing to do with it," she repeated dully. "Mr. Troy, promise that you won't tell anybody ... about me."

"I promise, unless ..."

"Unless what?"

Jeff frowned. "Unless Mac MacCormick is arrested for the murder of Isabelle Fleming."

## Chapter Thirteen

ON THE WAY BACK to Photo Arts Jeff explained to me how tired I was and that I should go home and have myself some rest. I appreciated his solicitude, but his reasoning left me cold. Then he was unsportsmanlike enough to appeal to me as a wife, suggesting that I go home and get a nice hot dinner ready for us. I knew he wouldn't be home for any dinner. Besides, it was nearly five o'clock; a girl should spend the whole day cooking for the man she loves, not just throw something together in an hour or two.

We found Kirk striding angrily up and down the studio, stopping only long enough to throw strong language at Wyatt and Lockhart, who were listening to his tirade with patient smiles stretched across their faces. Mac and Harry were watching Kirk's attack from the sidelines; they were agreeing, but silently.

"There are a lot of better things for you to do!" Kirk was shouting at the detectives. "For instance, you could find Julie instead of asking your darn silly questions over and over again! When, where, why! What does all that matter now? Why *don't* you find Julie? You've got the law on your side …"

Wyatt saw Jeff and me. "Well, look who's here!"

"The boy wonder!" Lockhart said. "And his wondering wife."

"What am I wondering about?" I asked politely.

"Aren't you wondering yet why you married all that trouble?"

"Lockhart should write for the radio," Kirk growled unpleasantly.

Jeff smiled. "It's a good thing for you, Wyatt, that I arrived. You and your assistant seem in line for some bodily harm." He looked from Kirk to Mac and Harry. "Mobilization, if I ever saw it."

"We're scared," Lockhart said. "Real scared."

Mac snuffed out Kirk's rising belligerency with a grin and a playful shove that sent him sprawling onto the sofa. "Just a moment! Before this develops into something. Everybody's in a nasty mood. I know I am; I'd welcome a good brawl. And I think I could take anybody here. Except maybe Jeff."

"Down at Al's Gym," Jeff said, "they call me the Ninety-third Street Cyclone. I'm dirty, too. I use sticks and stones."

"Troy's on our side, luckily," Wyatt laughed. "He's a detective."

"The point is," Mac went on, "we're all on the same side. We're trying to find Julie. And a murderer. So let's all be friends until we …"

Wyatt interrupted him. "We're all friends, MacCormick. There's bound to be a little misunderstanding when a murder's been committed." The irony in the detective's voice as he tossed that understatement at Mac plainly showed that Wyatt was not overly enamored with his career. Or at least, with this case. "Surely, MacCormick, you aren't taking anything I've said or done personally."

"Oh, no! Definitely no!" Mac said grimly.

"That's fine. C'mon, Lockhart, we're probably in Mr. Troy's way." Wyatt turned back to Kirk as he reached the doors. "About Julie Taylor, Findlay. I'm doing my best to find her. I've got a little girl at home just her size."

When the doors stopped swinging behind the two detectives, Jeff said, "What did he want, Mac?"

It was Kirk who answered. "He thinks Mac knows where Julie is. He's been hammering at him for an hour. Both of them, the dumb flatfeet!"

"That's what we taxpayers pay them for." Mac went to the cooler and got himself a drink; he could have used something much stronger than water. Crushing the paper cup into a ball, he flung it savagely into the wastebasket. "Listen, Jeff! Would you do this? Would you forget about the murder and spend your time looking for Julie? If you need money, I'll get it for you. Julie's got to be found, Jeff!"

"Nobody wants to find her more than I, Mac."

"I do," Kirk said quietly.

"You can't disconnect Julie's disappearance from the murder, Mac," Jeff said. "If we find the killer, I'm sure we'll find Julie. And if we find Julie, we'll find the killer. Maybe not in the same room. It might take some chasing."

"Then you don't think the murderer's got Julie?" Harry asked.

"She left town of her free will." Jeff beat Kirk and me to the draw. "I know, I know! She was tricked, she ... well!"

Robert Yorke was standing in the doorway, ready to pose for the liquor ad picture. He had obviously been spending the time since our arrival dressing for the part, a hunter just returned from a happy day in field and forest, his tongue hanging out for a swig of that good old rye, America's favorite for one hundred and forty years. If Mac's photography did Yorke justice, there would be a day of national swooning and a lot of housewives would be turning dipsomaniac. I have never seen a handsomer man. His lustrous black hair tousled as if by the wind, his beautiful eyes, his enchanting smile, the collar of the red and black checked lumberjack shirt open at the neck, hip boots and britches, the double-barreled gun held carelessly in the crook of his elbow all piled up to the male animal *ad summum*. Jeff glanced anxiously at me and well he should have.

"Will I do?" Yorke asked. He knew he would do and he'd have used that gun on anyone daring to say him nay.

"Hmm," Mac said, "yeah, sure. Yorke ... uh ... I know it's a dirty trick, but could we postpone the take until tomorrow? I don't feel up to any art work."

"Well ..."

"You'll be paid for both days of course."

"That isn't the point," Yorke said hastily, "I was just thinking ... yes, certainly I'll be available tomorrow."

"Thanks."

"Not at all." He leaned the shot gun against the desk and lit a cigarette. He was loath, I could tell, to get out of his becoming costume and I didn't blame him.

"Yorke," Jeff said, "are you married?"

The actor's eyebrows raised at Jeff's bluntness, then he smiled, a smile of non-resentment. "At the moment, no."

"You have been?"

"Oh, yes," Yorke said casually, "once or twice. Marriage didn't agree with me. Nor I with it. Why do you ask?"

"Detectives are supposed to ask questions. I haven't for about an hour; that's the only one I could think of."

Yorke laughed. "I see. Then I gather you aren't doing so well with this murder, Mr. Troy?"

"Not so well."

"What happened about Madge Lawrence, Jeff?" Kirk asked. "Did you see her?"

"Yes, but she refused to talk to me." He was keeping his promise to Madge. "I just haven't got that social touch."

During the pause that followed I happened to glance at Harry Duerr. He was going through what seemed to be the mental process of screwing up his courage. After two false starts and a throat clearing he finally said, "Jeff ..."

"Yeah, Harry?"

"I don't know whether this means anything and I don't want to get anyone in trouble, but ... well, this morning ..."

As Harry hesitated, Mac said, "C'mon, Harry, you're among friends."

"Well, it's probably silly but this morning I ran an errand for Erika ... up to the Fleming house."

"Go on, Harry," Jeff encouraged.

"I was talking to Mrs. Fleming's secretary for a little while. And she told me something ... something about Lee Kenyon."

"Kenyon?"

"Yes, but don't get excited, Jeff, it's nothing much. Just that Kenyon visited Mrs. Fleming on Saturday. Last Saturday afternoon."

"Last Saturday afternoon! Two days before the murder!"

"No, wait. Not that it makes any difference, but it was in the morning. The secretary told me that just as she was leaving the house to go to the bank, she heard the butler announce a Lee Kenyon to see Mrs. Fleming." Harry grinned. "Deduction, see? The banks close at noon on Saturdays."

"Was Kenyon still there when the secretary got back?"

"I don't know, Jeff. I'm sorry."

"Mac, what's this secretary's name?"

"Helen Thompson."

"I'll use the phone in the reception room."

When Jeff came back he made straight for his hat and topcoat. He seemed to have forgotten all about us, that we were there, all staring at him.

"Jeff!" I said. "What goes on?"

"I'm going up to see Lee Kenyon." He thought for a moment, then said, "Harry, I think I might need you."

"All right."

"I'm going, too!" Kirk said. "This studio haunts me. What are you going to do, Mac?"

"I'll take that picture after all, I think. All right, Yorke?"

"Are you sure you won't need any help?" Harry asked.

"No, everything's set. Beat it," Mac said. "Let's see what we can do, Yorke."

Mac was already critically surveying the various poses and facial expressions that Robert Yorke was exhibiting by the time we left.

Harry and I turned instinctively from the entrance of the Graylock Building toward a bus stop, but Kirk, the big spendthrift, would have none of that. We had to take a cab. Kirk explained that by dividing the fare by four it would only triple the price of a bus or subway ride. "Furthermore," he concluded convincingly, "it isn't fair for Jeff and Harry and me to ride subways. That means three women don't get seats."

While Jeff used the house phone at the Sherry-Netherland, Kirk and Harry and I again pooled our resources and bought a newspaper. A lack of further developments had pushed the Fleming case to the bottom of the first page.

There was an unhappy look on Jeff's face when he rejoined us.

"Kenyon has visitors," he said.

"Who?" I asked.

"Wyatt and Lockhart."

"Well!"

"I guess that means we'll have to wait," Kirk said.

"Oh, no. Wyatt insisted that we come up immediately."

And it was Mr. Wyatt himself who opened the door to Suite 422 and graciously bowed us into the living room. The furniture had all been pushed close against the wall and the big rug rolled up. A baby piano, cherry-red, impudently stuck out of the line of chairs and tables. Two wide full-length mirrors spanned almost one wall.

"Excuse the appearance of the place," Wyatt said. "Mr. Kenyon has been practicing the dance."

"You pronounce it dawnce," Lockhart said.

"Hello, you!" Lee Kenyon chirped. He wasn't at all perturbed by the visiting police. "Yes, I'm giving a recital early next month. At Town Hall. It's all arranged. Kirk, I'm glad you stopped in. I was wondering if you and Mack mightn't do some pictures of me for it." He smiled at Wyatt. "I hate to bother you and your crony with these details."

"His crony don't mind," Lockhart said, "if he don't."

"Of course I don't."

"Then it's a party!" Kenyon said. "Shall I send down for some wine? Champagne, perhaps? Mr.. Lockhart, what year do you like?"

"Any year the Yanks win the pennant I like."

"Lockhart," Wyatt said, "give Troy a chance to talk. He didn't come here to look at himself in the mirror. Go ahead, Troy."

Jeff grinned. "If I had come here on business, would I have brought my wife and friends?"

"I wouldn't be surprised," Lockhart said.

"I'm embarrassed."

"As your host, Jeff," Lee said, "I'll put you at your ease. Is there any little thing I can do for you?"

"Yes." Jeff smiled with charming friendliness. "Frankly, I'm broke. I thought maybe you could tell me where you got all your money. So me and my friends could take buckets and get some too."

"What makes you think I've got so much money?"

"New clothes, new luggage, you quit your job at the Barrel Room, you move into the Sherry-Netherland, a recital at Town Hall which you must be financing yourself ..."

"Is that a criticism of my dancing?"

"All that costs money. Plenty. You didn't by any chance get it from Isabelle Fleming when you visited her last Saturday?"

"You're getting hot, Troy," Wyatt said.

"Mrs. Fleming," Jeff went on, "didn't by any chance send her secretary to the bank to get the money which you are now using?"

"A detective!" Lockhart said.

"A mathematician," Jeff corrected. "Two and two and watch that sarcasm, you dumb baseball fan."

"Take a vacation, Lockhart," Wyatt said.

"How about it, Kenyon?" Jeff asked.

"Why would Mrs. Fleming give me money?"

Wyatt said, "She gave somebody money on Saturday. The secretary drew ten thousand dollars out of the bank that morning. It wasn't in the house when we went through it after the murder."

Jeff stepped toward Lee Kenyon. He was excited. "Thanks, Wyatt. That's cooperating. Kenyon! Isabelle Fleming knew that you were coming to see her. She knew that she was going to give you that money. The secretary had already started for the bank when you arrived at the Fleming house."

"All right," Lee said. "She sent for me. And she gave me the money."

"Why?"

"To subsidize my dancing."

"Ten thousand dollars! In cash and all at once!" Jeff shouted. "Oh, no. Isabelle Fleming was a businesswoman. She wouldn't give her own niece's husband any money outright. She was willing to buy stock in his company, but that's as far as her generosity went. She wouldn't lay out ten thousand bucks to back a dancer. She wasn't a patron of the arts and she wasn't big-hearted. She was tight and she was tough!"

"So?" Kenyon asked. His voice was casual.

"So you had a motive to kill Isabelle Fleming!"

"Such as?" His complacency was infuriating.

"Somehow you tricked her out of ten thousand dollars. She found out that you had tricked her. And she was a great one for taking things to court. And you're not."

Kenyon looked from Jeff to Wyatt. His complacency was beginning to waver.

"Troy's convinced me that you've got a motive, Kenyon," Wyatt said pleasantly. "Hasn't he convinced you yet?"

"For God's sake, how could I have tricked the woman!"

"Go ahead, Troy," Wyatt invited. "Tell him how."

Jeff went ahead with enthusiasm. "There are a lot of possibilities. For instance, you might have somehow got hold of proof that Amanda Lewis was not guilty of coercion when Sanford Fleming left her a fortune. You might have known that Isabelle had framed her."

"You sure get around," Wyatt said.

"My taxi bill is enormous. Well, Kenyon?"

Lee Kenyon studied his fingertips. "All right. I didn't know anything about this Amanda Lewis, you're crazy there. But I can see what's happening. By not telling the truth I'm going to get deeper in this mess than I really am." He suddenly threw back his head and laughed. It was genuine laughter. "Sit down, everybody. What I am about to tell you is really very amusing."

"A ten grand laugh, that should be funny," Lockhart muttered.

"Yes, it is funny. A joke that I'm in a position to appreciate more than anyone else, of course. Isabelle Fleming called me Saturday morning and asked me, commanded me rather, to come to see her immediately. When millionaires speak, poor little country boys obey. I didn't have any idea why she wanted me. I hardly knew her. Oh, I'd met her once when Erika dragged her to a place where I was dancing in the hopes that the old gal would sponsor me. But Jeff is right; Isabelle wouldn't spend a nickel to further the doubtful career of a dancer. Well, anyway, I went to her house. The minute I stepped into her study she informed me that she knew everything about Erika and me."

"What about Erika and you?" Kirk asked.

Kenyon shrugged. "I didn't know myself until she let me in on it. It seems that Erika had told her aunt that she intended to divorce Mac, that ..."

"Erika divorce Mac!" Harry Duerr was on his feet. "What are you talking about!"

"I'm simply reporting my interview with Mrs. Fleming."

"But Erika and Mac ..."

"Harry's right," Kirk said. "There's nothing wrong between Erika and ..."

"Go on, Kenyon," Wyatt instructed.

"Erika, she said, was in love with someone and she was going to divorce Mac to marry him. The old lady was furious. And Erika had made her more furious by refusing to tell her who the new husband was to be. She threatened to disinherit her, and Erika just laughed at her. Then, somehow, Isabelle decided that it was I Erika meant to marry, and she sent for me. She was livid with rage at the thought of her niece marrying a tap dancer. Let alone the scandal of a divorce. So, failing to dissuade Erika, she offered me ten thousand dollars if I would let Erika alone. I was to promise never to see her again."

"And you took the money."

Lee smiled jauntily. "Yes. So I took the money and bought myself some dancing shoes."

Kirk's face was dark with anger. "Erika never meant to divorce Mac! And she never meant to marry you! You blackmailed the old woman with a pack of lies ..."

Kenyon interrupted. "Of course I never meant to marry Erika. Nor Erika me. So it was no hardship at all for me to promise her aunt that I wouldn't. I was only too glad to do it. It was the easiest ten thousand I ever hope to earn."

"What made Mrs. Fleming decide that you were the man?" Jeff asked.

"I don't know. Perhaps because we've been together a great deal, Erika and I. But that was only because Erika believed in me, she thought that I had talent. She wanted to help me."

"Then who …"

"I have no idea. I was so surprised by Isabelle's accusation that I almost didn't accept the money. Listen, if you don't believe that there's nothing between Erika and me but a mutual interest in my dancing, ask her."

"And Erika … she'd tell the truth about it, Kenyon?" Jeff asked thoughtfully.

"I'd like it if you could prove you aren't the guy," Wyatt said.

"I wish I could accommodate you," Kenyon said slowly. The wrinkles in his forehead were ironed out as his face lit with pleased excitement. "By God, I can! I know I can!" With three long gliding steps he was across the room, beside the telephone. He was dialing a number. The dial swung back in place and Kenyon waited. Out of the corner of his mouth he said to Wyatt: "Jim Snyder and I have shared an apartment for years. He knows all about Erika and me, how often we've been together, how we feel about each other. He'll tell you that I'm not the man Erika wanted to marry, he'll …"

The detective was behind him. "You're telephoning Snyder?"

"Yes," Lee said tensely.

He lifted the mouthpiece an inch. Wyatt's hand shot out, taking the phone from him. Kenyon's long thin fingers closed over the hook, breaking the connection.

"There's no answer," he said.

With his eyes on the dancer, Wyatt replaced the phone. "I'll talk to him," he said, "and not over a telephone."

Lee shrugged. "I was just trying to help …"

Wyatt made no attempt to conceal the sarcasm in his words. "And of course you know that this Snyder will tell the truth."

"Of course!" Kenyon said earnestly. "Why should he lie?" The detective kept looking steadily at him. "Oh, all right. Do what you want. Talk to him before I have a chance to, if that's what you want. That'll prove it for you anyway."

"I will, thanks." Wyatt crossed the room. "Put Snyder on our calling list, Lockhart." He turned to Jeff. "And you wait down in the lobby for me, Troy. I'll be right there."

## Chapter Fourteen

KIRK, HARRY AND I stood uneasily in the lobby of the Sherry-Netherland and looked at Jeff. That seemed about all there was to do. His fierce scowl of concentration hardly invited the bandying about of words.

"Do you think," Kirk finally dared to say, "that he was telling the truth? About Erika and ..." He paused, then went on disconsolately, "Mac will ... Mac doesn't know anything about this. It'll knock him for a loop coming right on top of all the rest."

"I can't believe it," Harry said. "Erika and Mac. Why, they're ... Erika wouldn't do that to Mac. And Mac's such a wonderful fellow that no man would ... would steal his wife. It isn't true!"

"Parts of it, at least, are true," Jeff said slowly. "Isabelle Fleming gave Kenyon that money. She gave it to him because Erika was going to divorce Mac and she was buying off the man she thought was Erika's lover. But whether Isabelle had the right man or not ... that's something we've got to find out."

"By asking Snyder?" Kirk said doubtfully.

Jeff shook his head. "No. If Kenyon is the man he'll get to Snyder before we can. And Snyder will tell us exactly what Kenyon has dictated to him. There's only one person who might tell us the truth. Erika."

"Erika?" I had grave misgivings on that point. "I doubt if she'd admit even the fact, let alone name the man. Not now, with Mac in all this trouble. She wouldn't say that she didn't love him, that she wanted to divorce him. Erika's careful about the light she puts herself in ..."

"Oh, God!" Harry said softly. "If it's true, if everything Kenyon said is true ... Erika *mustn't* admit it!"

Kirk turned to him in bewilderment. "What are you talking about, Harry?"

"Don't you see what will happen if she does! It will prove conclusively to Wyatt that Mac's guilty. It would to anyone. Erika was going to divorce Mac, Wyatt will figure, and it was financial troubles that split them. So Mac murdered Mrs. Fleming for her money, not just to save the studio, but to save his wife as well."

I groaned. "He's right, Jeff."

Jeff said tersely, "Is Erika extravagant?"

"I would say so," Harry said.

"Hell, yes!" Kirk echoed. "She doesn't make a point of it; she doesn't think about money at all. It just doesn't mean anything to her. Money only matters to people who never had any."

"Or had it and lost it," Harry said unnecessarily.

"But if Erika and Mac are having trouble," Jeff said, "could it be financial?"

"I ... I suppose so," Kirk answered. "I don't know of anything else it might be."

"I've got to see Erika." Jeff was frowning furiously. "She's got to see me!"

"She won't," I told him. "She considers you unessential in this case. You know that."

"Suppose one of us calls her," Kirk said. "Harry or I. If we explained to her how important it is ..."

"You do it, Kirk," Harry said. "Erika's not especially fond of me."

Kirk looked at him strangely. "No, she ... well, all right. I'll telephone her."

"Hurry," Jeff said, "before Wyatt comes down."

Kirk ducked around a corner to a phone booth while Harry, Jeff and I kept our eyes on the elevators. In a few minutes he was back.

"She's not home," he said dismally.

I glanced at the clock above the desk. "Seven-thirty. She's probably out to dinner."

"Look," Kirk said, "I better beat it before Wyatt gets here. I'll keep calling Erika and when I contact her I'll call here and have you paged. I'll get her to see you as soon as possible, Jeff, and ..."

Wyatt and Lockhart stepped out of an elevator. Kirk sped in one direction and Harry, muttering something about going back to the studio, started in the other. Jeff and I moved to meet Wyatt.

"Troy," he said, "I'm going to take you and your wife to a little place I know and buy you a drink."

"That's mighty nice of you but ..."

"We've got a car outside. Let's go."

"I'd like to but ..."

"You don't mean you're refusing my invitation!"

"Well, it's like this ..."

Wyatt's eyes narrowed. "You were planning on being very busy in the next hour or so, is that it? Now that's another thing you can tell me about. What were you going to be busy doing?"

"I'd planned to take some spots out of an old vest."

"I'll bet there are a lot of things you can tell me about that you haven't. Come on, Troy. Maybe I'll buy you two drinks."

It wasn't disguised as an invitation any more. Wyatt was a policeman saying that he wanted a word with Jeff. And there was no way out.

"All right. But Haila ... Haila isn't feeling well ..."

I smiled wanly. "My head ... it's splitting."

"I'll put her in a cab," Jeff said, "if you don't mind."

Wyatt grinned at my headache, but he said, "No, go ahead. We don't need Mrs. Troy. At the moment we just want Mr. Troy."

Jeff took my arm and guided me to the sidewalk. Lockhart and Wyatt were right behind us. The doorman whistled for a taxi. Across the street the homicide bureau car was parked. The detectives started toward it. I got in the cab.

"Go to Erika's," Jeff said, his lips barely moving. "Camp on her doorstep until she gets there. Tell her to keep quiet until I see her ... tell her she's got to for Mac's sake ..."

Lockhart had stopped in the middle of the street. He was staring at us. In a voice pitched especially for his benefit, Jeff said, "70 East Ninety-third, driver!" He slammed the door shut and the cab pulled out.

As soon as we had rounded the corner I leaned forward and gave the cabbie Erika's address. We wove our way through the blaring theater traffic to the comparative serenity of the Murray Hill district. In front of the quiet elegance of the Stuart Arms Apartments we stopped. I wasted no time paying off the driver or getting into the lobby. There was no one there; it was dimly lit and very quiet. The elevators were just beyond the narrow staircase. The operator hadn't taken Erika up, but his colleague, he told me, might have.

The hall outside Erika's door was wide and bright and airy and there was a low bench squatting under a tapestry at the end of it. I was glad for that; here was where I'd have to keep my vigil until Erika returned. And it might possibly be hours before there would be any sign of her.

I stopped, nevertheless, in front of her door and went through the motions of knocking at it. At the same time I experimentally wriggled the doorknob with my other hand. It turned easily. I stepped into a vestibule, a smallish one, with a thick dark rug and a three cornered table. There were two other doors opening off it; both were closed.

"Erika!" I called, "Erika!"

The door opposite me opened and Erika stood there. She had already changed into a housecoat, a foamy green thing that ruffled down her slender figure. In her left hand she held a white portable telephone, in her right, the receiver, pressed against her cheek. With her eyes on me she moved the mouthpiece down to her lips.

"Just a moment, Kirk," she said into it. "I already have a visitor."

If punctuality counted for anything in this world, I thought, I'd get ahead. Here I was at my appointment a split second after Kirk had made it.

I said, "Erika, I've got to talk to you. It's ... it's very important."

She smiled. "Yes. Kirk's been telling me it was." She inclined her smooth blond head toward the vestibule's third door. "Would you wait for me in the library, Haila? I'll be with you in a moment."

Her door closed sharply and I went down a long hall both sides of which were lined with Mac's photographs. It was a nice room, that library. There was more of Mac in it than of Erika. Big, shaggy chairs and an old leather davenport, into which I plopped and lit a cigarette in an effort to work up some poise.

It was going to be hard to say to Erika the things I had to say. And she would make it harder. I wondered what her attitude would be while I stumbled through my mission. Perhaps she'd be indignant, angry. Or she'd be ashamed. But if I could make her understand that it was for Mac ... that whatever she did, it would be for Mac ...

A beautiful old grandfather's clock in the corner ticked heavily. I ground out my cigarette and moved restlessly around the room. Why didn't Kirk hang up and let me get this over with? Or had he hung up and was Erika letting me wait ...

At the sound of a door opening and closing I scurried back to my seat like a recalcitrant schoolgirl. This interview would leave me with an advanced case of nervous anemia. I took a deep breath and waited for Erika to float into the room.

Almost a minute passed before I realized that she wasn't coming. That door, then, what had that been? An almost certain knowledge of what had happened dawned on me. Erika didn't care to be talked to by me. She had slipped into street clothes and sneaked away, leaving me stranded in that library.

I started toward the door. It opened before I got there and Mac MacCormick stood before me.

"Mac!" I said, "Then it was you who just ..."

But Mac wasn't listening to me. He brushed his hand across horror-filled eyes, then teetered drunkenly and caught himself as he half fell against the door jamb.

I raced past him and down the long hallway. The door to Erika's room was open now.

She lay across a chair, her head hanging down almost to the floor. Her eyes were wide open and one hand was clutching a corner of the rug. There were long red marks streaking the whiteness of her throat and a trickle of blood drooled from one side of her mouth.

Things began to revolve in front of me. Circles of telephones, all white, chairs and tables, mirrors, lamps, Erika's dead body.

Mac's voice, coming faintly from the library, snapped me out of it.

"Police headquarters, please." Never had I heard a voice so deadly quiet. "This is Ralph MacCormick, 220 East Thirty-eighth Street. I want to report a murder ... the murder of my wife. She has been strangled."

## Chapter Fifteen

I AWOKE WITH A START. Bright hot sunshine was pouring full into my face, blinding me. It was a moment or two before I realized that I was stretched out on the studio couch in our living room, still wearing the same clothes that I had worn the day before; the clothes that I had worn to Erika MacCormick's murder. I remembered then that Kirk, at Jeff's request, had brought me home. He had dropped me at the doorstep and disappeared back into the night. The studio couch had been as far as I had been able to drag myself.

It was the phone that had awakened me. It rang again now, insistently.

"Hello."

"Haila?" Jeff's voice was so tired it made me want to cry. "Are you all right, Haila?"

"Fine."

"In case you're worried about us, Kirk and I are at the studio. Do you want to be with us?"

"I'll be right over."

"Bring me a shirt and razor, will you? People are stopping to stare."

"All right, Jeff."

I hung up and looked at the clock. Eleven-thirty. It was daylight, so that would mean eleven-thirty in the morning. Thursday morning, the morning after Erika MacCormick's death. I stood listening to the quiet ticking of the clock.

And I remembered how Mac and I had stood the night before listening to the clock's ticking while we waited for the police to arrive. In the room at the end of the hall Erika was no more motionless nor deathly still than we were as we stood there, waiting.

I remembered the police as they surged in, overflowed and stormed the place in a ghastly repetition of all that had been just two short nights before. But this was far worse. Then there had been nine of us to diffuse the barking questions of their relentless attack; now there was just Mac and I. Then there had been awe and panic that a life had been taken, but there had been none of this anguish. For that victim had been old and out of our world; Erika was young and she had been beautiful.

Detective Wyatt had made short work of me. He had pummeled me with quick hard questions and then brushed me quickly aside to clear the decks for his assault on Mac. Pushed into a corner I had tried to pull myself together, but I found it was more than a one-woman job. Fortunately, it was then that Kirk and Jeff had arrived.

I felt Jeff's arms around my shoulders and it was as though he had reached out and gathered all my ebbing strength and brought it back to me. His head was bent over mine and he was talking to me. I don't know what he said; it didn't matter. I knew that he was there beside me and my body stopped being made of water and the whirling dimness that had been closing in on me disappeared.

Then I saw Kirk Findlay, his face dull and grayish like one who had been anesthetized.

"She can't be dead," he kept mumbling. "I just talked to her." He repeated it over and over with the hopeless stubbornness that people feel when they are told of death and refuse to believe it because that same day, that same hour even, they had seen that person or heard his voice and he had been alive.

"We know you talked to her." Wyatt left Mac to beat at Kirk. "You telephoned her."

"Yes. Yes, I called her. I heard her talking to Haila while I was on the phone."

"And after that ... how much longer did you two talk?"

"A minute or two. Maybe not as long as that."

"Then you heard her scream," Wyatt barked. "You heard the telephone crash to the floor ..."

"No!" Kirk shouted.

"No!" I seconded. "She didn't scream; I would have heard it."

The detective smiled, almost malevolently. "Then it might have been her husband who came into the room. That wouldn't have frightened her. She wasn't afraid of him. She didn't know that he might mean to kill her."

"She didn't scream," Kirk repeated doggedly. "She wasn't frightened, not while I was talking to her ..." He stopped as he understood's Wyatt's reasoning. "No, Mac didn't kill her! Mac didn't come in while I was on the phone. She would've mentioned it! She told me when Haila came in. Someone came in after she hung up. He killed her. He sneaked back out again before Mac came!"

"No," Wyatt said. "There wasn't time for that. MacCormick came in only a few minutes after Mrs. Troy."

I pushed my way forward through the group of men. "You made me say a few minutes. It might have been five or six ..."

"Or two or three!"

"I can't be positive. I didn't watch the clock. One can't tell about a matter of minutes! You can only guess ..."

"MacCormick!" Wyatt wheeled away from me to Mac. And he hammered and hammered at him. Question after question. He kept repeating the same question until he got the answer that he wanted. When Kirk was taking me away, the last thing I heard was Mac saying in a completely defeated voice, "… all right, I didn't love Erika and Erika didn't love me. Our marriage was a mistake. But I didn't know she was going to divorce me …"

I tried to sweep last night's images from my mind, but the sound of those biting questions and Mac's desperate answers kept ringing in my ears all the way to Photo Arts.

Jeff was at the desk in the studio, his head on his arm. Kirk wasn't to be seen. Jeff looked like a bum; thirty-six hours without sleep or a shave made him look like a bum even to me.

"Jeff!" I said.

"They've arrested Mac."

"Yes, I knew they would."

"Arrested him and charged him with the murders of Isabelle Fleming and Erika MacCormick."

Neither of us spoke for a long time.

"Where's Kirk?" I asked at last.

"Out to get us some coffee."

"You need some."

"And a shower and a shave and a clean shirt." He took the package from me. "And then I'm starting all over again."

"To prove that Mac … that Mac …"

Jeff stopped at the door. "Haila, do you think Mac is guilty? Honestly?"

I couldn't answer honestly then. Before Erika's death I had believed implicitly in his guiltlessness. In spite of all that had happened, in spite of motive and means and everything else that pointed suspicious fingers at Mac MacCormick, I had known that he was innocent. It was nothing that I could explain. Just that something deep inside of me said with unshakable conviction that Mac would not murder. But last night a doubt, for the first time, had begun its creeping trek through my mind.

All I could give Jeff was a feeble, "I don't know …"

His shoulders drooped another inch as he turned away. I sat there miserably while the shower bath at the end of Photo Art's corridor splashed away.

Thirty minutes later Jeff looked fine. There was a fighting tilt to his jaw as he pushed the knot of his tie tight to his collar.

"Haila! Mac's innocent."

"Do you really think that, Jeff?"

"Yes."

At that moment I thought so too again. And I felt like a murderer myself for having ever considered Mac one.

"That makes two of us, Jeff," I said.

"You're not being the loyal wife? You can vote your own ticket, remember."

"That makes two of us."

"Four of us. There's Kirk and Harry."

"Four of us. Against Wyatt, the homicide squad, the district attorney's office and the state of New York!"

"Tough goin', huh?" Jeff grinned.

We heard footsteps in the hall and then Kirk shouldered his way through the swinging doors, walked across the studio to Julie's old desk and plunked down two packages.

"Coffee," he said.

He stripped the brown paper from the other parcel. It was a bottle of scotch, good scotch, as expensive as you can buy.

"One drink of that, Kirk," Jeff told him, "and you'll fold up in your condition. Sleep's the only thing ..."

"Sleep?"

"We'll get Mac out just as soon if you relax for a couple of hours."

"When you relax, I will. Haila, some scotch?"

"I'll try the coffee first."

"Jeff?"

"A little in my coffee."

Kirk went to the paper cup dispenser and punched it three times. He brought the cups to the desk and I helped him with the pouring. He filled his as full with liquor as I did mine and Jeff's with coffee. He sat on the edge of the desk and stared down into his cup.

"We used to drink bourbon, Mac and Julie and I. Good cheap bourbon. Photo Arts was weaned on it. We used to sit around and dream about the day we'd be able to send out for a case of this kind of scotch, then drink to those good old days of abject poverty. We all pretended that we liked being poor, that it was romantic. We even pretended we liked cheap bourbon. Maybe Mac did; he has a sense of taste like an alligator, but Julie and I ..." he laughed at himself, "Julie and I, we have a taste for the finer things in life."

"We all do, Kirk. It's no sin. But you and Julie stuck with Mac when ..."

"Who wouldn't! Except Erika," he said bitterly, then was immediately sorry he had said it. "I mean ... oh, what the devil! This Cottrell account was going to fix us up. Mac was going places. And then, look what happens. Murder rears its head all over the place. Photo Arts finally hits the jackpot and ... and Mac's in the hoosegow and Julie's among the missing ..."

"Drink up, Kirk," Jeff said.

Kirk shook his head. Pouring the scotch out of the paper cup back into the bottle, he replugged the cork. The scotch went into a drawer in Julie's desk. "On second thought," he said, "I'll have coffee."

He went to the machine and plinked himself out a cup, came back to the desk and filled it with coffee.

Jeff was staring at the paper cup dispenser. He punched it. A cup fell on the hook. Then he punched it again, three times in quick succession.

"Haila!" he almost shouted.

And like an echo a voice came booming in from the reception room, a masculine voice. "Anybody around!"

"Kirk!" Jeff said excitedly, "see who that is! Send him away or keep him out there. Don't let him in here if you have to beat him over the head! I think I've got something! Hurry!"

Scooting to the double doors, Kirk opened one of them an inch, then turned back to us. "It's Snyder, Jim Snyder," he whispered, "I'll take care of him." The doors closed behind him quickly.

"Haila, come here!" Jeff clicked the machine twice more and two more cups fell out. "Listen, Haila! Have you ever heard that noise before?"

"Hundreds of times. Every time anyone took a drink."

"No. Close your eyes." He banged the machine four times. "Think, Haila ..."

I thought. And suddenly it was dark. I was here in the studio ... I was alone. The horsehair sofa in the corner ... that's where I had been. A clicking sound had awakened me. I had sat up and listened while that sound had been repeated. I had shouted Jeff's name and the clicking had stopped and a figure had sped toward the double doors ...

"Jeff, of course! On Tuesday night! That person was working the machine!"

"How many clicks, Haila?"

"Oh ... five or six ... seven or eight ...

"Seven or eight! For a drink of water!" Jeff muttered. "A camel, maybe." He began working the machine furiously, removing the cups as they piled upon the hook. When he had started, the tower of paper cups reached halfway up in the glass cylinder. It had fallen to a quarter full when the machine jammed.

Jeff stretched up his hands to the glass cylinder and twisted it. Carefully, he lifted it out of its base and set it on the floor beside him. The pile of cups still balanced themselves upright even without their glass casing. One by one Jeff plucked them off and dropped them on the floor. A flash of silver caught my eye as he lifted the last one. He held up a small tin can. It had no label nor any marking on it.

With his eyes on me, he removed the cap and put the container under his nose. Then, quickly, he replaced the top and set the can on the desk.

"Chloroform," he said.

I ran to the desk and sniffed at the can.

"Yes, you're right, Jeff!"

"The chloroform that Julie smelled in the darkroom."

"But how ... how did it get in there!" I demanded. "Who put it in there?"

"And who was trying to get it out?" Jeff asked. "And why couldn't he?"

He began walking wide circles around the room. I sat on the desk and drummed my heels against its side. Neither of us said anything.

Jeff was screwing the cylinder back into place. He tested it to make certain it was secure. Then he turned to me.

"Haila!" he commanded. "Take it off again."

"Why?"

"Because of our beautiful undying love. Hurry or I'll mow you down."

I walked over to the machine and reached up. I stood on my tip toes and tried to turn the cylinder. I stopped and glanced around.

"What are you looking for?" Jeff sounded more excited than ever. "Do you need something to stand on?"

"I guess so. If this water cabinet wasn't in the way ..."

"All right! Don't bother!"

"What is it, Jeff?"

He was making his circles again. They grew smaller as he walked faster and faster. When he reached the point where he was revolving almost like a tightly wound whirling dervish, he smacked both hands together.

"Haila, I know who your visitor was!"

"You do!"

"And even more than that, I think! I hope! C'mon, let's go."

"Where, Jeff?"

I had to run to catch up to him. As we went through the reception room, Kirk and Jim Snyder looked up from a pair of dice that were rolling merrily across the velvet green carpet. We went in and out so quickly that Snyder was too surprised to even greet us. But we caught Kirk's wink and saw him hold up two dollars of what apparently had just recently been Snyder's money.

## Chapter Sixteen

THE TURTLES seemed a great deal more pleased to see us than Miss Frances Frost did. Jeff's pleasantry about being in the neighborhood and just dropping in went over with a thud. Miss Frost made it evident that only her good bringing-up prompted her to invite us in. Her sparse gray and black hair was tied in a businesslike knot that raised her height to all of five feet two. The dampness of her apron suggested that we had interrupted some dishwashing.

"How are you, Miss Frost?" Jeff inquired politely.

"Splendid, of course!"

"Stiffness all gone out of your lower limbs?"

"My ... my lower limbs!" She was horror-stricken at the realization that Jeff knew that she had lower limbs. And she was angry at the flippancy of the question. I hardly blamed her.

Jeff crossed the room to a chair on which a disarranged morning paper lay. He tore a strip off the front page and held it out enticingly to one of the turtles who was joining his mates in a spot of sun under a window. Jeff remained calm under Miss Frost's warlike glare. He got down on both knees in the terrapin's path and waggled the paper before it. The turtle stopped dead. He looked at Jeff for a moment then withdrew his head into his shell.

"What are you doing!" Miss Frost demanded.

I wondered, too. I knew that Jeff was getting at something, but his route was so devious that I could sympathize with Miss Frost's bewilderment and alarm.

"Don't turtles eat paper?" Jeff asked innocently.

"Mine don't!" she snapped. "I feed them properly."

"I guess a turtle has to be awfully hungry to eat paper. I know I do."

"My turtles never eat paper, they don't have to. And tearing my Tribune to pieces! Young man ..."

"Oh, haven't you read it?"

"No, Mr. Troy, you're behaving very much as if you were under the influence of alcohol!"

Jeff seated himself on the divan and crossed his legs. "Miss Frost," he said, "did you know that you and Haila had met before Tuesday night, when we were here?"

"I'm certain we never met before that!"

"Oh, yes, Miss Frost," Jeff insisted. "On Tuesday evening, a little earlier. In the Graylock Building."

"The Graylock Building! I wasn't ..."

"Photo Arts. The thirty-seventh floor."

"What are you talking about?"

"Of course, it was very dark," Jeff said. "You and Haila didn't get a good look at each other."

Miss Frost was getting a good look at me now. She said nothing. She withdrew into her shell as completely as her turtle had.

"It was so dark," Jeff continued, "that you couldn't find anything to stand on to reach over the cooling cabinet and take the glass cylinder off the paper cup machine. You got panicky. You started clicking out cups then, hoping that what you were after would fall out with them."

Frances Frost was staring balefully at Jeff. "This is absurd, absolutely absurd! What would I be after in ..."

"A chloroform can."

"And what would I want with such a thing!"

"You didn't want it; Julie Taylor did."

Miss Frost snorted and Jeff smiled.

"Julie had to be the one who wanted it," he said. "Anybody else connected with the case would have walked boldly into the studio—they all had an excuse to do that—and wait for the moment when he could sneak out the can. And if Julie hadn't disappeared she would have done just that, instead of using the more dangerous method of creeping around in the dark for it. However, Julie wasn't the creeper either. She wouldn't have dared to come back; she would have been recognized and reported by one of Wyatt's watchers in the lobby or by an elevator boy. Therefore this intruder must have been someone sent by Julie."

"Possibly," Miss Frost said frigidly, "but what makes you think she sent me?"

"The someone she sent was not tall. Bluntly, Miss Frost, she was short like you. So short she couldn't reach high enough to remove the glass cylinder on the machine."

"Julie has many friends." Miss Frost's tone was even more frigid now. "It may be that she knows someone even shorter than I."

"Could be," Jeff admitted. "But it also had to be someone who would do anything for Julie. And someone with whom Julie could get in touch."

"Since the telephone has been invented, young man ..."

"Right, Miss Frost. But there's no one on this earth that was easier for Julie to get in touch with than you."

"What do you mean!"

Jeff grinned. "Do you remember telling me about a note that you said Julie had left for you? A note concerning a cleaning woman?"

"Of course I remember!"

"And which, when I asked to see it, had been eaten by a turtle?"

Miss Frost rose majestically to her feet. "Young man, I ..."

"But," Jeff rushed on, "turtles don't eat paper. Not even when they're hungry. They would rather die than be caught eating paper."

"You are an authority on turtles, I presume?"

Now it was Jeff's turn to draw himself to his full height. "It may interest you to know that when I was at Dartmouth, a college, I got a 'C' in a

Zoology course. Turtles don't eat paper."

"Perhaps," I suggested meekly, "Miss Frost's are different."

"Turtles are alike the world over. I also happen to know that turtles eat only under water. Not liking paper in the first place, a turtle would hardly take the trouble of dragging it under water in order to consume it."

"This is a most ridiculous conversation, young man!"

"All leading to the fact that there never was a note. You made that up to mislead me … to keep me assured that Julie had left town. Where is Julie, Miss Frost?"

"I have no idea."

"She's in New York."

"Is she?"

"Has she been to see you today?"

"No!"

"Has anybody?"

"No!"

"You said you hadn't read that paper yet. Somebody has!"

Jeff suddenly strode across the room and flung open a door. Julie Taylor stood there. Her back was to us; she had started to retreat into the bedroom at the sound of Jeff's footsteps.

Julie turned around. She was wearing an old corduroy bathrobe which she held closely about her neck with both hands. Her lovely hair was rumpled into a tangly mop. Her face was white and strained.

"Hello, Jeff," she said.

"Hello, Julie. Won't you come in and sit down?"

Julie came in and sat down. She tried to smile at me but couldn't make the grade. She didn't look as if she had succeeded in doing any smiling for quite a while.

Miss Frost went to her. "Julie, I'm so sorry. I tried, but this young man …"

"It's all right, Miss Frost," Julie said.

Miss Frost glared at Jeff. "I thought he was a flippant and stupid young man; he fooled me." Her brows suddenly ceased beetling and her eyes went soft as they were meant to be. "He's a very clever young man." She turned to me. "And very pleasant looking."

"Thank you," I said.

"Well, Jeff?" Julie asked.

"You know that Mac was arrested."

"Yes." She nodded toward the newspaper. "Yes, I know."

"It looks bad for him, Julie." Her lips tightened; she didn't say anything. "Julie, you've got to help us prove Mac didn't kill Isabelle Fleming and Erika."

"Jeff, you shouldn't have looked for me!"

"You're our last chance, Julie, we've tried everything and everybody. Haila and I are licked unless you know something that will help us."

"You shouldn't have found me ..." Julie was sobbing.

Jeff went to her and crouched before her on one knee. "Julie, you've got to think, think back and remember something that will save Mac from the electric chair."

Julie shook the sob out of her throat, she straightened in her chair and demanded fiercely, "Do you think I can help Mac?"

"You've got to."

"Do you think I can save him from the electric chair?"

"Yes, you must, Julie."

Julie threw back her head and her laugh was harsh and mirthless. Miss Frost returned to her anxiously, but Julie brushed her aside and leaned close to Jeff.

"Jeff! If there's one scrap of evidence in Mac's favor, by telling what I know and remember, I can destroy that scrap of evidence. If there's the slightest doubt in anybody's mind ... yours or Haila's or anybody's ... that Mac is guilty, I can erase that doubt of his guilt with what I know. I can only prove one thing; that Mac is a murderer."

It was a long time before Jeff spoke. "That's why you ran away, Julie."

"Yes."

"By hiding you thought you could save Mac."

"I knew that sooner or later Wyatt would get me and ... and I didn't want to be the one who convicted Mac."

Jeff walked back to his chair and dropped into it. He looked tired and lifeless again.

"So you see, Jeff, you shouldn't have found me," Julie said.

"Wyatt would have found you."

"How? How did you?"

"The same way Wyatt will. He knows you're a smart girl, Julie, and it won't be long before he realizes that a smart girl like you, if she were sneaking out of town, wouldn't leave such an obvious trail of elevator boys and taxi drivers to testify that she went to Pennsylvania Station with a suitcase. He'll realize that it was so obvious that it was a plant, that you doubled back on your trail. After that it might take him awhile to here, but sooner or later he would."

"Yes, I suppose he would," Julie said. "You outguessed me and I suppose he would."

"Of course not being an authority on turtles might slow Wyatt up."

Miss Frost moaned. "I thought that lie about a note to the cleaning woman was so smart."

"Julie!" Jeff said suddenly. "Julie, do me a favor. Tell me everything. Start at the beginning and tell me all you can remember about the whole business. I might get something, some little thing that will help us clear Mac."

"Anything I tell you will only prove that Mac ... that he can't be cleared." The anguish in her voice sent a chill down my spine.

"Please, Julie," Jeff pleaded.

"All right." Now her voice was dead. "All right, it won't make any difference to Mac. It can't matter now. What I told Haila when I went to see her Monday evening was true. Everything that happened in the studio and in the darkroom was true."

"But you didn't think that it was Mac in the darkroom? That is was he with the chloroform?"

"No, oh, no! I never dreamed then it was Mac. If I had known then that ..."

"While you were at Haila's you got the phone call about the picture having to be retaken and you went back to Photo Arts."

"Yes. I had made up my mind to tell Kirk and Mac about it. And if they laughed at me, I'd tell Harry. Harry's less inclined to laugh at things. I stopped in the reception room to take off my things and light a cigarette. I didn't have any matches. Mac's coat was hanging in the closet and his pockets are always full of kitchen matches. I put my hand in his coat pocket. There was a chloroform can in it."

"In Mac's pocket," Jeff said slowly. "And then, Julie?"

"Then I knew what had happened. It had been Mac in the darkroom that afternoon ... Mac who was almost a murderer. You see, I knew how terribly he needed money, lots of it. Money to save the studio, money to meet Erika's extravagances. And there was only one way he could get it—through the death of Isabelle Fleming. So I knew that Mac had tried to kill her that afternoon. And somehow he had arranged to retake the picture so that he could try again tonight. I just had time to stuff the can in my pocket when Mac and Kirk bounced in."

"They were all happy and excited. Mac had just been up to see Mrs. Fleming and she had promised to finance the studio. Then I realized what that meant. He wouldn't kill her now; there wouldn't be another murder attempt. There was no reason for it now. But I had to get rid of that chloroform can and I had to make Haila keep quiet about what I'd told her. Then no one would know what Mac had done.

"I didn't know where to hide the can. I had no time to take it out of the studio and I was afraid if I slipped it in my purse or in my desk someone might smell it. Then I thought of the paper cup machine. It was airtight; no one would think of opening it until the cups were gone. I put it there meaning to sneak it out later."

"But you never got a chance."

Julie shook her head wearily. "No, I never got a chance. I tried, but the studio was never empty. Not once all evening. Even after the murder had been committed and everyone had been sent home, I tried again. I went back into the Graylock Building after I had talked to Haila in the taxi. But Wyatt was still there. He chased me home."

"And so you sent Miss Frost to get it because you were afraid of being seen."

"Yes, I sent Miss Frost."

"Young lady," Miss Frost said to me, "you frightened me half to death!"

"And vice versa," I said.

"And, young man, in case you're still interested, the stiffness *hasn't* gone out of my lower limbs. I never want to see another flight of stairs again."

"You and I, Miss Frost."

Jeff turned again to Julie. "Then after you had hidden the chloroform, Julie, Haila came. And she made things difficult for you by harping on that darkroom experience."

"I tried to tell her it was all a mistake. I tried to make her go home. But Mac put her in the picture and there was nothing I could do. Then, later, when she came to me and said that the plates had been broken, I ..." She stopped and put her hand over her eyes.

I tried to help her. "You told me that you had smashed them."

"I had to, Haila! I had to stop you from talking about it, from telling anyone. I knew that the plates had been destroyed deliberately; I found them before you knew about it. And I knew that Mac had broken them. But I thought that didn't matter now; I believed him, you see, when he told me about Isabelle Fleming's loan. I thought that ... that cancelled everything that had happened, that Mac no longer had any reason to murder Mrs. Fleming. I didn't think that he was going to try again. If I had known ..."

"Yes, Julie. We know."

"I was standing there with Haila beside the dining table, putting the silverware back in its case when ... when I noticed that the carving knife was missing. I ran into the hallway and opened Isabelle Fleming's door ..."

Her voice cracked as she tried to go on. With visible effort she controlled it.

"I knew then that Mac had lied about the loan; that he had said it only to put me off the track in case I had guessed that it was he in the darkroom. I knew that he had killed her."

She sat looking at us steadily. She didn't make a sound, her lips weren't trembling, but the tears streamed down her face. I don't think she was aware of them.

"And then, Julie," Jeff said, "you hid so that you might save Mac."

She nodded.

"Why, Julie?"

"Because I love him. I loved him long before he married Erika. I still do; I've never stopped."

"But Kirk!" I blurted involuntarily. "What about him?"

"Kirk? I … I'm crazy about Kirk. But it's Mac I've always loved. Oh, Jeff, Jeff, what can we do for him!"

"We'll do something, Julie. We'll do something. But, first, you're right about Wyatt. He mustn't get hold of you, not yet …"

"Then it is hopeless. Then I have proved that Mac is guilty."

"We're not admitting it yet," Jeff said sharply. "Now, listen, Julie. When you left Haila and went back to the studio Monday evening before the picture, who was there?"

"Just Mac and Kirk," she said dully.

"No one else?"

"I think … no. Harry got there right after I did. And then, later, the models started coming."

"Who arrived first? Which of the models, I mean."

"Jim Snyder was the first one I saw. I don't know what time he came; I didn't see him come in. But only a little while after I had, I think. I saw him coming out of a dressing room. He'd been changing his clothes, I suppose."

"And then … after him?"

"Kenyon and Robert Yorke. They came in together. And only a minute after that, May Ralston."

"How long had the boys been in the studio before you came?"

"I don't know. Kirk had come back first, Mac only a minute or two after him, I think they said. They couldn't have been there very long. Mac's coat … Mac's coat was still wet."

Jeff darted out of his chair and began to pace the room, frowning. "Listen, Julie, you've got to stay hidden for a little while. Long enough to give me a chance …"

"Could I go back to my own place, Jeff? They won't look for me there now, will they?"

"You can go back. Don't go out of the building; they're watching the front entrance now, I'm sure of that. And don't answer the door except for Miss Frost or Haila or me. Nor the telephone at all. If I have any reason to call you, we'll work it this way: let the phone ring for more than twelve times before you answer it. I'll keep right on ringing until you do."

"All right, Jeff."

Julie was looking slightly better now. From the mere action in Jeff's voice she had caught a spark of hope and it was starting to kindle in her eyes. Her effort to smile wasn't as dismal a failure as it had been the first time.

Outside in the corridor, I said, "Poor Mac! Now he doesn't have the ghost of a chance."

Jeff's head jerked around sharply to stare at me.

"He doesn't, doesn't he," he said.

## Chapter Seventeen

IT WAS DUSK when we walked past the Players Club and on around Gramercy Park toward Twenty-third Street. I began to peer anxiously at Jeff. He was marching along like a zombie with financial worries. When I dragged him from the path of a sanitation truck he looked at me coldly as though I had just spoiled a charming idea he had been nursing. There wasn't a hint of recognition in the glance he gave me.

I started to fret; perhaps this strain had been too much for him. But when he walked into the George Washington Bar, although he still retained that zombie quality, I was relieved. In the depth of his preoccupation he was mechanically reverting to type. He was still the old Troy heading for the nearest saloon.

The waiter shifted from foot to foot. Twice he had asked Jeff for his order. He tried again.

"What do you want, sir?"

"The same," Jeff roused himself to say.

"The same?" the waiter asked. "The same what, sir?"

"The same as Haila."

"Haila hasn't ordered," Haila explained. "Jeff, come to! He wants to know ..."

"Chloroform," Jeff said, not quite enough to himself. The waiter started violently.

"Two ryes and soda," I said hastily.

The man was halfway across the room when Jeff rapped sharply on the table. "Waiter! Waiter!" The man came hurrying back. "Will you please take our order? Two ryes and soda!"

The waiter cast a frightened look from me to him and crept away.

"Where have I seen that guy before?" Jeff asked.

"Oh, Jeff ..."

"Listen, Haila. After Mac left the Fleming house on Monday evening, he went home, didn't he?"

"Yes, for just a few minutes."

"And Erika … was she there then?"

"No. Don't you remember? Mac told Wyatt about it. Erika was out, he said, having dinner with some friends."

"Was anyone there when Mac went home?"

"I don't think so. I remember that he said he only stayed a little while. Just long enough to get a sandwich and to change his coat …"

"Because it had started to rain!"

"Yes. It started about six o'clock."

"And he left his house and came straight back to the studio and Kirk was waiting for him there. And after that … who came after that, Haila?"

"Harry. No, Julie came next. And then Harry, a minute or two later. He'd gone up to Times Square with a camera to take some pictures of the signboards."

"And then, Haila, who came then?"

"Jim Snyder, I think Julie said. She didn't see him come in. She just saw him coming out of his dressing room all ready for the picture."

"And then?"

"Then Kenyon and Robert Yorke together. Then May Ralston. All of them were there when I arrived. And after I came, Mrs. Fleming and last of all, Madge Lawrence. But what's all that got to do with …"

Jeff stood up so abruptly that the table teetered. He craned his neck to look around the place. "Where's the telephone?"

I pointed to a booth against the wall on the far end of the bar. Muttering about Wyatt … "got to call Wyatt," he hurtled across the place and disappeared in the telephone cubicle. I sat and wondered if Jeff had uncovered something that would save Mac and, if he had, what it could be. I lit a cigarette and smoked the first two puffs of it. The waiter returned with our two drinks and seemed vastly relieved to find me minus my escort. But he took no chances. He slid the glasses from the tray to the table with one sweeping motion and was gone. I toyed with my drink and waited some more, my eyes still on the phone booth.

"Haila!"

The voice came from directly behind me. Turning, I confronted only the top of a face across the high back of my booth. The rest of the face emerged and Lee Kenyon reached over to shake my hand.

"I've been wondering to whom that familiar voice belonged," he said. "I'd like to talk to you."

A moment later he slid into the seat beside me, putting his half-empty

Manhattan glass on the table before him.

I looked at him closely. This was not the Lee Kenyon we had talked to yesterday, smart and smooth and suave and cocky. This was a Lee Kenyon who had been drinking too much and sleeping too little. His bloodshot eyes were sunk deep above dark circles and his face was flushed unhealthily. When he lifted the cocktail glass and tilted it to his lips, his hand was unsteady.

He banged down the glass. "God!" he said. "I've just ... just heard about Erika." He turned to stare at me. "You know?"

"Yes. I was ... I was there when it happened."

"You were there! They didn't tell me that, the police didn't say that you were there! Then you must know ..."

"No," I said. "I was in another room. I didn't see anyone or hear anyone."

He gave a kind of a groan and, leaning forward, put his face in his two hands. His words came out muffled, thick.

"Erika dead! I still can't believe it. Yesterday she was alive, the most alive person I've ever known. She loved life so, it amused her so. Everything amused her, she laughed at everything. I was looking forward to telling her about what the police suspected, about our being lovers, you know. I wanted to hear her laugh at that. How *that* would have amused her, too! I wanted to see her face when I told her about the lousy trick her aunt was trying to play on her, and the one I played on Aunt Isabelle. And about the damn hot water I'd got myself into because of it ..."

"You never told her about that?"

"No. I never saw her to talk to alone after it happened. I wanted to tell her last night; I wasn't afraid to tell her. I tell you, she would have laughed at the whole thing. She wouldn't let me talk to her last night though because Kirk had called, she said, and made other arrangements for her for the evening. She was to see you and Jeff, I think she said. Anyway that was my last chance, my only chance. And now it's too late. She would have thought it was one hell of a funny joke; she would have ..." His voice rose and two solitary drinkers at the bar turned to look curiously at us. Lee gulped down the last of Jeff's rye and sat contemplating the empty glass with blind moroseness.

I had had enough of that. Murmuring something unintelligible about having to find Jeff, I got up and almost ran to the telephone booth. Three steps away from it I could see that it was empty.

I went slowly back to my table and Lee Kenyon. He hadn't moved since I had left him. He sat slumped over the table, his hands idly snapping matchsticks and tossing the pieces in a little pile before him. For some strange reason the sight of Lee Kenyon huddled there in his despair drove home to me the aftermath of murder more lucidly than anything else could have done. I wanted Jeff. I wanted to get Jeff and have him take me by the hand and lead me far away from all these murder-racked people, away from everything that had happened since last Monday night.

"My husband seems to have left me," I told Kenyon. "I'm going to find him."

He roused himself with difficulty. "Where'd he go?"

"I don't know. Back to the studio probably."

"We'll look there," he said. "I want to find Jeff, too. I want to help him solve the murder. I want to find out who killed Erika. I'll help you find him, Haila." He stood up and yelled belligerently for the check. I stood uncomfortably beside him while he paid for the ryes that Jeff had ordered and for his own Manhattans.

Riding up Fifth Avenue in a bus he started in again.

"I've some theories on this case, Haila. And one of them is that the first thing to do is find Julie Taylor. The murderer has got Julie Taylor. If we find her, we find the murderer. And when we get him …"

"That's right, Lee," I said soothingly, "you're right."

"I'll find them," he said grimly. "I'm going to stick my nose in this case now, and it's not coming out until I get the person who murdered Erika. I'm going to tear this case wide open. I'm going to crack it. I'm going …"

By the time we reached the Graylock Building, Lee Kenyon's detective ambitions had dampened somewhat. He walked through the lobby with me but then, at the elevators he made an abrupt about-turn.

"I'm going to stop in for a quick one," he said, indicating the Graylock Bar. "I'll come up to the studio later." Through the plate glass lobby window I watched him swing himself up on a red leather stool and hunch over the bar.

I opened the door into the studio and found myself in an eerie, shadowy semidarkness. There was no sound or movement in the big room. Then, in the dim twilight that clouded through the windows, I was able to discern two silent figures seated at Julie's desk.

"Jeff!" I said.

An arm moved out to the desk lamp and switched it on. The warm glow illuminated the faces of Kirk and Harry Duerr. They had been sitting quietly there, obviously unaware that it was time to turn on lights.

"Where's Jeff?" I asked.

They both shook their heads. Disappointed, I sat beside them. Neither of them spoke. It was as though the effort of making sounds was too much and too discouraging. I was glad I had my one little note of cheer to broadcast now.

I said, "We ... we found Julie."

Kirk was on his feet in an instant. Harry's hand reached across the table and clutched my arm.

"You found Julie!" Kirk shouted.

"Yes. She's been across the hall from her apartment. She's been there all the time."

"Is she ..." Kirk was almost afraid to say it ... "is she all right?"

"Fine."

"Thank God!" He was combing his hair with his fingers, trying to straighten out his mussed clothes and get out of the studio all at once. "I'm going to see her! I want to see Julie!"

"No, Kirk, not now."

Harry Duerr's eyes filled with apprehension. "She isn't all right. She ..."

"Julie's fine! Believe me."

"I'd love to see Julie," Kirk persisted.

"So would I," Harry said. "I'd like to talk to her. I'm positive that Julie knows something that could save Mac. I've felt that all along. Possibly she doesn't even realize that she knows it. But if I could see her, perhaps I could make her remember."

"Harry," I said, "Jeff doesn't even want the police to get hold of her yet. He doesn't want her to see anyone, and if everybody starts running up there ..."

"Who's everybody, Haila?" Harry asked. "It wouldn't be everybody, just ..."

"Kirk is dying to see Julie, you want to see her. I want to see her some more. And even Lee Kenyon ..."

"What about Kenyon?" Kirk growled.

"We came up here together on the bus. He's turning detective now; he wants to talk to Julie."

"Fat chance of Kenyon caring that Mac's in jail!" Kirk muttered. "I can't see Kenyon doing anything for anybody but Kenyon. Why does he want this case solved?"

"I think he was really terribly fond of Erika."

"Terribly fond of Erika ..." Harry repeated thoughtfully. "You know, we all believed Kenyon when he admitted that he had swindled Mrs. Fleming, that he had taken her money under the false pretense of being Erika's lover. It's an old trick. A man confesses to a lesser crime in order to convince the police that he is innocent of a more serious one. Kenyon's candor was disarming; we all believed his statement that he was not Erika's lover."

"No, Harry," I said. "I'm sure Kenyon wasn't the man Erika meant to marry. I've just been talking to him and, for some reason, I believe him. He says that Erika would have told the truth if she had lived; he says that there was nothing between them. He tried to get her to tell last night, but she wouldn't talk to him then. Kirk had called and she'd promised not to see anybody until she'd talked to Jeff and me. After that, of course, it was too late ..."

The look that sprang into Harry's eyes made me break off abruptly. "Haila!" His usual calmness had fled and his excitement left him breathless. "Haila, did you say that Kenyon wanted to see Erika, but that she refused him because Kirk had already made arrangements for you and Jeff to visit her?"

"Yes."

"But you were already there, Haila, when Kirk telephoned. You heard Erika talking to him ..."

"Yes, I did, I ..."

"So in order to know about Kirk's call," Harry almost shouted, "Kenyon would have had to talk to Erika *after* Kirk phoned. And it was *after* Kirk phoned that Erika was killed, just a few seconds or minutes after!"

"But, Harry ..." I started to object.

"Yes, I know. Kenyon might have talked to Erika over the phone. But, Haila, did you hear it ring?" Harry demanded. "I've been up there; there's an extension in the library where you were; you would have heard it. If Kenyon had telephoned Erika, you would have heard it ring. Did you, Haila?"

"No," I said, "the phone didn't ring."

"So Kenyon didn't phone her and yet he knew about Kirk's call," Harry said quietly. "He knew because he was in Erika's room. He was in Erika's room when she was killed."

"You mean that Kenyon killed ..." Kirk exclaimed incredulously. "No, Harry, not Kenyon; he ..."

"It's obvious, isn't it?" Harry's voice was threateningly calm. "I'm going downstairs to the bar. To see Kenyon. You two wait here for me. You'd better try to locate Jeff or Wyatt."

He moved swiftly across the studio and the doors swung closed behind him. Kirk turned to me; he was still shaking his head in disbelief.

"No, Haila, he's wrong. Not Kenyon. Not that little ineffectual ..."

"He's right!" The whole thing rose before me in one panoramic flash. I knew that Lee Kenyon was Erika's murderer. And the murderer of Isabelle Fleming. I knew how and why he had committed both those horrible crimes. And now I knew that he must be ...

"Kirk!" I said. My mouth felt frozen; I couldn't seem to form the words that I had to say so quickly. "Kirk, Kenyon's looking for Julie now ... he thinks the same as we do ... that Julie has a clue. He's got to get to Julie and manage to keep her quiet ..."

"Wait, Haila, you're ... Kenyon doesn't know where Julie is. How could he ...?"

"He might. He *might*! He was sitting in the next booth to Jeff and me in the George Washington Bar!"

"After you'd found Julie?"

"Yes. He must have heard everything that Jeff and I said."

"But, Haila, he's downstairs in the bar now; you saw him go in …"

"Yes! That's his alibi, Kirk! Don't you see! He was using me for his alibi …"

Kirk was already on his way toward the door. I chased after him.

He turned and caught me by both arms. "No, Haila. I'm going alone. It … it might be dangerous."

I wrenched myself free and followed him to the elevator. The boy obeyed Kirk's command and we plummeted to the street floor without a stop. I raced across the lobby after Kirk. He stopped so abruptly that I collided with him. Pushing me off, he ran into the Graylock Bar. In a moment he was back again.

"Kenyon's left," he told me. "And Harry's not there. He's probably looking for him. I've got to get hold of Jeff. Where is he, Haila?"

"He was talking about seeing Wyatt. Maybe …"

"I'll call headquarters. Get a cab ready."

I hailed a taxi and crawled into it. It seemed days before Kirk returned. I had prepared the driver. There could be no possible doubt in his mind now that my "matter of life and death" was not a figure of speech. He had the motor going.

Kirk stood with one foot on the running board. "Haila, get out. You mustn't come. Jeff would …"

I reached out for his arm and pulled him into the cab beside me. I nodded to the driver and we swung out into the traffic.

"Did you get Wyatt?"

"He hasn't been at headquarters all day."

"Then Jeff … Jeff hasn't found him."

"Probably not." Kirk put his head in his hands. "God! If only Jeff were here!"

## Chapter Eighteen

WE DIDN'T WAIT for the elevator. Kirk left me far behind as he rushed up the stairs. When I finally caught up to him he was beating frantically at Julie's door.

"It's happened!" he gasped. "It's happened already!"

"Wait, Kirk!" I pushed him aside and twisted the knob. "Julie!" I shouted, "Julie!"

The voice that answered me came from right behind the door. Julie's face must have been pressed up close against it as she said, "Haila! Just a minute, Haila!"

The sound of a bolt sliding smoothly and of a key turning in its lock followed. And then Julie Taylor stood in the doorway. She was wearing a gay little red apron with mops and brooms and dustpans printed on it over her corduroy bathrobe. In one hand she held a can of Maxwell House coffee. Tucked in the curve of her arm was the top of a Silex coffee maker. The sight of all that calm unruffled domesticity almost got me.

Kirk grasped her hand and held it tightly in both of his. He said at last, "Hullo, Julie? Have a good time?" And his voice quivered in his effort to sound serene and unconcerned.

Julie smiled at him. "Kirk! Kirk, darling. I didn't know it was you knocking. Until I heard Haila's voice ... Kirk, why didn't you say something?"

In his relief Kirk grinned idiotically. "I was too scared to talk. When you didn't open the door right away I thought ... you still look the same, Julie. You haven't changed a bit."

Julie closed the door behind us. "Jeff warned me not to open the door for anyone." She looked up at us and seemed to notice our strained faces for the first time. "Come on out in the kitchen," she said, "and I'll finish making the coffee. You both look as if you could stand a cup."

We followed her down the narrow hall, past the living room and bedroom, into her dinette. It was a nice little room with bright yellow walls and maple chairs and table, separated from the kitchen by two glass-windowed cabinets that were shoulder high. Kirk and I sat down while Julie measured coffee and water at the kitchen cabinet and plugged the Silex into the wall socket. She carried three canary-yellow cups and saucers into the dinette and set them on the table before us.

I looked around the cheerful room, at Julie's placid face and at Kirk's, that seemed now to be bursting with relief. I looked at the shining whiteness of Julie's kitchen and the bright figured oilcloth curtains at the one window above the sink. The Silex gleamed red and then began to bubble merrily. The fragrance of the coffee it was making was wonderful. Our chase began to seem silly and unreal; even our fears for Julie became remote there in her kitchen.

Kirk was telling her now about Lee Kenyon. She listened with a puzzled, half-horrified expression.

"He hasn't tried to see you, Julie, has he? He hasn't tried to get in touch with you?"

She shook her head. "No. But I ... I can't believe all this about him. And he hasn't been here or telephoned me. Nobody's called but Jeff."

"Jeff!" I exclaimed. "When?"

"About ten minutes ago. He said he was at police headquarters. He said that I was to stay here and that he and Wyatt would be down later."

Kirk said quietly, "I called police headquarters about ten minutes ago. Jeff wasn't there. Wyatt hadn't been there all day."

"But ..."

He leaned forward and his eyes held Julie's. "Julie, are you sure it was Jeff who called?"

There was perplexity in her gesture as she brushed her hand over her forehead. "I ... I think so. Oh, it must have been! He told me that if he called he'd let the phone ring more than twelve times. And when it had rung twelve times I answered it. So ..."

"Someone else might have let it ring that long ... if he knew that you were here to answer it."

"You mean that it was ... that it might have been Lee Kenyon?"

"Did he say anything that could make you sure that it was Jeff?"

Julie closed her eyes. "No," she said at last. "He was in a hurry. He said just what I told you. And if Jeff *wasn't* at police headquarters ..."

Kirk was on his feet. He gave his orders crisply.

"Haila, you get out of here. Now, right away. Try to find Jeff." I was already slipping my arms into my coat and reaching for my purse. "And Julie! You get into some street clothes and go up to the studio. Lock yourself in. Stay there until I call you."

I was in the hall when Julie spoke. I looked back at her. She was standing by the refrigerator, pouring cream from a paper container into a bright yellow pitcher. Her voice was very calm.

"I'm not going, Kirk. I'm going to stay here with you and see this thing through."

"Julie!" Kirk said. "Julie, you've got to go. It may be dangerous ..."

She came through the space between the cabinets into the dinette. She laid her hand gently on Kirk's arm. "Yes. That's why I'm staying. He ... he ought to be coming soon now."

I came back into the room and took off my coat. "I, also, am sticking around," I said.

Kirk looked from me to Julie with desperation. Then he shrugged helplessly.

"All right. You win; you both win."

Julie stepped into the kitchen again and disconnected the Silex. She poured three cups of coffee. She placed a sugar bowl and a creamer in the center of the table, then sat down opposite Kirk.

"The spoons are in the drawer by you, Kirk," she said in her high clear voice. "Will you get them out?"

The room seemed to grow suddenly cold and cheerless. I shivered involuntarily and looked down at my coffee. It didn't smell so delicious any more. I began to wish that I had taken Kirk's advice and gone to find Jeff. Julie could be brave, and so could Kirk. I was afraid.

In a tone that I hoped was matter-of-fact, I asked, "May I have a spoon, please, Kirk?"

Kirk's hand reached out toward mine. I half-turned to face him. And the scream that had started some place deep inside me surged up through my whole body and died strangling in my throat.

It wasn't a spoon that Kirk Findlay had extended. It was a small, shiny automatic. I lifted my eyes. The face above the pistol was one I'd never seen before. The eyes, without their laughing twinkle, were narrow slits of icy green. The mouth was an ugly gash across his face. Kirk rose and backed against the wall. He looked from me to Julie, then back at me again. His voice was harsh.

"I gave you your chance, Haila. I gave you two chances. You wouldn't take them. Now, you'll stay. You'll stay … with Julie." His eyes shifted across the table, but the gun remained pointed at a spot between Julie and me. "Julie, some towels. All that you have."

Julie didn't move. She stared at Kirk in a sort of dazed horror. A faint smile wavered on her lips, broke and was gone.

"You're fooling, Kirk? You wouldn't … you …"

"Get me the towels."

Slowly, like a sleepwalker, she rose from the table and moved into the kitchen. She brought back a neat pile of towels and tried to hold them out to Kirk. They slid from her hands to the floor.

"Pick them up, Julie. Take the big red one. Tie Haila's hands behind her."

"Kirk, I can't! I can't!" She held up her hands to show him. They were trembling violently.

"Do it, Julie."

Almost hypnotized, I put my hands behind me and around the back of my chair, and I knew that Julie's shaking ones were tying them together. I felt the strong linen tightening as it was wound around them.

"Tighter, Julie."

The knot that she made clapped my wrists together with such force that all circulation seemed to stop in them.

"Now her feet to the chair legs, Julie."

Julie was crying. Tears ran down her cheeks, her shoulders shook with great convulsive heaves. But nothing but a breathy, gasping sound came out. She stood up at last and looked at me. There was nothing in her eyes, not even recognition, as they swept over the knots that she had made.

Kirk's left hand was on Julie's shoulder; he pushed her down into a chair with firm gentleness. She offered no resistance. She sat, silent and wooden, as he placed his gun carefully in his coat pocket and then bound her hands as mine were bound. He dropped on one knee before her chair and tied her legs to it. With a quick hard movement he gagged her mouth with another towel. Walking over to me he checked my knots and then stood looking down at both of us, smiling a little.

I found my voice. Even to me it sounded choked and unfamiliar.

"Kirk! Kirk, no, you can't! Jeff's coming, he'll know! He'll be here any minute! You called headquarters, Kirk, you told them to come!"

His lips scarcely moved when he spoke. "No, Haila. Not Jeff. I didn't call the police; I called Lee Kenyon. It's Lee Kenyon who's coming here!"

"You couldn't have! He wasn't ..."

"Yes. He was. He was in the Graylock Bar. I telephoned there and had him paged."

"But Harry was with him," I said. "Harry will ..."

"Kenyon's going to break away from Harry and come up here. Don't worry, Haila." He was smiling again. "I won't get in any trouble; I've arranged it all. The police will think what you thought, especially when they meet Kenyon coming out of this building. And when Harry tells them how Kenyon sneaked away from him in the bar."

Panic hit me then, blind, raging panic.

"Kirk!" I said desperately, "you can't! I won't let you! I don't care if you shoot me, I don't care what you do! I'll scream, Kirk, I'll ..."

"Go ahead. Scream."

I opened my mouth. Kirk was advancing toward me. Slowly, deliberately, his face came close to mine; it grew larger as it neared me, as though my eyes were camera lens panning down upon him in a closeup shot. My scream wouldn't come. It was a nightmare scream, the kind that you drag and tear on with every living muscle of your body to no avail.

I hardly felt the coarse dry cloth that was being shoved into my mouth until, having drained up all the saliva, it began to choke me. I gagged and felt suddenly nauseous.

With a calm terrifying determination, Kirk moved into the kitchen. He reached out to the wall switch and turned off the light. One square yellow beam from some apartment across the court tumbled into the kitchen through the one small window. It was only a little light, enough to outline Julie's shining stove and refrigerator and Kirk's motionless figure.

Now, I told myself, now. It's to be now. I forced myself to close my eyes, to stop watching and thinking and feeling. Now it was going to happen. If it would only happen quickly!

I felt the rustle of him as he came close. My heart stopped beating. And then I felt him pass, I heard the door leading from the dinette into the little hallway close. Without realizing its significance, I knew that he had gone, that he had left us here. I heard a key turn in the lock, the sound of something being placed against the other side of the door. Not something hard, not a chair nor a table. Something soft that brushed against the bottom of the door as it was placed there.

His footsteps moved with unhurried caution down the hall; the door at the end of it, the outside door, opened and then closed. With my ears strained until the slightest noise was magnified to bursting loudness, I heard the clicking sound the door made as it locked itself behind him.

The cold sweat broke through my pores; I felt it icy on my forehead. Ungovernable shudders shook me. But they were shudders of great overwhelming relief. Julie and I were not to share the fate of Erika and Isabelle Fleming.

For Kirk Findlay had no key to this apartment; if he had he would have used it when he first arrived, he wouldn't have stood beating at the door. We had been bound and gagged to give him time for escape. He had locked the dinette door behind him as an added precaution. He had put things against it to ...

My eyes dragged dully back to the kitchen. I knew then what had been placed against that door. I knew what had been stuffed beneath it and around it, and I knew why.

The four small handles of white enamel on Julie's stove were clearly visible in the yellow beam, and they pointed straight out into the room.

Even as I looked I began to smell it. A sickening sweet odor tingling in my nostrils. What was it like to die by gas? It must be painless; it must be quiet and untortured. Old actors in cheap rooming houses were forever letting their coffee boil over while they slept. They died without even waking. The lethal chamber is the most humane means of execution; everybody knows that. It wouldn't hurt. If you didn't struggle against it, it wouldn't hurt. Don't fight, Haila. Fill your lungs with it, fill them quickly, easily. Pretty soon you'll get sleepy, your head will nod. ...

But I wasn't getting sleepy. Each breath I took burned in my nose, my throat, my lungs. My eyes were smarting.

I didn't want to die this way. I didn't want to die at all.

There was the window, tantalizingly close. One square of thin glass holding out the clean fresh air. If I could break it! I strained at the cloths that bound my legs. They gave slightly, almost unnoticeably. I tugged again and again.

Slipping my heel out of its patent leather pump I pulled my foot back as far as it could go. I swung it. The shoe flew off, described a pitiful little arc and fell to the floor. It had come nowhere near the window. Frantically, I kicked the other one. It went further, but not far enough.

Julie. If Julie could manage to get a little looser than I had, if she could kick a little further. I turned to look at her. Her head was sunk down on her chest; she seemed unconscious of my efforts. I moved in my chair until it teetered and made a jarring noise.

Julie's head jerked up. A strange, strangled sound broke from her throat. She turned in her chair to look at me and the shaft of light from the window caught her full on the face.

I knew then what that sound had been. It had been a laugh. Julie's eyes were wide and staring. Her whole body shook with horrible soundless laughter.

I knew then that Julie Taylor was mad.

It may have been that knowledge that made me tear at my bonds with new hard fury. I pulled until the blood pounded in my head. I could feel the cloth, drawn to sharpness now, bite and cut into my ankles and my wrists. The ties seemed a little looser. But there was so little time. The gas was burning agonizingly in my throat; I coughed painfully through my gags.

Putting everything that was left in me in one gigantic effort, I wrenched at the towels again. My chair seesawed. Then, with a creaking loll, it turned on its side. My arm hit the floor first and broke my fall.

Over the side of the chair I could see a sudden movement from across the table. Julie was straining at her bonds. There was a ripping sound. Julie was getting free. I lay there, paralyzed. If she got her legs untied before I did, then pray God the gas would get me first. Even there in the darkness I could still see those frantic eyes mocking me, still hear that burst of insane laughter.

I tugged again in desperation. The cloth split and my legs were suddenly free. I struggled to get up, my hands still tied behind me, my arm ablaze with pain where I had landed on it. Both legs were numb and dead.

For a fraction of a second I stood there, dizzy and bewildered. The room was spinning around me; I couldn't find the window.

I heard the sound of ripping cloth and the quick jerky movement in Julie's chair, and still I stood in that one spot, powerless to move. It wasn't until she had loomed up there beside me that I realized that she, too, was free.

I started to the door, then, remembering that it was locked, turned back into the room. Julie was between the cabinets, barring me from the window. I closed my eyes and rushed straight at her.

I only know that our bodies met with a sharp impact and then the passageway was open. I ran to the window. I couldn't open it; with both hands tied behind me I couldn't even use them to break it.

I turned sidewise to lunge my shoulder through the pane of glass. And as I turned I saw Julie's face in back of me. It was coming closer. I tried to push against the window, but her two tied hands raised themselves above me. They came down, swipingly, across the side of my head.

I staggered, fighting to regain my balance. And then I saw the sharp white corner of her refrigerator coming up to meet me as I fell.

## Chapter Nineteen

AT THE VERY FIRST I thought I was in my own bed in my own room and a wonderful feeling of peace and security paraded down from my eyes clear to my toes. Then I rolled over on my side and saw mauve-tinted walls and chocolate brown draperies. I sat straight up. My bedroom walls were yellow.

It was Julie Taylor's bedroom, not mine. But everything was all right; Jeff was sitting there in a corner smoking a cigarette and watching me.

"How do you feel, Haila?"

"My throat," I rasped, "my throat is burning … that gas! I'm still full of it."

"Don't worry. I've got you moored."

The sickly sweet odor of gas was still clinging to the place. I felt suddenly nauseous.

"Jeff, open the windows wider, please!"

"They're as wide as they'll go."

"Is the kitchen one open?"

"Relax, everything's under control."

"Julie! Where's Julie?"

"Take your time, Haila." Jeff was smiling fondly at me. "You know, you're cute."

"Is she in the hospital?" I persisted.

"No. She went downtown to greet Mac when the prison gates clang shut behind him, a free man."

"Kirk!"

"He's taking Mac's place in the hoosegow. Escorted by Wyatt and Lockhart."

"Oh." It was all over then. And Kirk … I couldn't believe it. Until I remembered his face as he pointed the automatic at Julie and me, then I could believe it.

"Don't think about it, Haila."

"How can I help it? Jeff, is Julie …" I couldn't ask it. "How did she recover so quickly?"

Jeff shrugged. "Maybe she doesn't breathe as deeply as you. Maybe getting to see Mac had something to do with it."

I closed my eyes and relaxed. Now I could take up my life again where it had been so rudely interrupted by the murder of Isabelle Fleming. I would start cooking for Jeff; in fact, I would learn to cook. I would darn his socks. If I could find them. And I could start being an actress again. And Jeff would find a good job. …

"Jeff, will that place with that publisher still be open for you?"

"No, but I've got another job."

"You have!"

"What do you think I've been doing all week?"

"Looking for a murderer, not a job."

"One of the Rothschilds told me once," Jeff said sententiously, "never to look for a job, but to create one for myself. I just did. I'm taking Kirk's place at Photo Arts."

"You and Mac! That'll be swell!"

"Sure. Come around; I might let you pose for a gas mask ad."

"Jeff, when did you figure out that it was Kirk?"

"When I was going down to see Wyatt. I met him just as he was arriving at Centre Street. We went up to the studio after Kirk. An elevator boy told us that he had rushed away with you. Then I knew that he must be on his way to get Julie. He'd been after her ever since she disappeared."

"After her to … to kill her?"

"Well, he knew that she had the facts to deduce that it was he who was the murderer, not Mac. He wanted to make sure that she'd never use those facts. That's why he was looking for her, not because he loved her. If she did use them, he would have to kill her."

"What facts?"

"These. That chloroform can was in Mac's raincoat pocket. His raincoat wasn't at the studio until seven o'clock that night. It wasn't there in the afternoon when all the models were around. And none of the models, nor Harry Duerr, had returned to the studio until after Julie found the can in Mac's pocket. So that limited the number of people who could have put it there to four: Julie, Erika, Kirk and Mac himself. Julie or Kirk could have put it in at the studio after Mac arrived, Erika at home before he wore the slicker out."

"But Erika wasn't at home when Mac was there that night."

"Right. But she might have put it there before he got home."

"That seems unlikely, Jeff. It would have been a terrific coincidence; Erika happening to select the raincoat to put the chloroform in, it happening to rain, Mac happening to stop for his slicker and wearing it back to the studio."

"Coincidences have been known to happen. I couldn't eliminate Erika. But I could Mac."

"How?"

"If he had been the person in the darkroom with Julie, he wouldn't be carrying around the can. It was evidence. He would have dropped it down a sewer. Or put it in someone else's pocket."

"But if he meant to use it again?"

"The can was empty, Haila. And that left Erika, Kirk and Julie. Erika's death eliminated her. And until I was on my way to Centre Street I thought it might be either Kirk or Julie."

"What made you choose Kirk?"

"I had been thinking how damn lucky Mac was to have a pal like him. He was working night and day to prove Mac's innocence, doing everything in his power, even lying and destroying evidence to help him. For instance, remember when Wyatt wanted to see the negatives of the evening pictures? Kirk realized that when he saw them he would know that the knife had been taken from the table *before* the final shot and that consequently, Mac's cartwheel alibi would be ruined. So Kirk hid the negatives to save Mac. There was a pal for you, I thought!

"Then something clicked! Why had Kirk, as clever as he is, been so stupid in his effort to save Mac? Why had he hidden those plates in the most obvious place in the studio, the very same wastebasket where the afternoon's pictures had been found and the first place where anyone would look for them?

"The answer is that Kirk *wanted* those negatives to be found. He wanted to spoil Mac's alibi. And since they made Mac look guilty he knew that Wyatt would think Mac had hidden them. And what if it should be discovered that it had been Kirk who hid them? Well, what? You heard what Kirk said to me when I discovered just that. He was protecting Mac! But at the same time he was subtly getting across that even he believed Mac guilty and, despite the risk he was taking, was trying to help him. Noble, see?"

"And, Jeff!" I said. "Kirk hesitated when Wyatt asked him if Mac had told him about Mrs. Fleming's loan. He made it seem as if he were lying about it to save Mac!"

"Sure. And it was things like that which gave me the idea that maybe Kirk was trying to put the blame on Mac because he, Kirk, was the guilty one."

"And how did you get along?"

"Fine. Nobody had an alibi for the time of Isabelle Fleming's death. Almost anyone could have done it, including Kirk. So that was all right. But when Erika was murdered ..."

"But, Jeff, just a second or two before she was killed she was talking to Kirk on the telephone. ..."

"No. Not on the telephone. He was there in the room with her. He heard you in the hall outside; he was afraid you might have heard Erika call him by name. So he made her pretend that she was carrying on a phone conversation with him. It was very clever; it made you give him an alibi."

I said, "Harry's theory about Lee Kenyon being the murderer involved something like that. Since Kenyon knew about Kirk's phone call, he said, he must have seen Erika afterwards, been in the room with her while I was there. ..."

"Harry was wrong. Kirk's actual phone call to Erika was the one he made from the Sherry-Netherland. He lied to us about not getting her; he wanted to hold us off until he got to her. Shortly after that, Kenyon phoned her, but that was much before you got there."

Jeff took a deep breath. "So, since he had the opportunity to kill both Isabelle and Erika, I took up Kirk's motive. Why would Kirk Findlay want to murder both these women? There was only one answer of course; money."

"But Kirk never cared a hoot about money!" I protested. "The way he ignored it was one of his charms."

Jeff nodded. "That's the way he played it. The trouble was he overplayed played it. Nobody can talk as much about money as Kirk did and be uninterested in it. Two or three times he got bitter about his lot. He hated cheap bourbon, remember; he liked the most expensive scotch. He hated his one room; he wanted something more, something like a suite at the Plaza with the Plaza's room service at his elbow. He hated subways; taxis were his meat. And for all his charming disregard of money and what it buys, he bought the most expensive clothes. It was he who talked Mac into renting and furnishing that elaborate studio. It was Kirk's tastes and Mac's generous acquiescence that broke Photo Arts. I don't mean that Kirk wanted money for itself or for the power it brings. He isn't a miser nor a financier. Luxury-loving, that's Kirk. Lighting cigars with thousand dollar bills.

"Well, he thought he had found those thousand dollar bills when he met Erika. He thought the Fleming millions were as good as in his pocket. And then he made his first mistake; he introduced Erika to Mac and there was a lot of love at first sight and she became Mrs. MacCormick. That was when Kirk started hating his pal, Mac.

"He pretended that it was all right with him; he made Mac think that they were still pals. But Kirk didn't give up. The minute the honeymoon was over he began working again on Erika and all that money that would be hers someday. He covered up by pretending he was in love with Julie and that he didn't give a damn for the material things in life. And poor Mac never dreamed that his pal was knifing him and stealing his wife."

"And Kirk," I asked, "didn't he ever really love Erika?"

"He never let himself get too romantic about it. He kept both eyes on the Fleming fortune, waiting impatiently for Isabelle to drop off of natural causes and leave it to Erika.

"And then something happened. Erika really fell in love with him, wanted to divorce Mac and marry him. Kirk couldn't let that happen yet; he knew that Isabelle would disinherit her niece. So he kept her quiet by saying that Mac was his friend, he couldn't bear the thought of hurting him. Rather than be so cruel to a fine fellow like Mac they would have to suffer bravely … and in secret."

"She must have thought he was wonderful!"

"Sure she did. But finally she got impatient. She went to her aunt and told her that she was leaving Mac for another man and that she didn't give a damn about being disinherited. And then she told Kirk what she had done. He realized that he couldn't hold her off any longer, but he didn't want her without her money. There was only one thing for him to do; he must kill Isabelle Fleming before she could take action.

"All this came to a head on Saturday morning after Erika had talked to her aunt and then to Kirk."

"But neither of them knew what Mrs. Fleming had done? That she had paid off Kenyon thinking he was Erika's lover?"

Jeff shook his head. "No. That was just an added complication. Just something that involved Kenyon in the murder picture."

"It was lucky for Kirk that Kenyon was one of the models," I said.

"Lucky? Uh-uh. Kirk planned it. On Saturday he knew that he would kill Mrs. Fleming. He had made Erika promise to keep quiet about their relationship until he could find another job and leave Photo Arts. His story was that he couldn't stand to see his pal suffer.

"It had already been arranged that Isabelle was to pose at the studio on Monday. That was when he would kill her. That studio was a good place for a murder. Lots of people around to baffle the police and lots of rooms and doors and confusion to hide the murderer. It was daring; I give him credit for that.

"So it wasn't a coincidence that Kenyon with his connection with Erika was one of the models. Nor Madge Lawrence with her motive for revenge. Nor even the silly business of May Ralston with her middle name of Fleming. I kept marveling at that coincidence until I realized that it wasn't one.

Kirk had handpicked those three models on Monday morning. He let Julie and Mac pick Robert Yorke and Jim Snyder."

"But how did he know about Madge Lawrence? That she was Amanda Lewis, I mean."

"Erika knew it. She had told him."

"Then Erika … why didn't she think that it was Madge who killed her aunt?"

"Perhaps she did."

"Then why didn't she say so? She didn't want Mac convicted; I don't believe that."

"Erika did say so. She told Wyatt. She wasn't speaking to me, remember. And if it hadn't been for Madge Lawrence's terrific motive, Wyatt probably would have arrested Mac long before he did." Jeff stopped to bend solicitously over me. "How do you feel, sweetheart? Gas all out of your lungs yet?"

"No. It'll take days."

"Wait here."

"As if in my condition I could do anything else!"

When Jeff reappeared he had a glass of water, two shot glasses and a half bottle of Four Roses with him.

"What you need is a drink, Haila."

"No, Jeff. But I would like a cup of tea."

"Tea?"

"Would you make it for me? I don't think I can manage yet."

"I can't make tea."

"Jeff, you boil water and …"

"Boil water?"

"Yes," I said patiently. "You put a little water in a pan and light the gas and …"

"I don't think I should strike a match in the kitchen yet."

"Oh, all right. I'll wait."

"You're cute, Haila."

"Not so cute. I thought Kenyon was the murderer."

"For a while I thought it was Snyder. And all because he had alibied Erika that first night."

"I remember. He said that he hadn't seen anyone in the reception room. Why?"

"Because Snyder is just a little gentleman. He wanted to do Erika a favor. He thought that Erika might do him a little favor with all her aunt's money."

I said sadly, "I guess my grandmother was right; all men are alike. I'll never trust another one."

"You shouldn't; not after Kirk's rudeness."

"Jeff, it was horrible! I know he wanted to kill Julie, but ... but me!"

"He tried his damnedest to keep you from coming with him, didn't he?"

"Yes."

"And he tried to trick you into leaving Julie and him alone together, didn't he?"

"Yes."

"But you wouldn't listen, would you, sweetheart? You wanted to stick around."

"I was being brave. Jeff, tell me, how did Kirk do it? He was the man in the darkroom with Julie, wasn't he?"

"Yes. He was waiting there for Mrs. Fleming. He had asked her to meet him in the third room on the left side of the corridor, that he had something important to tell her concerning her niece. She didn't know that that room was the darkroom; she'd never been in the studio before. He expected her to walk right in.

"He picked the darkroom because there was less chance of being interrupted there. Julie and Mac and Harry were the only people with any reason to go in it. And if one of them should happen to come in, there would be a chance of his getting out without being seen. Just as it did happen when Julie walked in on him."

"And Mrs. Fleming? Did she ever go in it?"

"He headed her off. He said that he would tell her the next day."

"He was lucky that Julie didn't talk about it."

"Yes. He didn't know why Julie was keeping quiet any more than Julie knew herself. But when she didn't say anything he knew that he was safe; he knew he could go on and try again.

"The first thing he did was trick Mac into putting off the developing of the pictures until later. Mac agreed and asked him to be back at seven. Then Kirk hid the chloroform some place; he would need it again. He went out and walked the streets; he had to think. By six-thirty he had his second attempt planned.

"He rushed back to the studio, smashed the plates and threw them in the wastebasket. It would be no more incriminating to have them found broken than for them to be missing. Now the picture would have to be retaken. Mrs. Fleming would be at the studio again. This time he wouldn't need the chloroform; he would use the carving knife. He poured the remaining chloroform down the drain and started out of the studio to get rid of the can. That can would be incriminating. But before he could get out Mac came in. He was bursting with the good news of Isabelle's promised loan.

"That was Kirk's first tough break; he couldn't get rid of that can. He and

Mac were both in the reception room. Mac hung his coat in the closet and went to the darkroom to start developing the picture. Kirk quickly hid the can in Mac's pocket. He'd get rid of it later. And, in case it was found, it would be found in Mac's pocket. That wouldn't hurt Kirk.

"Mac didn't find the plates even though Kirk was helping him look for them. And he finally persuaded Mac that they were really lost and the picture must be retaken at once." Jeff paused to pour another shot of rye. "How do you feel, Haila?"

"Some better. I'm going to sit up."

"Do you think you ought to? Consolidated Edison puts out a nasty gas."

"I'm going to try." I sat up and put my feet on the floor. I felt surprisingly good. "Go on, Jeff."

"After the test negative Kirk slipped the carving knife off the table and started for Fleming's dressing room. But in the hallway he met her coming out. He would have to momentarily postpone the deed. He waited until the coast was clear, then sneaked into her room and hid the knife there. That much, anyway, was done.

"His chance didn't come until after the final shot when Mac handed him the plates and asked him to start working on them. He took them into the darkroom, left them there, and went immediately to Mrs. Fleming's room. You and Mac and Julie were in the studio. Harry had gone to the storage room. The models were all changing in their dressing rooms, except Jim Snyder who was in the reception room with Erika.

"It took Kirk only a minute to retrieve the knife, come up behind Isabelle Fleming and stab her to death. He held the knife with a handkerchief; no prints of his were on it. He didn't know, of course, that a print of Mac's and a print of Julie's were still on the part of the blade that didn't penetrate Isabelle Fleming's body. That was just another hunk of velvet for Kirk.

"He slipped quickly back into the darkroom. He hadn't been seen. When Mac finally joined him there, Kirk was well on his way with developing the plates. To Mac, Kirk had obviously been there all the time.

"Now all he had to do was to get rid of the chloroform can. The first opportunity he found he went to get it. It was already gone. Someone had found and surreptitiously removed it. Only one person would have done that … the person who had been in the darkroom that afternoon and knew that chloroform had been used. Julie Taylor. And then he guessed, and rightly, what had happened. Julie thought it had been Mac in the darkroom and had hidden the chloroform to protect him. It was then he got the idea of framing Mac. But he had to keep an eye on Julie. She might all of a sudden stop thinking that Mac was the murderer. And if that happened, she'd know who the real murderer was. But Julie cooperated nicely with him by putting herself out of reach the next morning.

"The only other person who could tip his hand was Erika, if she should come out with her intention of divorcing Mac to marry him. But he pointed out to her that with her aunt's threat of disinheritance hanging over her head, it would be wiser for her to keep quiet.

"She almost ruined things down at the Barrel Room though. She wired him to meet her there; she had to talk to him. And he was afraid not to go, for he had to keep an eye on Erika too. Of course, he didn't know that Lee Kenyon was dancing at the Barrel Room. If he had known that he would have found some way out.

"Then you and I banged into the place and he knew that before long we'd see him. If he got up to go out we'd see him. So he pulled out the spotlight plug and pasted me when I got in his way in the dark. Erika covered him after he'd left.

"Kirk rushed back to his room, changed from the dark suit that I'd seen a corner of, into a light tan one. Then he waited for us on our doorstep. He was all done in from spending the night looking for Julie Taylor. The only reason he ever wanted to find her was to make sure she kept her mouth shut and didn't use her brains."

I said, "And I thought he loved her, that her disappearance had him sick with worry."

"Darling, you'd better lie down again. You'll have to take it easy for a week or two."

Maybe Jeff was right. I had heard of people catching pneumonia after experiences like mine. I got back in bed and pulled the covers over me. Jeff took another slug of rye. Then he stretched out beside me and pulled my head onto his shoulder. Neither of us spoke for a minute.

"Jeff," I finally said, "how did Kirk kill Erika?"

"It started up at Kenyon's place when I told Kirk that I wanted to talk to Erika about her and her boyfriend, remember?"

"Yes. He went to call her right away but he told us she wasn't home."

"But she *was* in and he arranged to go right down and see her. He told her that you and I were coming down later and he had to talk to her first. He knew that if I could scare her into telling me that it was Kirk she loved, it was his head. He got to Erika just a few minutes before you did. And then when you arrived he did some fast thinking and turned your coming into a break for him. He made Erika pretend that she was talking to him on the phone. He made her send you into the library. Maybe that automatic was already in his hand and that's how he made her do those things. Or possibly she didn't know yet that he was her aunt's murderer. He might have told her after you got there and she refused to become his accomplice in the crime.

He couldn't use the gun for you would hear it. He strangled her."

"She didn't make a sound," I said. "If she had screamed ..."

"Would you like to see if you can make a sound that can be heard in the next room with my hands around your throat?"

"No, thanks, sweet."

"Well, then, Kirk slipped out of the apartment. He was going down the stairs while Mac was coming up in the elevator."

"What if Mac had got there a moment sooner?"

"He would have killed Mac. Then you. And he would have gone on killing until he got killed."

I thought about what an amusing and charming and thoughtful young man I had always considered Kirk. It just went to show. It certainly did. And I thought about Mac and Julie and the tragedy it had taken to bring them together. And I wondered if they would get over it and make a life for themselves. It might take years but ...

"Mac's lucky to have Julie," Jeff was saying. "It isn't as if all this happened because they love each other. It'll be tough but they'll get over it all right ..."

"Jeff, how did you know I was thinking that?"

"Mental telepathy."

I scoffed; Jeff smiled.

"You don't believe in that sort of thing, do you, Haila? Mind over matter and ..."

"Mind over tommyrot!"

"All right. There was a man once in Milwaukee ... perfectly healthy ... and he got the idea that he ... Wait a minute till I get it straight. He was a violinist. And he lived in constant fear of losing the use of his right arm. And he brooded so much about it that his arm became paralyzed. That's mind over matter."

"And it always happens to someone in Milwaukee. Somebody you can't possibly check on."

"I can tell you about a case. A case that you can check on. Somebody you know."

"Go ahead."

"All right. Julie has an electric icebox, you know."

"Yes."

"And a brand new electric toaster. And a brand new electric Silex for coffee and a ..."

"Jeff, what are you ..."

"She never cooks, except toast and coffee, so she never uses her stove. It isn't connected."

"What!"

"Julie closed her gas account with Consolidated Edison just last week. You were asphyxiated via mind over matter."

"No, Jeff!"

"Her gas isn't turned on. Mind over matter."

"Why didn't Julie tell me?"

"She had a gag over her mouth. And she did keep you from hurting yourself when you were going to crash through the window."

"But, Jeff ... I can still smell the gas!"

"You're cute, Haila."

"It wasn't mind over matter!"

"Your mind! And what does it matter? You're awful cute, Haila. Kiss me."

THE END

# About the Rue Morgue Press

"Rue Morgue Press is the old-mystery lover's best friend, reprinting high quality books from the 1930s and '40s."
—*Ellery Queen's Mystery Magazine*

Since 1997, the Rue Morgue Press has reprinted scores of traditional mysteries, the kind of books that were the hallmark of the Golden Age of detective fiction. Authors reprinted or to be reprinted by the Rue Morgue include Dorothy Bowers, Pamela Branch, Joanna Cannan, Glyn Carr, Torrey Chanslor, Clyde B. Clason, Joan Coggin, Manning Coles, Lucy Cores, Frances Crane, Norbert Davis, Elizabeth Dean, Constance & Gwenyth Little, Marlys Millhiser, James Norman, Stuart Palmer, Craig Rice, Kelley Roos, Charlotte Murray Russell, Maureen Sarsfield, Margaret Scherf and Juanita Sheridan.

To suggest titles or to receive a catalog of Rue Morgue Press books write P.O. Box 4119, Boulder, CO 80306, telephone 800-699-6214, or check out our website, www.ruemorguepress.com, which lists complete descriptions of all of our titles, along with lengthy biographies of our writers.